To Jason

With

Suzie

Oct
2012 .

Our Josh

Suzie Litton-Wood

Bloomington, IN Milton Keynes, UK

authorHOUSE®

AuthorHouse™
1663 Liberty Drive, Suite 200
Bloomington, IN 47403
www.authorhouse.com
Phone: 1-800-839-8640

AuthorHouse™ UK Ltd.
500 Avebury Boulevard
Central Milton Keynes, MK9 2BE
www.authorhouse.co.uk
Phone: 08001974150

First published by AuthorHouse   10/19/2006

ISBN: 1-4259-4177-X (sc)

Printed in the United States of America
Bloomington, Indiana

This book is printed on acid-free paper.

Our Josh

It was early one mornin' when these two men in uniform came marchin' over the bridge and down the towpath towards our boats. We'd been moored up at the Barge Inn for the night 'cos they always gave us good dry stablin' for Hercules, our horse. We'll as I was sayin', these two uniforms came marchin' up to our boat and they knock on the cabin side like............

...........An evocative story set on the canals of England at the turn of the Twentieth Century. An intimate window on the day to day life of one family in particular, who were deeply affected by the time and tides of War, the prejudices, the sense of community, the isolation, the hardship and the sheer joy of a working narrowboat family in the early 1900's.

Acknowledgements

My grateful thanks to Mr. R. J. Hutchings, who was at one time the Curator of the British Waterways Museum at Stoke Bruerne for his permission to use photograph nos: 1, 2, 3 & 4.

Also Mr. Clive Hackforth, previous curator of the Kennet & Avon Canal Museum at Devizes, for his enthusiastic support of my search for canal history and for permission to use photograph number 5.

Special gratitude to my youngest son Jay, with whom I share a love of working narrowboats, for his fine drawing.

I would like to dedicate this book to all those men, women and children who have lived and worked on the Canals of England since their inception. To all those narrow 'boaties', living and dead who have inspired me to write this amazing story. Also special thanks to Rose James, a wonderful lady who was born on the horse drawn narrow boat 'Persia' and her husband Bill for their wealth of first hand knowledge of life on the canals throughout the early 1900's. And to my friend Dave Wright, known on the Cut as 'Shrimp', from whom I bought the 100 year old ex Fellows, Morton & Clayton Butty Longton, which became the portal for my connection with hundreds of Dirty Boaties! To my wonderful husband Lit, for his loving support and understanding. And most importantly of all, to Jessie for entrusting this, her own story, to me.

Contents

Preface

Since early childhood I have had the ability to communicate with the Spirit World, possibly inherited from my Father's Romany family, or rather, Spirits communicate with me. I am not clairevoiant, in the usually understood way, I do not 'summon up' the Spirits of dead people simply to pass on messages to anxiously waiting loved ones. I have no control over the Spirits, I see, or speak with, they choose me. I believe this gift is called Claireaudient, which simply means that I am 'open' to the possibility.

My interest in canals and their history, began whilst on holiday with a large group of mad, fun loving, folk singers and musicians. There were thirty or so of us in four narrow boats, hired from a popular canal holiday company. The trip was organised by Tony O'Neil, a lovley man, known affectionately as 'The Admiral' and we 'did' the Cheshire Ring, a circuit of several canals in the the Midlands. Our holiday culminated in a visit to the British Waterways Museum at Stoke Bruerne, where they had a special exhibition of old sepia photographs. It was here that I met for the first time, faces of long dead 'boaties', their boats and families, and so the love affair began.

For months afterwards I was literally 'haunted' by some of those faces, and was 'inspired' to write songs about some of them. Never having written songs before, I was amazed at how five or six verses would suddenly 'appear' in my head. Sometimes complete with a tune, as though it was being handed to me, quite literally, on a plate and I would struggle to get it all written down, before the 'window' closed. Although a seasoned folk singer, I have only a very limited ability to read music, therefore I had to sing or hum the tunes I was 'given' into a tape recorder and play them to my dear friend and singing partner John Meleady, who then played them on his guitar. At first they sounded so familiar I was convinced they had to be traditional tunes, but after searching many collections and performing the songs to folk audiencies up and down the country, I had to conclude that they were indeed unique.

My love of the canals and their history continued on. I bought my first narrow boat, Ladhra (A celtic name pronounced Lara) and began my adventures on the navigable waterways of England. Not satisfied with spending all my weekends and holidays afloat, I dreamed of changing my whole lifestyle and going to live perminantly on a narrowboat. Then one day the opportunity was again 'handed to me on a plate'. I was made redundant! Without a second thought, I put my house up for sale and began searching for the boat which would become my new home. I had by this time formed a canal folk band 'Keepers Lock' and we were singing our 'self penned' canal songs and telling stories at the many waterways festivals up and down the country.

It was at one such festival, Canal Cavalcade in Little Venice on the Paddington Arm of the Grand Union Canal in London that I met Dave Wright, the owner of a pair of ex Fellows, Morton & Clayton narrowboats, 'Lupin and Longton'. As luck would have it he was looking for a suitable enthusiast to buy the 'butty' Longton, an unpowered, originally horsedrawn boat. He told me she was a 'Josher' built in Saltley in 1898. I was immediately hooked and even after seeing her, moored up on the North Oxford Canal, in a very dilapidated state, I was totally smitten. She needed a lot of work to make her habitable, but I decided I could live on 'Ladhra' while the renovations were being carried out.

I soon realised just how special Longton was and that I was not the only person living aboard her. Initially it was just the strong smell of pipe tobacco pervading the back cabin, then tools and other items which became 'lost', only to reappear again in the back cabin. The feeling of a 'presence' gradually gave way to the actual manifestation of a man in his mid-thirties, dressed in a short jacket and flat cap, living in the back cabin of my boat. We began to communicate, a sort of thought transferance, he told me his name was Jack , he'd been born on a narrowboat and had lived and worked all his life on the canals. I often used to see him tightening the ropes that fastened over the cloths, along the entire length of Longton's hull, over our 'non existant' cargo. Later came three children, two girls and a boy. I never knew the name of the older girl but the boy was Thomas and his younger sister, a child of about four years of age, with a mass of blond curls, was named Flossie. They played hopscotch between the knees of Longton's stripped out hull and skipped along the keelson beneath flapping cloths. I saw this so clearly on many occasions even though Longton had now been converted to a live aboard with every modern convenience!

It became a fairly normal occurance for me to be wakened in the early hours of the morning by various 'boaties' all anxious to tell me their stories. Some I would see in total physicallity and I was able to interact with them, some were just swirls of energy, their voices speaking into my head and others gifted me with complete songs or stories that I would hurriedly scribble in my now ever present, bedside note book. As time went on, I began to see many more spirit people and not always when I was on my boat, although I believe that Longton was the catalyst or portal for these visitations. Most of their stories seem to reflect some kind of deep sadness or injustice during their lives and I feel that by performing the subsequent songs, I am some how addressing these issues and helping to heal them by making them known. It was while I was compiling songs for a new album, 'Memories', which portrays the effects of War on the people of the day, living and working on the canals, the material for which had mostly come from my long dead 'boatie' friends, that I was first visited by 'Jessie'. She gave me a 'vision' of two men dressed in typical First World War uniform, marching down a muddy towpath and knocking on the cabin side of a boat moored there. I saw and heard the entire conversation, Jessie standing in the well deck beside her mother, the two soldiers demanding to know where her brother Josh was, and later, Josh leading Hercules down the towpath from the Barge Inn, which was just visable above the hedgerows. I hurried to write down every word, knowing that I only had that one opportunity to capture the poignant scene and when Josh was eventually led away by the soldiers, I felt all of Jessie's pain and frustration.

Two weeks later Jessie visited me again and left me with two verses of a song about her brother, the tune of which evokes thoughts of the old Musical Halls. After the album was produced and we began to perform it's many songs, I felt a strong presence of 'Jessie' beside me on stage, every time I told her story and sang about her beloved brother Josh. Often she would just appear, where ever I was, at home on Longton, in the supermarket, in a pub or while walking my dog Rauney along the towpath. She would smile and say "I have more to tell you" and when I asked her to continue she would say "Not just now" or "In a little while".

When difficult circumstances forced me to sell my beloved Longton and move away from the canals, I was heartbroken, fearing this would terminate my connection with the 'boaties'forever. It was almost a year I guess, before my mind again found that inner peace and stillness, which I now know is necessary for me to be 'open' to a spirit's presence. 'Jessie' came to me one night in what seemed like a dream, she told me she was ready to tell me her story. I got out of bed and went straight to my computer and began typing frantically, in an effort to keep up with her dialogue. After several hours I returned exhausted and very cold, to my bed. Next morning I could not decide whether I had actually spoken with 'Jessie' or whether it had just been a haunted dream. But my computer confirmed the truth of it, thirty or so pages of a story I had never heard or had any recollection of. 'Our Josh' is not *my* story to tell, I am just fortunate enough to be the vehicle by which 'Jessie' conveys it to the living world.

Suzie Litton-Wood.

CHAPTER ONE

The Two Uniforms

It was early one mornin' when these two men in uniform came marchin' over the bridge and down the towpath towards our boats. We'd been moored up at the Barge Inn for the night 'cos they always gave us good dry stablin' for Hercules, our horse. Well, as I was sayin' these two uniforms came marchin' up to our boat and they knocks on the cabin side like.

"Hey up Missus" says the one to me Ma, "We've come about Joshua Ridley"

"Our Josh, what would you be wantin' with him?"

"We've been told he's a good man with the horses" says the other 'un.

"Aye our Josh knows about horses, but he's no man, he's now't but a lad" says me Ma.

"We've made enquiries, and the clerk at the Company tells us that Joshua Ridley is   seventeen years of age, and drawing half pay – that's man enough for us!"

"You can't be thinkin' of takin' him away for the Army," me Ma says, getting' all upset like.

"We need men who are good with horses at the Front and the Company has agreed to release him" the uniform said.

I could see Ma was getting' in a state, she were pressin' her 'ands down the sides of 'er apron, a sure sign she were getting' worked up!

"But we can't manage without our Josh, he works the horse, and now with the two boats and me man still getting' over the monia, well we can't be doin without our Josh."

"Look Missus," says the other uniform "King and Country comes before the likes of you! We have a paper here, signed by the Company, what says Joshua Ridley is released to us, so stop tryin' to prevent us doin' our duty and tell us where he is!"

"Why, he's up at the stables behind the Barge Inn, tackin' up our horse, we're due in Nuneaton by six o'clock tonight, me husband's meetin' us there with a return load."

"Well Missus, I suggest you look lively and pack up your son some snap for the journey, 'cos he's comin' with us......Now!"

And with that the two uniforms turned on their heels and walked back up the towpath towards the Barge Inn. Ten minutes later they came back with our Josh leadin' the horse.

"Is this right Ma, I have to go away to the Army, with these two, leavin' you and the kids to get to Nuneaton on yer own?"

"Oh son! I don't want you to go, is there nothin' to be done?"

Ma wrung her hands and stood between our Josh and the two uniforms, as though that would stop them from takin' him away.

"No Missus," says the uniform, "Papers is all signed".

Then he looks at our Josh "Now look lively lad, we've wasted enough time here. Get your gear together and some snap for the journey. It's a good walk to the railway station an' another six hours 'til we joins up with your unit. I just hope we make it in time before they embark for Flanders.

Our Josh just looked about him, 'elpless like, almost as though he 'alf expected someone to say it'd all been a big mistake, but it weren't and there was now't for it, he had to go. I swear he were more upset at leavin' Hercules than he was the rest of us, for he had tears in his eyes as he patted the 'orses 'ead and pulled his ears. The uniform tried to sound cheerful like, but whatever he said made things worse. Then finally he said,

"I'm sure your Son'll write to you Missus, when he gets settled".

"Can't write" says Josh

"Weren't no good if you could" Ma said "None of us can read!"

And with that the two uniforms marched off up the Cut with our Josh between them. He never looked back. And that was the last we ever saw of our Josh!

****

"Don't stand there gawking girl!"

Ma was shoutin' at me now and it brought me to me senses. The two uniforms had long since disappeared up the tow path with our Josh and it were rainin' again. I turned and led Hercules to the front of our lead boat 'Isis' and began to attach 'im to the rope, which was attached to the mast. We'd a fair way to go today and with a pair of hands short, working the horse and the locks was gonna be 'ard whichever way you looked at it! Havin' attached Hercules I turned back to see if Ma was ready for the 'off'. I could see she 'ad attached the snatcher to our second boat 'Bluebell' and she was wavin' me back to her. I looked down the two boat's lengths and saw that our Sammy was standin' in the well deck ready to steer. I walked back to where Ma was, and holdin' out an old flour sack, she said to me

"Better put this over yer 'ead girl, this lots 'in' for the day"

I took the empty sack which had been slit down one long side, and slipped it over me head. Ma handed me a length of string which I tied around me neck to stop the sack from slipping off. Then without another word I trudged back down the towpath to where Hercules was standing.

"Stand to Boy" I cried out, before I even reached him, then I watched the muscles in his neck go taut as he leaned forward to take up the slack. Then slowly every muscle and every sinew rippled right through his entire body as the strain of hauling 60 tonnes of dead weight took its toll. Then all of a sudden, like magic, the strain seemed to disappear as the two boats started to swim very slowly. They seemed to glide on the glass like water, tiny ripples extending from the bow of the lead boat right down its 70 foot length to join with the ripples of the second boat which, tied to the first, was being drawn along behind. Hercules' whole body sort of shuddered,

"Steady boy" I said as I came along side of him and I patted his rump to let him know where I was. Then I said, more quietly now, "Walk on Boy" and he set off at his steady rhythmic 'clip clop' pace which would take us the fifteen or so miles to Nuneaton. All around the leaden sky was ousing rain in long freezing streaks, each one stinging like nettles as the wind whipped and lashed our bodies, now soaked through despite the sacks, two across Hercules' back and one over me 'ead. I hardly saw the flooded fields and dripping trees, as I never looked up from the deep muddy pot holes made in the towpath by the horse's heavy hooves, as we ground our way south. It wasn't long before we reached the first pair of locks. I was tryin' to get it straight in me 'ead, why Mr. Griffiths, the owner of our boats, would want to be sendin' our Josh off to the War. It didn't make no sense, our Josh 'ad never wanted to be a soldier, 'E was a boatman through and through. 'E 'ad been so excited when we got our other boat Bluebell, 'E'd talked of nothin' else for weeks and weeks after. It seemed to make 'im feel more important like, cos Da had written 'im down as number two steerer, and Mr. Griffiths had agreed to givin' him half pay. What a difference that was goin' to make to all of us! But to our Josh most of all, 'cos now 'E was like a real man, 'E said, and earning too. I was so proud of our Josh. I don't know if 'E ever noticed, but I even used a bit more elbow grease when I polished his boots these days. Well I was strugglin' along through the mud, beside Hercules and had just decided in my head that it must all be a huge mistake and the Army would send our Josh back 'ome when they realised, when a change in Hercules step made me look up into the blinding rain. I hooked me icey fingers into the horse's mane, 'ardly able to feel the course hair as I said quite unnecessarily "Wait up Boy", but Hercules 'ad already stopped and as 'is head went down to the tufts of rough grass at the canal's edge, our two boats glided past us. Ma was standing in the 'well deck' of the 'Isis', as Sammy pushed past her and leaped across to the towpath, lock key in hand. He hung on to his cap as he raced the twenty or so yards up to the lock gates. We was heading towards Atherstone and although most other boats that morning had been going the same way, we had just passed a 'Joey' boat going in the opposite direction, so the lock was 'set' for us. By easing the rein up over the lock gates and encouraging Hercules to eat the grass at the far side of the lock, Sammy & I managed to manoeuvre 'Isis' into the lock leavin' 'Bluebell' tied up on the bollard. The canal was fairly narrow and only had single locks so we 'ad to put each boat in separately. Ma disappeared into the cabin even before we had the gates closed, reappearing two minutes later with mugs of steaming hot black tea laced with sugar. What a sight for sore eyes that was! I took me mug and wrapped both hands tightly around it to take advantage of the warmth, at the same time taking tiny sips of the scalding liquid. I knew I had fifteen minutes at least in which to enjoy every mouthful, while the lock filled up and I was not about to waste a single drop. Rain dripped steadily from the sack to me hair, from me hair to me nose and cheeks, eventually running from me chin. The sleeves of me blouse were soaked and stuck to me arms, as was me skirt to me legs, which hung heavily from me waist, weighed down by six inches of mud around the hem. Me boots was heavy with the caked on clay and me bare feet squelched in the inch deep water soaking up through the leather soles. Once Isis was through, we had to repeat the 'ole process again, first emptyin' the lock then bow-haulin' Bluebell in and refilling the lock. By the time we was ready to set off again the rain had eased off, but I felt thoroughly cold and miserable, soaked and shivering I couldn't get the thought of our Josh bein' taken off by those two uniforms earlier that morning, out of me 'ead.

"I'll spell you 'til we get to Atherstone flight Jessie" shouted Sammy across the lock, "So you can dry off a bit"

"Ta, I think a wringing out is what I need" I called back to my younger brother. " If you close the gate on that side I'll 'old Hercules until you get across, then I can hop onto 'Bluebell' and warm meself up a bit"

"I'll see you at the bottom lock" Sammy called as he set off with the 'orse down the tow path, our two boats gliding along behind. His short legs stuck out from under his sack, gave him a strange, almost unreal appearance. It was good of our Sammy to give me a chance to dry off 'cos leading the 'orse was not his favorite job.

I climbed over the gunn'al and stood in the well deck of Bluebell. If I was to have the chance to get inside the cabin to dry off a bit, I would have to 'tie off' the tiller arm so the elum wouldn't flap about, as this would make it more difficult for Ma, steering up ahead on 'Isis'. Down in the cabin I shook off the soggy sack, fighting with the wet string which was now tied tightly 'round me neck. A large red wheal had appeared where the string had chaffed and I made a mental note to rub some lard into it when I had dried out a bit. Standing as close as I could to the heat from the range, steam began to rise from me clothes sending delicious warm streams down me arms and legs. I took an old shawl from the bed'ole and wrapped it around me head and shoulders, rubbing me 'air as I stepped out of me boots. I pushed and wriggled me freezing feet in between the strips of rag, which made up the tiny cabin rug in front of the range and the warmth was delicious. I pulled the slide and the cabin doors closed behind me until just a slit of daylight was visible, in an effort to keep the rain out. In the darkness of the warm cabin I curled up on the floor, staying as close to the range as I could.

After a while I reached into the coal box and carefully lifting the top ring, placed three large lumps of 'Barlow's Best on top of the already glowing embers. Snuggling back into me now damp, but warm shawl I was just starting to nod off when a shout from Ma on 'Isis' told me we were approaching the next set of locks which would take us up into Atherstone. So it was back on with me cold wet boots and soggy sack and out into the pouring rain once again. Sammy had brought Hercules to a stand still some way off from the lock and through the lashing rain I could just make out the figures of similarly clad people working the lock with their two boats up ahead. Sammy was now soaked through to the skin, as I had been, and Ma again produced mugs of steaming black tea. There was no point in our getting back inside the cabin, cos wet is wet whichever way you looks at it and we had eleven locks to work in this flight. We stood together, drinking our tea and sayin' nothin'. Since the two uniforms had marched off with our Josh, I could not think of a single word to say. Well that's not exactly true, I could think of lots of questions, like 'Why our Josh? And where was he now? And how was we gonna manage without him? But I was sure that Ma would be askin' herself the same questions, with no more chance of getting' an answer than me, so I just kept me thoughts to meself. Da was gonna be mad, I thought, when we gets to Nuneaton without our Josh, he'll likely go off to the Company office and put them straight, then they would realise it was a mistake, our Josh would be let off and things would get back to normal. Da would never let anyone get away with interferein' in people's lives, at least Ma always said so. I had this picture in me head of our Josh arrivin' at the barracks to be told he was the wrong man and he could go home after all.

Just then Hercules started to move off and I looked up and saw that the first lock was now empty. Givin' me mug to our Sammy I says

"Put these back on board and I'll see you up there".

I thought to meself 'He's a good boy, our Sammy, not yet eleven years of age, it'll be a hard winter for him if we has to go on without our Josh'. The rain was still comin' down in 'Rods' as we worked the locks and continued our way up to the summit, through the town, and on 'til we was out in the countryside once more. We didn't 'ave no clocks and the sky was very dark and grey, but me stomach was tellin' me it was long past mid-day when Ma called out to me from the back deck, where she had been stood all mornin' steering.

" Tie up alongside of that tree for a bit and we'll have a bite and a cuppa."

Numbed by the cold and continual rain, I took two or three paces before Ma's words sunk in and I had to run up alongside of Hercules to say

"Wait up boy".

The wind was howlin' and as this was not a usual stoppin' place, the 'orse wouldn't 'ave stopped here of his own accord as he did at lock gates, bridges and the like. I ran back down the tow path 'til I was level with Ma and she threw me a rope, at the same time Sammy jumped the two feet between the back deck of 'Isis' and the front deck of 'Bluebell'. I pulled 'ard on Ma's rope to stop 'er and to bring her in closer to the bank. As 'Isis' slowed, Ma slipped the snatcher and pushed against Bluebell's nose and she nudged alongside of 'Isis' . The two boats was still movin' quite fast so I had to work quickly. I took a turn with the rope round a tree then ran up to the front just as Bluebell's nose was comin level, Sammy threw me his rope which landed at me feet, pickin' it up I pulled for all I was worth' til both boats came to a stop. Sammy was on the front deck of Isis now and we lashed the two boats together. Meanwhile Ma was lashing the two back ends together across the studs. Once I was certain we was tied up secure, I reached under the cloths and took out a nose tin for Hercules. Rain water had already soaked the oats through, cos the cloth at this end of the boat never seemed to stay tied down and the rain always got in. Me Da was careful when loading the boat with cargo at this end, so it wouldn't spoil in the rain. We was carrin' nigh on 50 tonnes of China Clay in both boats down to Wedgewood's at Barlstone. Our Josh, Ma and me doin' all the loadin'. and unloadin', as well as getting' the stuff there. Da had been in the sanatorium in Nuneaton for three weeks 'cos he was real bad with the 'monia'. We 'ad to keep goin' with the boats, even though Ma was so worried she could barely think straight. But if we didn't carry on we wouldn't get paid for the load and Mr. Griffiths, the owner, was not about to let two of his best boats lay over for a week or two. Keeping going was the only choice we 'ad. Da had been bad ever since he jumped in the Cut to fish Lizzie Higgins little'un out when 'E fell in head first, off the cabin top. We was just mooring up behind 'em on the colliery arm, ready to unload the mining' supplies the followin' mornin' when I see's little Jimmy sat on top of the cabin roof. As we got closer I could see the leather belt tied round his little body, attachin' him to the smoke stack, with a cushion in-between. Lots of boatie families did this as a way to keep the little 'uns safe while they was going along. Kept 'em warm too, up alongside of the chimney. But Little Jimmy was on his own, no sign of either Lizzie or that daft husband of hers. I remember thinkin' 'You didn't oughta leave a little un' like that, on his own, he couldn't be more than a year old'. But I had work to do and I turned to take the rope from Ma ready to pull 'Bluebell' alongside when little Jimmy fell in, chimny and all! Da was tyin' up at the front of 'Isis' while Josh was unhitchin' Hercules when we hears this splash, Da looks up just in time to see the babby disappear under the water. No sign of life on the back end of Lizzie's boat, Hercules is throwin' up his 'ead as if he knows the danger, Josh is hangin' on to quiet the horse, so Da jumps in. By, it weren't half cold, it 'ad been snowin' on and off all day and we'd all had a dose of 'flu. Lizzie and her 'alf baked husband Freddy appeared at their cabin door when they heard the second splash and surveyed the scene as though it had now't to do with them, til Da pulled the little'un out and shoved him over the side of their boat. Lizzie screamed when she saw it was her Jimmy, she grabbed the babby from Da's 'ands then disappeared back into the cabin wailin' and screechin' while daft Freddy just stood there in a daze. Josh and I rushed to help Da out. The towpath was icy and I slipped and nearly went in meself. Da's boots were full of water and the old flour sack tied to his back was a dead weight. 'E was coughin' and hackin' all night after that. Ma said they was really lucky, if Da hadn't of been there to jump in and pull the babby out, 'E would 'ave drownded, an they'd 'ave been done for murder, like our poor Great Aunt Annie.

Next mornin' Da could 'ardly get out of bed he was so weak and Ma was mad as hell when she found that Lizzie and Freddy had moved off early with never a word of thanks nor nothin'. Da was so bad on the following day we tied up early and he went straight to bed. Then in the night Josh came and woke me to say he was off into town to fetch the doctor as Da's fever was up! I had our Flossie as well as Sammy on Bluebell so they could get a good night's sleep. Our Josh had stayed to help Ma with Da on Isis 'cos he had no strength and could 'ardly stand let alone walk'. I left our two young un's asleep and puttin a shawl over me night dress, walked up the towpath and climbed into the back cabin of Isis. By the light of small oil lamp I could see Ma bathin' Da's head with a rag soaked in water. His breathin' was rough and he kept on coughin'. "Mend the fire lass" Ma had said without looking up and I'd pulled out the coal box from under the back step, "And mash some tea, the kettle won't take long to boil" she had added. We waited and waited for our Josh to come back with the doctor. Eventually when he did come, he was on his own. I could tell by the look on his face that 'E was real mad, if it hadn't of been that Da was so ill I know our Josh would've ranted on. But 'E spoke very quite like as 'E said, "That Bloody Doctor won't come Ma, he said we was dirty boaties and he didn't want to catch nothin'. 'E said we most likely didn't have no money to pay his fee neither. I told him Da was bad but he didn't take no notice. I could've hit him Ma, smug bastard!! "That's enough of that!" Ma had said.

She never liked to hear any of us swearing, not even Da. I could see, even in the dim lamp light, the nerve in the side of our Josh's cheek twitching as it always did when he was angry or upset. His knuckles was white an' all as he clenched his fists, gritting his teeth as he spoke. "He said he'd see Da in his surgery tomorrow if we took him, as long as we had the three shilling fee." I could see Ma's face in the lamp light, she was mad too, but I knew then that Da must be real bad 'cos she never made no fuss, she just said we should all get some sleep and we would take Da first thing in the mornin'.

Next mornin' Da was much worse. Josh and Ma did their best to get him up onto Hercules' back. The horse didn't like anyone on his back, but he seemed to know it was serious 'cos he didn't buck nor fidget. I stayed with the little'uns and the boats. There was nothin' we could do so I spent the time cleanin out both cabins. When I saw our Josh come back up the towpath, leading Hercules some hours later I was real scared. The fact that he was on his own meant that Da must be in a bad way.

"Doctor says Da's got the 'monia, says he's real bad and they're sendin' him off to the Sanatorium. Ma's goin' to stay with him there tonight, settle him in like, then I've to go back and fetch her in the mornin – all bein' well."

I knew what 'All bein' well' mean't but I did not want to think about it. and I couldn't find no words to say neither. Josh said we was to stay tied up here for the rest of the day, as it wouldn't do no good if we carried on up the 'Cut' we'd just be further away from the town and Ma would have further to come. 'Cos of Da bein' so ill we hadn't set any snares the night before, so we had no chance of a bit of meat for supper and we'd eaten the last of the rabbit stew two days before. But we had plenty of flour and drippin' as well as tea and sugar and I had kept the fires goin' on both boats all day, so I decided to set about getting' us something to eat for supper. 'Isis' had the larger cooking range and all of our cooking pans on her, so I took the little'uns and we moved onto her. Josh was sure he had seen cows in the field across on the other side of the 'Cut' and tatoes in the field, so he went off to see what he could find. The tow path was slippery with ice as it had been for the past week or two. My little sister Flossie had only soft shoes on so I carried her the short distance up to 'Isis'. Sammy carried the extra buckby can so we would have plenty of clean water for tea. Josh had left Hercules tied up against the hedge for shelter, with his blanket tied 'round his back and neck. We was miles from anywhere, so there was no friendly Inn keeper offering stabling for the night. But if Da was to be off work for a while we would have to watch every penny we had and stabling could cost as much as 5d per night, with or without oats. Both boats were fully laden with earthenware now and we had to get to the City Road before noon on Friday else we wouldn't get unloaded 'til Monday mornin'. That would mean no pay and no food for two whole days! Ma always eaked out the money and food to last each stretch and Da would always make sure we got a return load, even if the Company hadn't laid one on for us.

"I'm hungry!" Flossie whined as soon as I set her down inside the back cabin of 'Isis'

"Well you'll just have to wait 'til our Josh gets back, even he doesn't know what he'll be able to get, with the ground all frozen, diggin' up a few tatoes ain't gonna be easy".

Flossie gave an irritating cry and curled up in the corner of the bed'ole, with her thumb stuck in her mouth, this was her answer to everythin' when she was not happy or not getting' the attention she thought she deserved. I ignored her and set about mashing some tea. Black Tea with plenty of sugar would keep us going 'til I could sort us out with some food. It must have been mid afternoon, but it was beginning to get dark as it does so quickly in winter and the wide open sky threatened yet another heavy frost. I left Sammy sitting opposite the range fiddling with a bit of string. Flossie had fallen asleep and her thumb had dropped from her mouth as I covered her with Ma's old shawl. She was just four years of age, Ma had lost two babies, one still born and the other to whoopping cough at the age of two, so when Flossie came along she was sort of precious and we all 'baby'd' her much more than normal. Ma had been so distracted at the death of the other two it was as though we all had a duty to make sure nothing happened to this little'un. Nothin' was ever said of course, we just did! I pulled me shawl around me shoulders and over me head as I stepped up into the well deck, closing the cabin doors behind me. The gunn'all was already slippery with frost and the cloths that covered the whole length of the cargo were crisp and hard, as I lifted one corner and took out Hercules' nose tin. He had eaten earlier in the day as our Josh always scooped up any remains from the previous night's feed from inn stables in the mornin' before tacking him up and bringin' him back to the boats. Although our Josh prided himself that he was the 'horseman' 'cos he loved animals, I knew he would be tired, after the trek into the village and back with Da and Ma, then having to go and forage for food. So I pulled the bag of oats from off the top of the half empty sack of coal and shook some into the nose tin. I poured in a little fresh water from the 'buckby can' and mashed it together with me hand, then while that was 'steepin' I fetched the 'Dipper' from the back deck. Then lying full length across the frozen tow path and extending the handle as far as I could, while still keeping a firm grip on it, I scooped up the canal water for Hercules to drink. Like most boat horses he preferred to drink canal water than fresh any day! I managed to wedge the 'dipper' in between the branches at the bottom of the hedge, so that Hercules wouldn't kick it over. Then as I was attaching his nose can to his head harness I heard a familiar whistle and looking up could just make out the shape of our Josh coming back across the fields from the direction of the farm we had passed the day before.

"What yer got?" I called out to him as he climbed over the fence and jumped down to the tow path. I knew he had managed to get something for us to eat as his pockets were bulging and he was carrying a small can.

"Hey sis, you wouldn't believe it. Do you remember back last summer when we were working this stretch, an' I helped a man to catch his runaway horse, well would you believe it, he's the farmer! The ground was so hard, I knew there was no way I could dig up even a few little tatoes. So I thought there was now't for it but to go straight up to the farmhouse and see if there was any chores I could do in return for some veggies. And who should come to the door but the very man. He had said at the time, if there was 'owt we needed next time we passed by, to stop at the farmhouse and ask. He were that pleased to see me!"

"Lets get inside before we both freeze to death" I said "I've some tea mashed and you can tell me all about it in the warm!"

Our Josh could see what I'd done for Hercules so he just patted the horse on his neck and pulled his ear a bit then followed me into the back cabin. Flossie was still sleeping in the bed'ole and Sammy had nodded off, on the day bed, the red glow from the range reflecting on his face, but he stirred as soon as I slid back the hatch and climbed in.

"Eeh our Josh, I thought you was never comin' back!" he said as he rubbed his eyes with the back of his grubby hand.

"Move over and let us get in then" I said as I stepped down into the warmth.

Sammy moved over to the bed 'ole beside the sleeping Flossie to make room for Our Josh and me. I poured two mugs of strong stewed tea from the pot and added three spoonfuls of sugar to each. As I did this our Josh put down the small can he had been carrying and began to empty his pockets. There were three large potatoes, two carrots and a big turnip. Well at least we'll eat well tonight I thought, then I set about cleaning them off and cutting them up and all the while our Josh was going on with his story of good luck, having met up with the farmer he had helped earlier in the year.

"He said he wouldn't hear of me doin' any chores and brought me straight into the kitchen. He made me sit at their table and drink tea. His wife poured it for me from a china pot and we had milk in it!"

Josh's face shone in the firelight as he went on with his tale.

"I told them about Da jumping into the Cut to save Lizzie Higgin's babby and how they had just gone off the next mornin' without a word and how the doctor wouldn't come to the boats to see him when he got ill unless we could pay his fee, and how he had to go off to the sanatorium and we didn't know how bad he was, but that he had the fever!"

Josh paused for breath and to take a deep draft of the hot sweet tea.

"The farmer remembered me!" he went on "Said he'd looked out for me when he saw other boats goin' past. I told him we hadn't stopped on this stretch of Cut since then, well not since Mr. Griffiths had got the regular contract carrin' for the potteries ".

Our Josh looked real pleased with himself as he went on.

"Well, he tells his wife to bring some vegetables from the pantry and sent his daughter out to the dairy for a can of milk, can you believe that, just for us! He said I was to take the can back to the farm after milking first thing tomorrow and he would fill it again"

Josh was grinning from ear to ear 'cos 'E was so pleased with his good fortune and so was I. It wasn't every day that a farmer or a 'townie' would pass the time of day with us boaties, let alone give us anything! It was always 'ard to get hold of food, especially on a long haul. We had to eak out the pay from the previous load to last us for our next. And with tolls to pay along the way and every day away from our destination meaning another day without pay, we had to make every penny count. Our Josh and Da would set snares each night, once we was clear of the towns, to catch rabbits for the following night's supper. Ma always bought in vegetables from the market, before we set off, and flour and tea and sugar. Drippin' she would get from the butcher along with the odd bones for stock, if he were feelin' generous. Ma would never pay for bones! She made bread every evening, two loaves, one for supper and the other for breakfast. Not with yeast like the townies eat, but with soda, like her Ma had always made. Sometimes we would have dumplings in the stew, we loved these 'sepcially when she found herbs growin' along the way and she would hang them upside down over the range to dry out. Then she would chop a few up and add them to the dumpling dough – this was heaven! But if the 'run' took longer than Da had expected, or if money was a bit short, then our Josh would look out for 'tatoe' fields or any other veggies growing in the fields alongside the canal. He would dig up one or two from each row, hopein' the farmer wouldn't miss them. We didn't do this all the time, only when we was desperate! Some farmers whose fields were along side of the canal put up boards called 'trespass notices'. We didn't know exactly what they said 'cos none of us could read, but the Company men told us to stay clear of fields with these in, as it meant the farmers didn't like us and would 'prosecute' boaties found on their land. We weren't even to walk across these fields to get to the farm or the village as this was called 'trespass' too. Mostly we tried not to meet up with townies or farmers and we relied on other boaties to tell us how the land lay when we was workin' a new stretch. Boaties stuck together, that was the way of it. Not all boaties was kind though, I can tell you! Oh no we had bad'uns in our community too. Some as spent all their pay in the boozers, even when they had families to keep, men and women alike. Some who would push past you into a lock when you was settin it for your own boats and shout abuse if you tried to argue with them. Da wasn't afraid to take on any man who tried to prevent us from doin' our days work, but he would never take on a drunk. He said you never got nowhere fightin' a drunk! Da liked a drink with his mates like any man, but he never spent all the night in a pub and never more than the one or two he could afford.

Sometimes, 'specially in the summer when the evenings were warm, we would sit out, if we was moored up close to a pub, Da would walk back down the tow path with a glass of stout or porter for Ma and we would all have a sip! Ma never went into a pub herself and she never had to send any one of us to fetch Da out, not like lots of other boaties did, we was very lucky that way.

I had finished making the loaves and put them into the tiny oven to bake, the stew was bubbling away merrily on top and I was getting' out the bowls when we heard foot steps and there was a knock on the cabin side. Our Josh jumped up pushed back the hatch and opened the doors. He climbed up to the well deck and I could hear a man's voice talking low. Then our Josh stepped back down into the cabin and closed the doors

"Well, that was Matthew from the farm, he says his master, Mr Trenchard, the farmer, has to go into Nuneaton tomorrow. He'll call at the sanatorium and bring Ma back with him in the cart if everythin's all right. He told Matthew to say it will save me havin' to go all that way to get Ma and if Da is any worse, well he can bring us back the news".

Neither of us wanted to think that Da would 't get no better, we just gave one another an embarrassed look and I carried on cooking and dishing up our meal.

"Come on Flossie, supper's ready" I said gently shaking the sleeping little body, whilst pulling off the shawl to help her wake up.

Sammy was already stirring and our Josh was helping him to sit close to the drop down table so he could eat his meal without spilling it. I pulled out the strip of wood, which served as a bench between the drop down bed and the day bed. Flossie and I sat on this to eat our meal. She could 't quite reach to the table so I had sat her on a bolster and now her chin just rested on the table. For the first time in ages we sat in silence eating our supper, dipping the warm bread into the greasy gravy and spooning up the hot vegetables. I wasn't a bad cook even though I didn't get much practice, as Ma generally cooked our meals. Now that we had the two boats I usually worked our second boat Bluebell, steering her up behind 'Isis', while our menfolk worked the locks. Our Josh did everything for Hercules our horse, he fed and watered him, tacked him up, checked his feet and shoes, brushed and curried him morning and night, stabled him when we were able and talked to him all day, every day. In fact we said he thought more of Hercules than he did of any of the rest of us. Our Josh said he got more sense out of Hercules than he did any of the rest of us! That was our Josh, he just loved animals!

Back Cabin of N.B. Lupin showing the traditional
boatman's stove and 'drop down' table.

CHAPTER TWO

Dirty Boaties

Now our Sammy was a different kettle of fish altogether! He was into everything, wantin' to know about everything. Every time you looked round, there was our Sammy asking 'Why?' and 'When?' and 'How?' Da said it showed an 'inquirin' mind' I just thought he was irritatin'. Though to give him credit, he always did his share of the work. He might have been small for his age, but that never stopped him from working alongside the rest of us, he could help with the sheetin' up, bow haul the boats, work the locks and was handy with a shovel when we was loadin' or unloadin'. He was quite happy to run errands when we was tied up and would walk miles into the nearest town or village, even after a hard day's graft. But the one thing Sammy didn't like doing, was taking care of Hercules. In fact he was scared stiff of horses altogether. Couldn't blame 'im really as E'd been kicked badly when E was barely four years old. It'd happened one evening when we was mooring up on a Colliery Arm, just off the Coventry Canal, ready to unload next mornin'. Being the Colliery, it was a busy stretch of Cut, and you could have as many as twenty to thirty coal boats all waiting to load or unload at the same time. Well, Da and our Josh was tying up and Ma were down in the cabin seein' to our supper. It was Summer time so the evenings was light and we boat kids took advantage of a bit of play time before bed. I took our Sammy who'd just 'ad his fourth birthday, up the tow path to where the Boswell kids was playin' with a puppy beside their boat. We didn't have no pets as Ma said she had more than enough to do with looking after us, without adding to her chores.

Well Sammy was very taken with this puppy, he picked it up and tried to cuddle it. We all laughed 'til we cried as it wriggled and writhed, first licking Sammy's nose, then biting it, then peeing all down the front of his shirt with excitement. We was so taken with the puppy's antics that we never took no notice when Charlie Hawkins tried to lead his horse past us, to go up to the stables.

"Hey up you kids, get yourselves outta the way now" called Charlie.

It all happened so quick it's hard to remember exactly what happened next, but the Boswell kids started to stand up to make room on the towpath for the horse and Charlie to pass, then one of them slipped and fell against our Sammy. In the crush, he dropped the puppy but was quickly on his feet and running after it. The puppy, with not a brain in its head and no sense of danger, ran between the 'orse's legs. Our Sammy with eyes only for the puppy, lunged after it. The 'orse, suddenly aware of something moving between its legs, got skitish and reared up, hooves flying in all directions. I didn't 'ave no time to think I just rushed forward, caught hold of our Sammy and dragged 'im clear, but not before the 'orse had clobbered him with a flying hoof on the side of his head. What a to-do! There was our Sammy screaming and bleeding all over the place, Maizie Boswell shreiking that the puppy was squashed, Johnny Boswell howling 'cos Maizie was shrieking and Tom Boswell was crying 'cos his dad had just cuffed him! People came running from their boats, Charlie Hawkins was trying to calm the horse and everyone was shoutin' and asking questions all at the same time. All I remember next was sittin' on the ground, cradling our Sammy in me arms and rockin' him backwards and forwards when Ma and Da and our Josh came running up and knelt down beside us. They never shouted at us, Da just lifted our Sammy and gave him over to Ma who wrapped him in her shawl and took him back to our boat. Then Da lifted me up too and looking 'round at the small crowd that had gathered, quietly asked if someone would go and fetch the doctor as quickly as they could. I never saw who it was wot ran off up the towpath to fetch the doctor 'cos I had me head buried in Da's shoulder. I was so scared that our Sammy was dead like the poor little puppy, now lying lifeless in Maizie Boswell's lap.

When we got back to our boat, Ma had laid our Sammy in the bed'ole and was batheing the blood away from the side of his head. Our Josh was stood beside them holdin' a basin of water. I waited for the tirade I expected to come from Ma, directed at me, for my part in this terrible event. But Da sat me down on the side bed and went to the range to push the kettle over the flame to bring it to the boil. Ma carried on batheing Sammy's head and only looked up when Molly Aitkin put her head through the hatch to ask if there was 'owt she could do.

Da looked up gratefully and said "Aye Molly you can come on in and mash some tea" and taking his baccy and pipe from the shelf behind the range, he climbed up to the well deck making room for Molly to step down and into the cabin.

"Eeh lass," she said to me, "You're as white as a sheet" and she laid her hand against me cheek, "And cold with it!" Molly pulled off her shawl and wrapped it around me shoulders.

"You alright there Flo?" she called to Ma.

"Aye, I will be when you get that tea made!"

Nothing more was said until Molly had poured the hot black liquid into our mugs and added three spoonfuls of sugar to each. She handed one out to Da who was sat smoking his pipe on the back deck.

"Here you are Josh" Molly said as she handed our Josh his tea "Give me the bowl lad, you go out with yer Dad an' I'll help yer Ma with little Sammy"

Our Josh looked glad to be relieved of his job, probably he didn't like the sight of all that blood, boys is funny like that. Just then I heard someone outside shouting

"Here come's the Doctor, he's the one from the colliery."

And with that Molly pulled me up from the seat saying "Why don't you come back with me for a bit lass, give the doctor and your Ma some room to breath in".

We passed the doctor who was hurrying along the towpath with his huge black bag and a small crowd following behind, to show him the way! We took our mugs of tea to Molly's boat and her husband Arthur said he would go down to see if my Da needed anything doin'. They had no kids yet, being newly married, so it was just Molly and me in their back cabin. I sat on their day bed, too frightened to speak incase it broke the spell and then I would be for it! I felt I truly deserved punishment for having let this awful accident happen to our Sammy. We drank our tea in silence and I leaned back against the cushions. It was hot inside the cabin, with the stove goin' full belt and it being a warm evening an all. I must have dropped off to sleep 'cos the next thing I know'd was I was wakin' up and it was dark.. Arthur and Molly were just finishing off their supper as I sat up and rubbed me eyes.

"Hello there Jessie lass, we've saved you some pie" said Arthur grinning at me.

I felt I must still be dreaming as they placed a warm dish into my hands filled with meat 'n' tatoe pie and gravy. This was me favourite.

"You've got a bit more colour in you now lass" said Molly seemingly pleased as I tucked into the pie.

I saw Arthur squeeze her hand as he said to her, "She'll be fine now Molly, you'll see".

I had eaten every bit of the wonderful meal when Molly said she would take me back to our boat as it was getting late. Da was still sitting on the back deck smoking his pipe, but he obviously had not been there all the time as he handed Molly three clean plates sayin'.

"Thanks for the grub Molly, that was real kind of you to feed us"

"Oh that's no trouble Joe, you'd do the same for us if it were needed.

"How's the lad now?" Molly said

"Our Sammy's sleepin', but the doctor said he should be fine now except for the bruisin' and the 'con-cushion".

"Oh my brother Tom 'ad 'con-cushion' once when he fell out of a tree, 'E were a bit bruised and 'ad a bad 'ead ache for a few days, but no permanent damage, thank God"

Molly came from a big family and had a brother or sister to suit almost any occasion. Da thanked Molly again and said that he and Ma were real grateful for all she'd done and for looking after me.

"Aw its no trouble" Molly said "And as I said, I know you and Flo would do the same for me and my Arthur, if it were needed"

Then she was gone, back up the towpath to her own boat. I just stood there in the darkness and waited to receive me punishment, which I knew I deserved. Da held out his hand to me saying

"C'mon Jess, its been a long day."

And pulling me across the gunn'all, he lifted me down into the cabin.Ma was preparing for bed but she looked round when I stepped in, she looked tired but she put her arms 'round me and hugged me to her

"Our Sammy's gonna be alright, the doctor says he's got 'con-cushion' but the wound will heal up. He'll have to stay in bed for a week so you'll have to help your Da and Josh with the unloading tomorrow."

"Yes Ma" I said, still not understanding why I wasn't getting a pastein' or at least an earful for letting our Sammy get injured.

Our Josh had gone to his bed in the hold, where he slept on top of a pile of sacks, wrapped in blankets, under the cloths. Which was fine in the summer, it gave the rest of us a bit more room in the cabin. Ma and our Sammy and me in the bed'ole and Da on the floor where he said he could stretch out. In minutes we was all in bed.

"Give us a shout if you need 'owt lass."

Da said as he rolled up his coat and put it under his head for a pillow.

"Aye I will, night luv."Ma said and she put her arm around me.

I was so glad at not being told off and so 'appy that our Sammy was gonna be all right that hot tears slipped from beneath me closed eyelids and ran sideways past me ears and soaked into me hair.

I hardly saw our Sammy the next day as I was kept busy working alongside of Da and our Josh. It was always the same when we was loadin' or unloadin', the job had to be done as quick as possible so we could get underway again. Time spent tied up was time wasted Da allus said. We had been carryin' flour and oats all packed in sacks, for the colliery's company shop, for the last six months, so we knew the routine. All the other boaters was like us, the sooner they was unloaded, they was away, no time to stand around mouthering. There was a large wharf so three or four boats could unload at the same time. Each berth had a contraption with a huge wheel with coggs and a sort of lifting arm with a huge hook on a long chain which you could swing out over the boats, lower it down into the hold and then with a great double handle that two people had to turn, lift the sacks up and out onto the wharf side. Most of the boats was there to collect coal and they got 'priority' and proper 'wharfingers' to load up for them, but we was just delivering supplies to the colliery stores, so we 'ad to do all the unloadin' ourselves. Me first job that day was to help our Josh to strip back the top sheets and to fold them neatly while Da set up the lifting contraption. Then I was sent down into the hull where Our Josh was sortin' out any of the sacks that looked old or damaged 'cos these might split if they was attached to the hook. These he put to one side as they would have to be lifted out by hand, 'cos to lose any part of the cargo would mean we would be 'docked' on our payload. We only got paid for full sacks delivered in good condition. Our Josh and I dragged any of the damaged sacks to the back end of the boat and Da came over to help to unload these first. There was only seven bad'uns and these we laid on the wharf side careful like, so as not to spill the contents. Then Ma came out from the back cabin to help Da to wind the handles, as it was a 'two man job.' Josh and I spent the rest of the mornin' attaching the sacks so Ma and Da could 'winch' them off. We had to work our way up and down the length of 'Isis' hull, as you have to be real careful to unload the cargo evenly, 'cos if you takes too much out from one side or the other the boat could roll right over. I'd seen a boat roll once, at the dock in Limehouse Basin. A big ship was unloading great long lengths of Deal in huge bundles straight into the hold of this barge and the load shifted as it was lowered over the side. The bargee was struggling to get his barge lined up straight against the side of the ship but had 't quite made it when the load was dumped into his hold. Totally unbalanced, the barge just turned on its side, then as the cargo of Deal spilled into the water the boat 'turned turtle'. The Bargee's wife and babby got drowned in that accident 'cos they was trapped in the back cabin when the boat went over.

All mornin' I was thinkin' of our Sammy, curled up in the bed'ole with his head in bandages, so me and Our Josh was very careful with the unloadin'. We'd had no time for breakfast that mornin' for as soon as it was day light, Da sent our Josh off to get Hercules from the stable so we could get in position, ready for unloadin'. The colliery gaffer never allowed the boats to moor up on the wharf over night, so we all had to wait our turn outside of the gates on the other side of the bridge. They was such a big company, they'd built their own arm and wharf so boats could load and unload and not clog up the Cut too much. Fred Minchin ran a Farrier business just outside of the colliery gates, they had big Shires to pull their wagons, so he had plenty of business from them and from the boat horses. He also kept stables for the boat horses and didn't charge us too much for showing the horse neither! There could be as many as thirty boats a day into this wharf specially in the summer when there was more daylight.

Well we finished unloadin' and Ma went into our back cabin to mash tea, while Da went off with the tally clerk to get his ticket signed and to get paid for the load. Our boat belonged to Griffith's Carryin' Company and the 'Gaffer', Mr. Griffiths, had contracts all up and down the Cut to deliver all kinds of cargo. Mostly he would assign certain boats to a particular run and they would stick to that stretch for as long as they worked for him, or as long as the contract lasted. We got our orders from Mr. Griffiths'man Smiffy. He would tell us where and when to pick up the cargo and where to deliver it. As well as wot price they'd all agreed for delivery. He wrote out the laydin' tickets which Ma would put in the 'ticket drawer', over the range in our cabin, for safety. If you lost your 'ticket' you was in real trouble 'cos no one would let you load or unload without a ticket! Da told us that we was our own 'men' once we'd loaded, it was up to us how quickly we got to our unloadin' point and the more loads we took, the more we got paid. On this run, Da would get paid direct, by the tally clerk at the Company shop, for each sack we delivered. Most of this money was then put away for Mr. Griffiths. We would take out an agreed sum for ourselves to live on and to feed Hercules, we also had to pay the tolls out of 'our' money. Not all companies worked this way, some boaties never 'andled no money at all except for their own wages that is. But Da had worked for Mr. Griffiths since he was a lad and would often be sent to sort out other boaties who had got into 'difficulties' or who was just not able to complete a run. Smiffy said that next to him, Da was Mr Griffith's best employee, that we never gave him no trouble.

Ma needed some drippin' and a cake of carbolic soap and as the colliery allowed us boaties to buy stuff from their company shop, our Josh and me was sent with 3d and a small clean sack to fetch the goods. The gaffers at the colliery were very strict, no one was allowed to cross through the wharf where the unloadin' was done unless they was doin' just that. So to get to the Company shop we had to walk across the field at the back and round the whole works. We was hot and sweaty from the mornin's work, but we knew there was a horse trough at the front gates where we could splash our faces and get a drink.

The Sun was high in the sky with not a cloud to be seen as we picked our way through the long grass 'round the high fence, to the main gates and the Company shop. All 'round us towered huge slag heaps like enormous black mountains and massive pit wheels. It was never a place I liked to go, specially with the colliers with their black faces and foul mouths. Even as a child when I didn't really understand what was bein' said I knew they was bein' rude to us boaties. As we came 'round the corner, we saw that some of the 'top' workers was takin' their ten minute break and eatin' their snap beside the trough. I couldn't take me eyes off them, they looked so queer, with their eyes all white and their mouths all pink, gapeing eerily out from their black faces.

"Look out! Boaties!" cried one young lad.

"Dirty Bargee's!" cried another.

Our Josh pulled me closer to him as we walked past."Don't look at 'em Jess" he commanded me in a whisper, as he stepped up his pace. I had to almost run to keep up with him. But I couldn't help gazing at the trough and longed to plunge me hands and face into the cool water.

"Stare Cat, stare cat, wot'cha lookin' at" shouted a girl of about my own age who was now standing beside the trough with arms folded across her chest.

Defiantly I looked away, just as our Josh reached for my hand and cried 'Run for it!'.

I 'eard the first lump of coal, as it landed just behind me heel, then another and another. Luckily they was all bad shots 'cos none of them actually hit us, but we was glad to reach the wooden veranda and quickly climbed the three steps up to the Company Shop door. There was quite a queue of people inside the small cramped shop, they turned to look at us as the little bell over the door rang as we walked in, breathless. Our Josh and me just stood in the line sayin' nothin' until it was our turn to be served. Da had told us that the shop was run by the mine owners and all the workers were paid in what they called 'Tommy Notes', not proper money like we was. This meant they had to buy all their food and clothes and everythin' from the Company Shop. Ma said they 'paid through the nose' for the priviledge. I wasn't sure what she meant, but I knew it wasn't good, just by the way she said it, all dignified like. I gazed 'round the shop as we waited our turn to be served. You couldn't see any part of the ceiling for all the things what was hung up there. Pots and pans, kettles, buckets, and tin baths of all shapes and sizes., oil lamps, coils of rope, picks and shovels, scrubbing boards and even a bicycle! All 'round on the floor, sat forty or fifty large sacks all full of wonderful things like sugar and flour and beans, dried fruit, fresh vegetables and the like. I stood on tiptoe to see behind the counter, there was large marble slab upon which was displayed hams and tongues and cheeses, the like of which we had never tasted! I felt my mouth begin to water as I gazed at all these untried delights that smelt so delicious! They kept the tea in a large chest behind the counter and I watched as Mr. Crabtree, the Company shop manager, with never a smile on his face, not for no one, weighed out 2oz of tea on his shiny brass scales, bein' careful not to give as much as a single leaf over the exact weight. At last it was our turn, and our Josh asked for the drippin' and handed over our small sack to carry it in. We both watched the scales to make sure we got good measure, as townies often tried to swindle us boaties, if we was not watchin'.

"And a small cake of carbolic please" I said as politely as I could.

"That'll be thruppence all together" said Mr Crabtree, lookin' over the top of his spec's and down his long thin nose at us.

Our Josh gave over the three pennies and we turned and walked quickly out of the shop. Once outside, we looked longingly across to the front gates and the horse trough and we was relieved to see that the workers had finished their break and had gone back inside.

"If we're quick we'll get a drink before anyone else comes out" Our Josh said as he pulled me down the steps and across to the trough.

We both stuck our heads into the cool water and coming up coughing and spluttering, we heard,

"Oye, get outta that trough you dirty boaties!"

But never looked back to see. Hand in hand me and our Josh ran for all we was worth round the corner and back across the field to the safety of the Cut and our own kind. I never could understand why they called 'us' dirty when all of them at the colliery was as black as soot!

Da had turned the boat 'round when we got back and we was moored up out on the Cut opposite the bridge, ready to go back the way we'd come. Ma made us sit on the cabin roof to have our cuppa tea and slice of warm bread straight from the oven, 'cos our Sammy was sleepin' and she didn't want him disturbed. The sweet stewed tea tasted so good and so did the bread as Our Josh and me sat together enjoying the moment's rest. We never said nothin' about the colliery kids, Ma and Da had heard it all before, it was one of those things that we boat kids had grown to expect from townies. Not that it was confined to us kids, we had often witnessed bitter scenes outside of shops and public bars when townies had tried to stop our kind from goin' about our business. They always called us 'Dirty' which was fine comin' from the likes of them, who looked no cleaner than us! Da said he wouldn't give a 'tinker's cuss' to live in a filthy town, where the night's slops was thrown out into the streets.

Da had arranged to pick up a small load from the Charity Dock on the following day, so as soon as we had finished our meal we was on our way. Our Josh leadin' Hercules, Da steerin' and Ma down in the cabin with our Sammy. I decided to walk along the towpath with Our Josh, enjoyin' the sense of closeness, following our shared experience at the colliery. We walked along in silence, Our Josh not bein' a great talker like. Now me, I could chat the hind legs off a donkey, or so Ma would say, but I held me tongue so as not to spoil these moments with Our Josh, he was my big brother, my hero. Later that day, as we crossed from the Coventry to the North Oxford canal, the countryside opened out and we could see green fields and low hills for miles and miles. Hercules knew this stretch so well he would just plod on and on. But you couldn't let a horse go on his own down the towpath 'cos the path only went down one side of the Cut. So when you passed a boat comin' the opposite way you had to be there to make sure the lead reins didn't get all tangled up. Our Josh spent most of his day walking beside Hercules our horse, he loved animals and said you could trust them more than people. This hurt me a bit 'cos I loved our Josh and I so much wanted him to trust me!

In no time at all Ma had nursed our Sammy back to health. Although he always had a scar on the side of his head, which made his hair grow funny, we soon forgot all about his accident. But not our Sammy, he lived all his life with a fear of horses. Which was difficult for a lad growing up in the 'Boaties' community in those days, when everyone was workin' horse drawn barges and narra'boats.

CHAPTER THREE

The Day Our Flossie was Born

I'll never forget the day that Our Flossie was born. We was carrin' a load of pig iron and strawboards from Brentford up to the Paddington Arm, not our usual run. Smiffy 'ad come along on 'is bike some weeks before, to where we was moored up, and asked Da if 'E would do a couple of short runs, as a favour to Mr. Griffiths. At the time I never gave it no thought, well I was just turned eleven at the time, but when I did think about it much later, I realised that Mr. Griffiths was doin' 'is best for Ma and Da. 'E 'ad always been good to us, but then Da was one of 'is best employees, Smiffy 'ad allus said so. By askin' Da to change from 'is reg'lar run to 'do a couple of short runs' it meant that life would be a bit easier for Ma, 'cos 'er time was near and we wouldn't be too from help, should she need any during 'er 'lyin' in'.

Everyone on the Cut knew that Ma 'ad lost two babies, one still born and the other, a beautiful baby boy we called Issac, to the 'oopin cough when 'E was just eighteen months old. We 'ad all been upset for months after, but Ma took it real 'ard. She 'ad nursed little Issac for weeks, three times the doctor 'ad come out from the town to give our little brother medicine from a brown bottle, but 'E didn't get no better. His little body was racked with the coughin' and whenever that stopped 'E was so exhausted, he just lay on the 'drop down' 'ardly breathin'. Ma would get so scared that she'd 'ave to pick 'im up again to make sure 'E was still alive and that would start 'im off coughing all over again.

Then one mornin' we woke up and there was no more coughin', there was a strange silence and I couldn't think what it was. Then I 'eard Ma sobbing into 'er pillow in the bed 'ole. Da went to get our Josh up, to send 'im to fetch the doctor out again. But it weren't no use, little Issac were gone. We 'ad to 'ave a buryin' for 'im and Da asked one of the other boaties, Albert Wheeler, to knock up a bit of a coffin for our little brother. Albert was 'andy with an 'ammer and nails and people often got 'im to make up bits of furniture, stools, coal boxes and the like.

Molly Aitkin brought round a beautiful nightgown to dress 'im in. She said it was new and that she'd been savin' it for when she and Arthur 'ad children, but that she would like our little Issac to wear it for 'is buryin'. Ma washed out the woollen shawl that Issac 'ad been given before 'E was born by Old Ma Thomas, who lived in a cottage beside the Cut near Stoke Bruerne. Ma said she was a seamstress, she made shirts and blouses and bonnets and such, for us boaties. We 'ad gone to see 'er before our little brother Issac was born and Ma 'ad got 'er to make two baby nightgowns and a new smock for me, out of a white cotton sheet what Ma bought cheap at a market just off the City Road. When we called back on our return journey to collect them, Ma Thomas gave Ma the shawl as a present for the 'new 'un'. She 'ad crocheted it 'erself. Ma was so pleased, she said she'd wanted to make one, but with all the work she'd just never got round to it. I asked Old Ma Thomas to teach me how to crochet and she laughed and said that if we ever tied up along side 'er cottage for long enough, she would. And now Ma wanted to wrap our little Issac in the shawl when she laid 'im in 'is little wooden box that Albert Wheeler 'ad made. We 'ad to do the buryin' quick as none of the boaties could afford to stay tied up for too long, but they all wanted to come to 'show their respects'. I didn't know what that meant exactly then, but that's what everyone said as they gathered on the towpath outside of our boat the next mornin'. Da 'ad got up early, wakened our Josh from 'is bed under the cloths and 'ad gone off by 'imself down the towpath, I watched 'im through the gap between the two cabin doors, 'is 'ands deep in 'is pockets and 'is cap pulled down around 'is ears. We didn't know where 'E was goin', 'E didn't say. Ma was speakin' quietly and I could tell she was real upset 'cos she 'ad to keep wipein' 'er cheeks with the back of 'er 'and. I got our Sammy up and dressed while Ma kept fussin' with little Issac as 'E lay lifeless in 'is wooden box at the bottom of the 'drop down'. She 'ad dressed 'im in the pure white nightgown and wrapped 'im in the fluffy woollen shawl. When Da came back 'E was carryin' a tiny bunch of primroses. 'E looked so stiff and awkward, this big man with 'is iron 'ard 'ands, clutching a tiny bunch of wild flowers. That was one of the few times I ever saw Da shed a tear and it broke me heart!

There was a crowd of boaties all standin' on the towpath beside our boat, many 'ad only tied up that mornin'. Someone must've told them about our little Issac, dyin' of the 'oopin' cough, and they 'ad stopped off on their way up or down the Cut. Joe Cotter 'elped Da out of our cabin with Issac's little wooden box. The lid 'ad not been nailed down at that time and all the boaties came up one at a time, the men mostly doffed their caps and the women touched the side of 'is cold little face. No one spoke. Then when everyone 'ad 'paid their respects' Albert Wheeler stepped up to nail the lid in place. Da took the 'ammer and nails from 'im and did the job 'imself, not looking at anyone's face and even when Ma began to sob loudly, 'E just carried on. Mary Ann Cotter came up alongside of Ma, put 'er arm 'round 'er and gave 'er a white lace edged 'ankerchief. I felt real sad as we all walked in silence the two miles behind Da, carrin' our Issac to the church in the nearby village. The weather 'ad been bad, rain and snow for weeks, but I remember thinkin' 'ow good it was of the Sun to take the trouble to 'pop' 'is 'ead out of the clouds and shine down on us on the day we took our little brother Issac for 'is buryin'.

* * * * * *

Well, as I was sayin', I can remember the day our Flossie was born. It was hot and sunny, as it 'ad been for weeks. The ground was good an 'ard and the water level in the Cut was well down! This meant 'ard work for Hercules our 'orse and much slower goin' as the fully laden boat would sometimes scrape the bottom of the Cut in places where it was real shallow. We 'ad actually run aground the day before and Da 'ad to use our long wooden pole to get us movin' again. Hercules was knackered that night when we unhitched 'im and tied 'im to a tree beside the towpath. There was an 'ole in the hedge and it was just big enough for 'im to shove 'is nose through to nibble the sweet fresh clover hay growin' in the field beyond.

Ma was findin' it 'ard goin' in all the heat. She 'ad told us she was near 'er time and our Josh who was thirteen at the time and me, I was just eleven, knew full well what that meant. Da 'ad told us that as soon as Ma's pains started 'E would stop the boat, unhitch Hercules and send our Josh on the 'orses back into the village to fetch Mrs Stewart the midwife. Da 'ad wanted to stay tied up close to the village for a couple of days, but Ma said we would lose too much money if we missed a run altogether. Besides which, Mr. Griffiths was relyin' on us and 'E 'ad allus been good to us, so Ma was not about to let 'im down. We knew this was just 'er way of tellin' Da that she didn't want no fuss makin'. But me and our Josh knew that Ma and Da wanted everythin' to go right with this baby real bad, and that Da was doin' all 'E could to make things easier for Ma.

All of us kids 'ad extra chores to do, to save Ma's strength. Not that we minded, oh no, all three of us knew we was so lucky to 'ave a Ma and Da who looked after us and who didn't spend all their time and money in the boozer, like some poor souls we know'd.We 'ad been just comin' up to a wide stretch in the canal when Ma puts 'er 'ead out of the cabin door 'ole and asked Da real quiet like, if 'E was able to tie up soon. Da was steerin', our Sammy and our Josh was walkin' up the towpath behind Hercules. I was sittin' on the cabin top, enjoyin' the sunshine, polishin' up the brass bands on our chimney, as it was one of the few days in the year when Ma 'ad let the fire go out, as the weather was so hot!

Da looked ahead of us up the Cut and said "Are you all right for ten minutes or so? I'd like to get us nearer to Tubney's bridge, if you can hang on Flo".

"I'm fine Joe, I just thought I'd better give you a bit of a warnin' like, that's all" Ma said and disappeared back inside the cabin, as we carried on up the Cut for a bit.

Then just as we rounded the bend and Tubney's bridge came into sight Da said to me "I think we'll all be needin' a cuppa tea very soon Jess,"

So with that, I climbed down from the cabin top and stepped down into the darkness of the back cabin. Ma 'ad 'dropped the bed and was lyin' in the bed 'ole on top of the covers.

"You alright Ma?" I asked, adjusting me eyes to the cabin's dimness after the bright sunlight outside.

"Aye lass, I was just 'avin' a bit of a rest, you makin' a brew?"

"Yes Ma" I replied "We're comin' up to Tubney's now and Da sent me down to put the kettle on."

"Good girl" Ma said, but then she clutched 'er stomach and turned 'er 'ead to the cabin wall, makin' a sort of whining noise in 'er throat.

The stove 'avin' been 'let out' now 'ad to be lit, but it wouldn't take too long as Ma 'ad cleaned it all out inside and laid in the small bits of kindling wood. I reached into the coal box under the back step and took out a few lumps of coal which I arranged carefully on top of the wood. I was just reachin' for the matches from the shelf above me 'ead when I 'eard Ma again makin' sort of moanin' sounds. She was never a one to complain when she was feelin' poorly, but I wasn't surprised neither 'cos I knew this birthin' thing was a painful business. I couldn't remember our Sammy bein' born, I'd only been about four then, but I certainly remembered the 'still born' baby, that 'ad gone on for days and poor Ma was wore out with tryin' to birth it. We didn't have no money for hospitals or maternity 'omes so she just had to stay on our boat. I remember bein' so afraid, I thought she were goin' to die! I think Da was scared too, but 'E kept on tellin' us that she'd be all right once the baby came out. We'd been on a different run then, somewhere up north, and Old Ma Gilbey had been the only sort of midwife we could get to come to the boat – witch Da 'ad called 'er!. He blamed 'er for the fact that the baby 'ad been born dead, said it were the foul potions she 'ad given to Ma when the terrible pains 'ad gone on for days and days. So when I realisied that Ma's pains 'ad started this time, I was a bit fearful and 'oped everythin' would turn out right this time. I concentrated on lighting the fire as I felt the boat coming to a halt, I could hear Da shouting to our Josh to untie the 'orse as I poked the kindling sticks and blew hard into the stove through the grill at the front. Then when it began to catch nicely, I put on more lumps of coal and opened the damper.

Because we'd only been doing short runs this last few weeks we 'ad plenty of fresh water in our buckby cans. I filled the large copper kettle which 'lived' its entire life on top of the stove, removed the hob ring and pushed the kettle over the flames, then I heard Ma let out another sort of moan, but this time it was much louder.

"Ma, you all right?" I asked stupidly "Shall I get Da?"

"No lass, I'm fine" she replied, "Wait til we're all tied up. You get on and mash the tea now"

I pulled down the drop table and took out our tin mugs, then putting two heaped spoonsful of sugar in each. I sat on the side bed and pushed open one door so I could look out to the well deck and beyond. I heard Ma again and turned to see her draw up her knees tight to her stomach as she lay in the bed 'ole. I wanted to go and jump off the boat and run far away so I wouldn't 'ave to stand by and see Ma go through this awful pain. It didn't seem right to me............I didn't understand.

The kettle seemed to be taking a lifetime to boil. Normally we would 'ave the stove lit all day, every day and the kettle sittin' on top, would never be far from boilin'. But what with the heatwave, Ma had complained that she was too hot in the cabin and it was sappin' all 'er strength, so Da had let the fire go out the night before and we'd been drinking cold water ever since. Not that I minded drinking water, especially as we 'ad plenty 'cos we could fill up the buckby cans every other day on this run. I heard Ma breathing in and out heavily, as though it were gonna be 'er last breath. She seemed to hold onto it for ages before she let it out again and when she did it came out like a sort of growl. I didn't want to annoy 'er by askin' if she were 'alright' again, but I wished that Da would come inside 'cos he'd know what to do. I busied meself with getting' out the teapot and mashin' the tea, carefully countin' out the right number of spoonfuls of the precious leaves and pouring on boiling water. Ma allus said the secret of a good cuppa was makin' sure the water was freshly boiled when you poured it over the tea leaves.

The tea made, I glanced across at Ma who was curled up in a tight little ball, her breathing sounded real rough and she 'growled' a few more times. Just when I was feelin' real scared the cabin door behind me opened and Da stepped down into the cabin.

"How is it Flo?" he asked as he crossed to the bed 'ole and gently smoothed Ma's brow.

"I think ….this one's….. in a hurry…. t-to get born". Ma gasped between sharp intakes of breath.

"I've sent our Josh to fetch Mrs Stewart" Da said as he took hold of Ma's hand and began rubbing it gently. "What can I do for you?" He said again, lookin' all worried like.

"There's clean sheets and things in there" Ma said indicating the cupboard over the bed 'ole. "Get Jessie to boil up the kettle again, and if that's my tea, help me up Joe, me mouth's as dry as a bone!"

I didn't need any tellin' I was on me way out of the back doors while Da helped Ma to sort of sit up and drink some tea. I filled the kettle up from the buckby can and was on me way back into the cabin when Ma let out a muffled scream in the back of her throat. I banged the kettle back onto the stove and shot Da a look of pure panic!

"Take Sammy out a cuppa tea Jess, then keep a look out for our Josh comin' back with Mrs Stewart." He said.

Glad to escape I quickly did as I was told. Sammy was leaning over the bridge a few yards further up the Cut. He was busy throwing stones and watching them 'plop' into the water below when I came up beside him.

"Is it all over then?" he asked nervously.

"No Sammy, the midwife's not come yet" I replied "Though I think she

oughtta get 'ere pretty soon!".

When the other two babies had started to be born it had been in the middle of the night and though we'd been moored a long way from the nearest village, ther'd been other boaties tied up alongside of us, so there was plenty of help from the other boatwomen, most of whom knew exactly what had to be done, or even if they didn't, they'd 'ave an opinion on it. Ma should 'ave let Da lay over and tie up for a couple of days I thought, then we'd have been close to the midwife and anyone else who could help. And now, here we was, miles from anywhere and not another boat in sight!

Sammy didn't seem to share my worries, he just carried on dropping stones over the side of the bridge parapet and watching them plop into the water. Irritated by his apparent lack of concern and because I couldn't think of anything else to do, I walked slowly back to the cabin of our boat 'Isis'. As I climbed back into the cabin I could see that Da had got Ma into her night gown and she was resting back against the pillows.

"Here Jessie, come and bathe yer Ma's forehead with this damp cloth, while I sort out these sheets" he said.

I tried to look cheerful as I approached the bed 'ole to let Ma know I thought everything was fine, but I don't think it worked 'cos Ma said

"It's alright Jess, don't look so worried, its just yer new baby brother or sister wantin' to be born"

"I know Ma" I replied, trying to sound grown up.

Then another pain gripped her and she screwed herself up into a ball again and let out such a cry! Da pushed me to one side as he bent over her anxiously trying to scoop her up into his arms.

"It's coming Joe!" she gasped "It's coming now!" She let out another cry then lay back groaning and clutching her stomach.

Da stood up and pulled me gently towards the cabin doors, "Run along the tow path Jess and see if you can see our Josh coming with the midwife".

I didn't want to leave Ma now, but I knew better than to argue, so I quickly climbed out of the boat and ran off in the direction of the village.

It must have been about half an hour later when we all arrived back at the boat. Our Josh had gone twice 'round the village before he eventually found Mrs. Stewart, who had delivered two other babies that day and was making her way back home when he found her. Hercules was not an 'orse for riding, our Josh was the only one who could ever get up on 'is back. Not that it would 'ave made any difference, Mrs. Stewart was not a woman for riding 'orses!!, she went everywhere on 'er bicycle. However as luck would 'ave it, it 'ad a puncture that day so they 'ad walked the two miles across the fields when I caught up with them. Our Sammy 'ad seen me running off and 'ad followed me down the towpath. We was nearly into the village, all hot and sweaty from the running when we spotted them coming through a gate on the opposite side of the Cut.

"Better hurry up" I called out to our Josh and the midwife, "Ma says its nearly there!"

Despite my chiding , progress back to our boat was slow and I knew we were too late to help Ma with the birthing when I heard the baby's crying as we turned off the bridge and onto the path that ran alongside our boat. Mrs. Stewart was the first to go into the cabin and she immediately threw Da out! We all went to sit in the shade under a huge oak tree with out flung leafy branches, where our Josh was tying Hercules. Da put his arms awkwardly round Sammy and me but I knew everthin' was alright 'cos he was smiling as he said

"You've got a new baby sister!"

"Can we go and see her?" I ventured to ask.

"Probably not just yet, well not 'til Mrs. Stewart says so".

Now it was my turn to smile, seeing Da's face look all kind of helpless, 'E wasn't used to not being in charge. Fancy Mrs. Stewart throwing Da off his own boat! and I smiled again. We must have sat there in the shade for quite a while. I lay back listening to Hercules munching the long sweet grass and smelling the strong scent of tobacco from Da's pipe as he sat with his back against the tree, contentedly drawing in and puffing out the pungent smoke. Then at last he said

" Go and pop yer head through the door Jess and ask when we can all come in to see yer Ma and the baby".

I didn't need asking twice, I was up and runnin' to the boat like a dog after a rabbit. Mrs. Stewart gave me an imperious look as I stepped into the well deck, then relented and said that as I was a daughter, I could come inside and make some tea, but the menfolk would have to stay outside until Ma and the new baby were settled...... whatever that meant.

I felt very important as I carried out my given task. Onto the fire went more coal and back went the kettle over the flames. I tried to sneak a little look past Mrs. Stewart, as I hurriedly prepared the tea things. The midwife was fussing over the pillows and covers and the little white bundle lying in Ma's arms as she sat propped up, looking exhausted in the bed 'ole. I plucked up the courage to approach the bed once the tea was mashed, only to be sent away with a bowl full of blood stained water with orders to 'get rid of this!'. I took the bowl and struggled to lift it up onto the back step. Da, who must have been watching the back doors like a hawk, came striding over and lifted the bowl from my hands.

"Every thing alright Jess?" he asked as he poured the contents of the bowl into the Cut then leaned over and rinsed it out with canal water.

"Yes, fine Da" I replies "I've made another brew".

"Good lass" Da said and sort of patted the top of me 'ead. "D'you want to pass it out and we'll drink it in the shade?"

I thought this was very strange behaviour for my Da, asking me if I'd like to do this and that, all polite like. Normally he'd just say do this or do that, not in a nasty way, but he just seemed to be acting strange. I supposed it was 'cos of Mrs. Stewart and his not being allowed into our back cabin until she said so. It also felt very strange to be tied up in the middle of a hot sunny day, doin' nothin' it was sort of like a holiday, like Christmas in the middle of the summer! When finally Mrs. Stewart decided that Ma and the new baby could be left to the mercy of their family, she stood on the back deck and handed Da what looked like a bundle of stained rags

"I suggest you burn these Mr. Ridley as the foxes will only dig them up if you try burying them. But not on the boat, the fumes won't do your wife or the baby any good at all. There's no more for me to do here, you have a healthy child and your good lady has paid me my fee, so I'll be off". And with that she climbed over the gunn'all, and was away up the towpath and over the bridge without a backward glance.

I felt real important like, as I made sure Ma was comfortable and ready to receive the rest of the family..... self appointed matron that was me, or at least that's what Da said over the next few days.

"Can we come in now and see?" it was Sammy calling from outside.

Ma smiled at me and nodded and the whole family crowded into the 8ft x 6ft space we all knew as home, the back cabin of Isis. We gazed in awe at the tiny red faced bundle swathed in clean white sheets and shawl, lying in Ma's arms.

"Can I hold her?" I asked tentatively

"What's 'er name?" Sammy demanded to know

"You alright Ma?" our Josh inquired

"Now yer Ma's going to need lots of rest" Da said, as he sat down on the

drop-down bed, "So you'll all have to do a bit more to make sure she gets it."

We all nodded in agreement, non of us wantin' to see Ma go down hill as she had after the death of little Issac. We were all 'willing' this baby to live and be healthy and for Ma to get back to her usual robust health.

"So what are we gonna call it?"

It was Sammy again, ever impatient to have his questions answered satisfactorily. Ma looked at Da

"I'd like to call her Florence after you Ma" he said quietly.

Ma reached out her hand and took Da's in hers and they sat for a moment just lookin' at each other. I wanted to stay like that forever, it was so special, you could sort of taste the happiness in their faces, I wanted to draw it or bottle it up and keep it forever , moments like that didn't happen often. Years later when I looked back on that scene, it would always bring a lump to me throat and a tear to me eye. I never heard Ma and Da tell one another that they was loved, but you only 'ad to look at 'em now to know they was. Life was 'ard for all of us in them days and there was rarely time for shows of affection, but moments like these lasted a lifetime.

"You look tired Flo" Da said at last as he patted the back of her hand. "Why don't you have a little nap while our little Florence here is asleep, she'll be awake soon enough, demanding to be fed, then we'll all have our hands full".

Ma smiled weakly and Da helped her to tuck the little bundle, that was our new baby sister, beside her in the bed. Ma sighed and laying back on her pillows closed her eyes. Da took the boys off to help him make a bonfire, while I set to and peeled some vegetables. Josh had caught a rabbit in one of his snares the night before, skinned and cleaned it for our supper. And as I added the vegetables to the stew pot, I thought strangely, how much a skinned rabbit looks like a new born baby!

The Bed 'Ole on the N.B. Lupin.

CHAPTER FOUR

Family Life.

Grey light filtered through the gaps in the door 'ole and I lay in the darkness listening to the sound of my family sleeping. I couldn't quite see 'is face, but I knew 'E was lyin' on 'is back, as 'is rhythmic snoring told me that 'E at least, was still fast asleep. Da was lyin' wrapped in a blanket, full out on the floor, with 'is short coat rolled up for a pillow under 'is 'ead, , right up close to the stove and 'is feet under the drop down bed. Da had mostly slept on the floor of our back cabin for as long as I remember, well at least ever since our Sammy grew too big to sleep between 'im and Ma in the 'drop down'. In them days it 'ad been our Josh who slept on the floor and me on the narrow side bed which ran along under the gunn'al, opposite the stove. We never really thought about it as being cramped like, it were just the way it was! We was no different from all the other boatie families we knew, and better off than some I could mention! But now 'E were eleven, it were our Sammy what slept on the side bed and our Josh had made his self up a bed in the hold. 'E said 'E was good an' comfortable there, that 'E could stretch out and snore as much as 'E liked and not risk an elbow in the ribs! I knew this were probably true when the weather weren't too bad an' dependin' on the cargo we was carrin', 'cos sacks of sugar and flour would make a good soft bed to lie on. But in the winter, even when the hold were all sheeted up an' lashed down good and tight, I knew it must be as cold as ice, for there weren't no stove to keep 'im warm, just the two blankets 'E wrapped 'is self in.

I turned onto me back, slowly like and stretched me legs out full length in the bed'ole, not wantin' to disturb our Flossie who was sleepin', all curled up in a ball with 'er thumb stuck in 'er mouth, 'er blond curls spread across the bolster. How could a small four year old child look so much like and angel while she was asleep and create such havoc when awake. There was times when I wished we could go back to before she were born, when the five of us 'ad lived together without no arguments. It seemed to me that since our Flossie 'ad come along we 'ad never 'ad a day's peace, she was completely spoiled!

In the dim light I could just make out the figure of Ma lyin' on 'er side with 'er back against the cabin wall on the other side of our Flossie. 'Er thick plaited hair laid across 'er shoulder with one hand under 'er cheek and the other resting lightly on our Flossie's shoulder. When had she begun to look so old and tired I wondered. I couldn't really say how old she was, she was just my Ma. We never made much fuss about birthdays and such, well only for the little'uns. Life was tough, every day on the move, up and down the 'Cut,' loadin' unloadin' the cargo, cookin' cleanin' and washin', just keepin' ourselves clean and fed was 'ard enough. But to be honest, we never really thought about any of it, it was just our way of life.

Just then Da stopped snoring and 'is breath became lighter, as I turned me 'ead towards the stove, 'E began to sit up.

"Give the fire a poke Da an I'll make us a brew" I said without moving.

"Aye Lass" 'E replied as 'E got to 'is knees and opened up the damper on the stove, then reachin' into the coal box under the back step, 'E took out some small lumps of coal, then taking a poker from beside the stove 'E began to carefully rake out the ashes under the still hot embers. We allus 'banked up' the stove overnight, so it kept us nice and warm and it didn't take too long to get it going again in the mornin'. Da then lifted off the hob ring and pushed the large copper kettle over the hole through which bright yellow flames had now begun to flicker.

I swung me legs over the side of the bed as I pulled me shawl around me shoulders, over me nightgown. As I slipped out of the bed and put me feet onto the wooden floor boards, I could feel the warmth, from where Da had layed all night. 'E was just struggling into 'is coat and reachin' for 'is pipe and baccy

"Kettles on" 'E said over 'is shoulder and with that 'E pushed open the two back doors and stepped up into the well deck. Bright white light and a blast of icy wind whipped through the gaping door'ole and almost took me breath away. I stood blinking in the bright light and pulled me shawl tight up around me neck.

"By we've 'ad a frost last night" Da said "Get yerself dressed lass, while I go and give our Josh a shout" and with that 'E pushed the two back doors together and immediately the cabin was plunged once more into darkness. I reached under the blankets and pulled out me clothes what I'd placed there the night before to keep 'em warm. Then pulling me nightgown over me head I quickly replaced it with two petticoats, me heavy cotton blouse, and long blue serge skirt. Over this I tied a clean apron and again pulled me shawl tightly round me shoulders.As I waited for the kettle to come to the boil I unbraided me hair and ran a comb through it. Then satisfied that I had removed all the tangles, I rebraided it in one long plait which hung down me back to me waist. Just then I heard movement behind me,

"Move over Jess and let me get outta this bed" It was Ma, now fully awake and ready to start the day. At the same time hot water began to splutter from the kettle's spout and I quickly pulled it clear of the flames and poured the boiling liquid onto the dry tea leaves in the large enamel teapot.

"Real heavy frost last night Ma" I said over me shoulder as I stirred up the strong black brew.

"Aye I'm not surprised, you could see every star in that sky a'fore we went to bed" Ma replied as she wasted no time in getting into her clothes

"Give our Sammy a dig, then we can get this lot put away" Ma said and indicated to the bed and its bedding.

I pulled the blanket away from Sammy's head at the same time pushing one of the cabin doors open ajar, immediately a strong blast of icy morning air came in with the bright morning light.

"Aw our Jess, let me be" Sammy protested as he pulled the blanket back over 'is 'ead. 'E was a strange one was our Sammy; at night 'E never wanted to go to bed, then in the mornin' 'E never wanted to get up!

"C'mon Sammy, get yerself outta there!" Ma's voice sounded sharp behind me. Our Sammy knew it was useless to argue with Ma, even though he'd 'ave given me enough lip, 'ad she not been there.

"Just a bit longer" 'E ventured recklessly

"Sammy, don't let me 'ave to tell you twice............."

"Aw Ma, it's cold............" He began to complain.

"The sooner you starts movin' the sooner you'll get warm Sammy, now move!" And with that Ma whipped the blanket off as she spoke. "Now lets 'ave no more nonsense from you, young fellow, me lad!"

"How come our Flossie gets to stay in bed!" he grumbled as 'E struggled into 'is clothes.

"You leave Flossie alone, she's only a bairn" Ma said as she picked up one end of the blanket and motioned for me to pick up the other. Together we folded all the blankets, save one, into a neat bundle which Ma then stowed away into the bed'ole. Then wrapping the still sleeping Flossie in the remaining blanket, Ma gently slid 'er up onto the bolster while I pulled out the mattress from beneath 'er, rolled it up and stowed it away in the drop down.

Just then I heard Da and our Josh climbing over the gunn'all, so I went to pour hot tea into our mugs and stirred in the sugar.

"Just what we need!" Da said as he took the two mugs I handed out through the door'ole. He and our Josh stood in the well deck, hands clasped around the steaming mugs, savouring the warmth. I could see their breath coming out in puffs of steam as they stood together discussing the day ahead. I looked round to where Ma was still fussing over our Flossie, tucking the blanket around the sleeping figure of my little sister. And pulling the 'modesty' curtain across the bed'ole she said "Let her sleep." And I had to admit it seemed like a very good idea to me too. For as soon as Flossie awoke she would be fussin' and frettin', makin' sure she had everyone's undivided attention, then whining and complaining if she discovered that she didn't actually have it.

I reached into the cupboard and taking out half a loaf of bread I began to cut it into thick slices. These I spread with butter from a small wooden tub. We each had a slice with our tea every mornin' before the day's work began. I handed them out to Da and me brothers, then as I took a bite of my own I bent down and reached under the stove to pull out me boots. Several pairs of thick hand knitted woollen socks were hanging on the brass rail over the stove. I grabbed a pair and in between sips of tea and bites of bread I pulled them on over my now very cold feet, the warmth was pure luxury.

"You'll need an extra pair of those for yer 'ands" Ma said as she handed me an old blanket which she'd cut in half crossways, to wrap over the top of me crocheted shawl. Breakfast over and now suitably clad for the cold winter morning, I left Ma to clear away and stepped up to join Da and our Josh on the back deck. Everywhere I looked was sparkling with thick frost. The grass felt stiff and crunchy under foot and the ground iron hard as I jumped down from the gunn'all and landed on the towpath, just managing to stop meself from slipping between the boat and the bank. The trees and bushes had taken on a strangely magical appearance, each leaf and branch all glittering like crystal in the early morning sunlight. Mist was rising from the water in the Cut and this seemed to mingle with the steam and hot breath coming from Hercules and our Josh as they seemed to step right out from the Sun as the two of them walked from the stables, down the towpath towards our boat. The hedgerows too where covered in glistening spiders webs, the fine filigree seemingly spun by pure magic overnight. The surrounding fields were completely white and shining brightly and it seemed almost unreal as I stood there feeling that me and my family were the only beings alive that morning.

Our Josh was hitching Hercules to the lead rein and soon I was untying the ropes and we were on our way once more. Da was steering from inside the two back cabin doors and our Sammy was sat on the cabin roof beside him with his legs dangling down through the open hatch, into the cabin. Ma's voice carried across the still mornin' air and from inside the cabin, I could hear her as she tried to sooth the now fully wakened grizzling Flossie! This was good enough reason for me to walk up alongside of our Josh and Hercules, rather than getting back on board our boat. Besides which, I loved to be close to my big brother, even if he didn't have much to say to me.

We walked along the deserted tow path in companionable silence for nearly two hours before we came to the day's first set of locks. We was coming off the 'summit' so we was going down in all the locks. Fortunately for us, another boat had passed us goin' in the opposite direction late last night, as we was tyin' up and nothin' had passed us since so we 'ad a good road as the locks was set in our favour. I was very glad of the extra pair of socks, now covering me hands, as I attached the lock key to the gate paddles. The heavy frost had not abated and the woollen socks stuck firmly to the iron gate as I wound up the paddle with all me might. Me boots slipped on the iron hard ground as I put all me weight against the great wooden gate and fought to heave it open.

All day we worked our way up the Cut in the freezing cold, stopping only to fill or empty the locks and just long enough to drink the many mugs of hot sweet tea Ma kept us supplied with.

"Want to steer for a bit Jess?" Da had called out to me at one of the locks, but I knew that steerin' the boat, standing inside the back cabin doors, even with the streams of warmth coming up from the stove inside the cabin, wouldn't fill me with the same warmth I felt from just bein' close to our Josh.

"It's alright Da" I replied "I'm quite happy workin' the locks with Josh".

And so we continued on for the rest of that short winter's day. The temperature never rose above freezing and as the darkness threatened in the late afternoon, it found us still a day's journey from our destination. We had passed few other boats on the way and the Cut remained eerily silent as we tied up. From inside the cabin the delicious smell of rabbit stew invaded our nostrils and my mouth was watering mercilessly as I finished off my chores for the day, before stepping down into the cosy warm cabin. Light from the fire and the oil lamp lit up everyone's face as we crowded round the tiny drop down table and waited for Ma to dish up our supper. The tantalising smell wafting from the huge enamel pot simmering on the stove. I pulled off me boots, tucking them under the shelf beside the stove, where they'd stay nice and warm for the mornin'

"Here Joe, Josh, take these plates, they're hot mind!" Ma passed round our plates piled high with steaming stew and none of us needed tellin' to get it down us, I can tell you! All you could hear was the scrap of spoons on our tin plates as we savoured each delicious mouthful.

"You got room for a bit more Joe?" and Da laughed as he passed his plate back for a second helping

"Ever known me to refuse more of yer stew Flo?"

"Not so as I can remember!" she replied and covered his plate once again with the steamy broth.

"Any more dumplin's Ma?" it was our Josh this time with his plate held out.

"I s'pect I could find an odd one" Ma laughed as she spooned up more stew from the pot on the stove. Then satisfied that 'the men' had all been given their fill, she ladled one last spoonful each onto the rest of our family's plates. We all ate on in silence until,

"Maaaaaaaaaaaaaaaaaaaaa!" it was our Flossie.

"What's the matter pet?" Ma inquired.

"It's Our Sammy, 'e's pinchin' me!" my spoiled little sister wailed.

"Sammy, leave 'er alone!" Da commanded.

"I never touched 'er" Sammy retorted

"'E did Ma" Flossie continued whining "'E did, 'E pinched me leg!"

I stood up and lifted Flossie from her place at the table and sat her beside me in an effort to save our Sammy from further trouble.

"Maaaaaaaaaaaaaaaaaaaaaaa!", Flossie cried out again "Our Jessie's interferin' again!"

"Look, both of you, get on an eat yer supper and leave Flossie alone"Ma said sharply.

"I was only tryin' to calm 'er down" I replied indignantly.

"That's enough from you Jess." Ma was getting cross now, and I was just about to proclaim my innocence yet again when I felt a heavy boot coming down hard on top of my bare foot and looking up I caught sight of our Josh's face lookin' very serious at me. He was slowly shakin' 'is 'ead from side to side and so I bit me tongue. But not before hot tears stung the back of me eyes and I had to turn away from our Josh's gaze. We all got blamed for doin' or sayin' things to Flossie which were just not true. That child was so spoiled, she always got her own way! I had to swallow down the injustice and the lump in me throat along with the remainder of me supper.

When we had all finished I began to clear away and taking the 'dipper' from off it's hook over the stove, I steeped the plates in hot water poured from the kettle.

"Here Sammy, you can dry" I said as I pushed a clean dish rag into his hands.

"Can't I wash!" he exclaimed, "I always 'ave to to the dryin' up"

"That's because you never clean the dishes properly" said our Josh as he squeezed past us and pushing open the back cabin doors, stepped out into the cold night air.

"I'm just off up to the stables, to settle Hercules in for the night" he said.

"How would you know our Josh, you've never washed up in yer life!" Sammy called after him.

"That's enough!" Da intervened, "Just get on and do the job Sammy"

"The sooner you gets started, the sooner you'll be finished" Ma chipped in.

Da reached for his pipe and baccy, then putting his short coat on and taking his cap from the pocket followed our Josh out of the door. "I'm just going to treat Our Josh to a half at the Barge Flo, and one for meself of course". And with that he followed our Josh up the towpath to the Barge Inn.

When all the pots had been washed and put away, I filled the kettle and put it back on the stove to boil for yet another cup of tea. In the meantime, Ma had pulled down the 'drop down' bed and made it up for our Flossie to get into and she now lay fast asleep, thumb in mouth, looking for all the world like an angel once more! Our Sammy must have read me mind 'cos he looked up at me, then across at our Flossie, raised his eyebrows and just shrugged. I managed a sort of lop sided smile, more because I wanted Sammy to know I'd understood . I mashed the tea and Ma, Sammy and me settled ourselves beside the stove.

"Have you finished that piece of embroidery yet Jess?" Ma asked

I had been trying to finish a length of 'spiders web' embroidery on a piece of Irish linen for nearly three months now. I wanted it to make a proper boatman's belt for our Josh, for 'is birthday. But we rarely got the time to just sit of an evening, and so it was taking longer than I'd expected. I reached up into the cupboard over the bed'ole and pulled out a small cloth bag in which I kept all me sewing things. Ma reached out her hand as I pulled the linen out of the bag, wantin' to inspect me work.

"That's real fine our Jess, don't know where you gets that talent from, not my side of the family and that's a fact. I can 'ardly see to thread a needle these days, let alone sew with it." And she handed the needlework back to me.

"I need's some strips of leather and two buckles for it when we goes to that little market just off the City Road Ma" I said as I continued on from where I had left off a week or so ago.

"You'll 'ave to remind me when we're there next, 'cos I'm bound to forget. You'll need a bit of sacking to stiffen it with an all" Ma said.

She was toastin' 'er feet, restin' them on the shelf underneath the stove and I could tell she was nodding off when she didn't quite finish 'er next sentence

"Remind me in the mornin' Jess to get yer Da to................"

The next thing I knew, she was snoring softly, chin on chest, arms folded.I looked across at our Sammy and 'ed fallen asleep too. I don't know 'ow long I'd sat there in silence sewing me rainbow coloured spiders webs until I 'eard the sound of footsteps and low voices outside on the towpath, then the boat gently rocked to one side as Da and our Josh came back onboard 'Isis'.

"By its fair freezin' out there!" Da said as he pushed back the hatch and opened the back doors, Ma stirred and sat bolt upright, tryin' to pretend she 'adn't been asleep at all.

"Come on in Joe and get warm, what you and our Josh want to be doing up in the pub on a cold night like tonight I'm sure I don't know" and she fussed around Da, helpin' 'im off with 'is coat with one hand whilst pushin' the kettle over the hob with the other.

"We saw Jacob....... up at the Barge, didn't we Da" It was our Josh's turn to get fussed by Ma as he stepped down into the back cabin, closing the door and then the hatch behind 'im.

"Oh yes, and what did 'E 'ave to say for 'imself" demanded Ma.

"Well I must say, I was surprised he spoke at all. In fact I thought 'E was ignoring us when 'E went past the other day, when we was sheetin' up at the bottom of Itchin'ton flight, but no, give 'im 'is due, 'E came right across the bar when 'E saw me and our Josh walk into the Public.

"Well Mary Ann looked real sheepish when they passed us the other day" Ma said "Not surprising when they still owes us that shillin' you lent 'em a month back".

"Jacob could 'ardly ignore us when we was there in the bar, right infront of 'im" Our Josh added.

"No, but like I said, give 'im 'is due" Da said again "'E did come straight over. I could see 'E were a bit embarrassed like, but he's promised to let Smiffy know about the shillin' so we can collect it when we're back at the wharf".

"Just so long as 'E does!" Ma said.

While all this were going on I mashed yet another pot of tea and poured it out into four cups, Sammy having gone to sleep long ago, and Ma 'ad covered 'im with 'is blanket.

Then Ma spoke again "Did you see Henry Jordan goin' by this afternoon Joe, when we was waitin' to go into the bottom lock and you was tightening up the ropes?"

"I did Flo, and I was more than surprised to see 'im. I'd 'eard he was givin' up the boats an' taking 'is family up north to live with 'is sister."

"Well who could blame 'im" Ma replied "After what 'appened to 'is Violet, fallin' down between their two boats in Buckby top lock like that".

"Don't remind me Flo, that were one of the worst days of me life, 'aving to help Henry pull 'er out and worst of all, avin' to drag 'im away from 'er when we all realised she was dead."

"Aye" Ma sighed "And those poor bairns 'aving to stand by and watch the 'ole sorry business. Who'd 'ave thought it could 'appen to someone like poor Violet, she were born on a boat, and her Ma before her!"

"Don't make no difference, all the experience in the world couldn't 'ave prevented 'er fallin' in. With the snow comin' down so thick an' fast an' the gunn'all all froze, she didn't stand a chance!". Da said as he packed his pipe for his last 'smoke' of the day.

"She shouldn't 'ave been out there!" Our Josh put in hotly.

Ma and Da turned to look at our Josh, real surprised like. It wern't like 'im to 'ave an opinion, and even less like 'im to voice it.

"What makes you say that son" Da said, still surprised at our Josh's outburst.

"Jimmy should've made sure the front sheets was secure before they went into the lock and not expect

Violet to 'ave to walk along the top planks to fix it once they was in there. 'E never even shut the paddle down to stop the water floddin' in!" Our Josh was getting' quite fired up…..and we was all surprised.

"Well it wouldn't be the first time someone 'ad to do that to stop the water from pourin' over the bow and spoiling the cargo lad!" Da replied.

"No Da, I'll grant you that, I've done it loads of times meself and so has our Jess, but you wouldn't ask Ma to do it would you?, and Violet was eight months gone wi' a bairn!" And with that our Josh stormed out of our back cabin!

Well! we all sat there in stunned silence…………….. our Josh 'ad never expressed opinions on anyone, he saved all 'is sympathy for animals. In all me life I'd never known 'im to get so het up. 'E was a dark 'orse, our Josh and no mistake.

CHAPTER FIVE.

The 'Ealth Inspector

It wasn't often that we ever 'ad 'visitors' on our boat. Mostly we was on the move from morn 'til night, 'keepin' the boat's ahead' was what Da called it. I took that to mean that we was allus trying to get ahead of our selves, with the cargo and such. If you thinks about it, the more trips we did, the more money we earned, 'cos we got paid by the 'load'. So if it took us ten days to get from Limehouse to the City Road and ten days back, then we 'ad to live for the 'ole twenty days with no pay 'til we got back to our 'ome wharf. But if we could do the same trip and knock off two days either way, then we 'ad the same money to last for sixteen days. That's of course if we was comin' straight back to our 'ome wharf.

Occasionally if our Gaffer, Mr. Griffiths 'ad a real important job come in, 'E'd get Smiffy to cycle along the tow path to give us a 'sub' while we went on somewhere else to load up and deliver. But we never spent more time tied up than we absolutely 'ad to. Of course at Christmas time and at Easter and Whitsun the local church goers got the canal companies to lock up the Lock Gates so we had to stop. That's when we boaties 'ad what Ma called 'our gatherings'. I s'pose it was the nearest thing we ever got to 'olidays. Then we'd 'ave one or two days all tied up with other boaties with nothin' to do. Well except that it was a golden opportunity for the women to get all the washin' done, beddin' aired and the back cabin's scrubbed out. People would make a big effort to get to a particular set of locks or wharf so they could all tie up together and spend time with family and friends and of course the menfolk would go to the 'public' for a pint or two of beer.

We rarely got involved with people what lived in the towns and villages, so it came as quite a surprise when one day we was 'visited' by a man from the 'Government' wot said 'E was an 'Ealth Inspector. 'E said 'E 'ad the right to come and inspect our back cabin and see exactly where we all slept.

"Nosey Bugger our Josh called 'im, but not in Ma's hearin'. 'E was all official like, asked all sorts of personal questions!'E said it wasn't legal to have boys and girls mixed together in a boat's back cabin, that it weren't 'ealthy neither! Ma had said there were nothin' unhealthy in her cabin,   that you could eat yer dinner off the floor, it was so clean. But the man was havin' none of it. 'E 'ad a big black bag and from it 'E took out 'is clip board and a fancy fountain pen! , then wrote down everythin' we said. He asked me and our Josh, and our Sammy how old we was. We told the truth, we had now't to 'ide. Our Josh said he was seventeen and that Mr. Griffiths had agreed to put him on the company's books, to pay him half pay and to write him down as our boat 'Isis' number two, Da being the number one, captain or steerer. Ma allus said she was the 'Mate' but she wasn't wrote down and didn't get no pay neither.

"And where do you sleep?" the man said, not taking much notice of what our Josh was tellin' 'im. Josh told 'im that he had a bed made up under the cloths, that it was good and dry and comfortable on top of the sacks. The man sort of coughed and wrote on his paper. Then he asked me how old I was and where I slept, I told him it wern't right to ask personal questions, but Ma said "Just answer the man Jessie and don't make no trouble". I didn't want to make no trouble, but I didn't think it was right for him to come into our cabin and sit there like Lord Muck with his nose turned up, like he had a bad smell under it, askin' us about our private life. Ma gave me one of her 'looks' and so I says to this man

"I'm fifteen Mister, and I sleeps there, where you're sittin', in the bed'ole".

He looks at me real hard like, then writes on his paper. Then he looks at our Sammy who was sittin' on the step fiddling with a bit of string.

"And you" the man said pointin' 'is finger at me younger brother.

"I'm Sammy Mister" me brother answered proudly.

The man wrote on his paper. "How old?" 'E said not even lookin' up

"He's nearly eleven Mister, well 'E will be, its 'is birthday come Sunday and we're all gonna ride on the carousel".

I was about to tell the man that we were going into Nuneaton next Sunday, that we had heard there was a fair and Da had promised our Sammy, as a birthday treat, that we could all go.

"I am not interested in what you are doing on Sunday" the man said in a funny sort of clipped 'posh' voice. "Kindly let your brother answer my questions".

Our Sammy looked real pleased with 'is self as he said "I'll be eleven this coming Sunday Mister".

"And you sleep where?" the man went on.

"Sometimes I sleeps down there" our Sammy replied, pointin' to the floor "Under the drop down, or sometimes if Da wants to stretch out, he sleeps down there and I sleep there where our Jess is sittin, on the side bed".

The man again made a sort of coughing noise in the back of his throat. I could tell he disapproved of what we was tellin' him, but at the time I didn't know why.

"But then sometimes I sleeps in the bed'ole and our Jess ...."

"I think the man's 'eard quite enough from you Sammy!" Ma cut our Sammy short. I think she was feelin' a bit peeved 'cos we kids 'ad all been asked before 'er like. Well she was the 'Mate' after all. Later she told us that she thought we'd given more than enough information to use against us. I couldn't see the problem, we'd only told the truth. We was no different from any other boat family, well cleaner than some! But all the boats had back cabins more or less the same size. There was some boats, we'd seen 'em, had another cabin, upfront. Da had told us this was 'cos the 'Government' insisted that girls should sleep separate from their brothers when they was a certain age.

Da said he had spoken to Mr Griffiths about it but he had said that it was too costly to put another cabin on his boats 'cos it took away valuable cargo space, not to mention the cost of wood for the cabin and the time to build it. No Mr Griffiths wasn't in favour of extra cabins. Our Josh had been sleepin' in the 'hold' for ages, well long since before our Flossie was born. He had made 'is self quite cosy lyin' on a pile of sacks, on top of the cargo. Ma had stitched up the sides of a good wool blanket and he had another one to put over the top and Da had let him have a small oil lamp, as long as he promised to be real careful with it. I quite envied our Josh, havin' his own bed space. But I never thought there was 'owt wrong with my bedspace neither. I liked to sleep on the side bed right opposite the stove and even though I had to sleep with me knees curled up, since I was gettin' taller, I was very cosy with me own crocheted blanket and a cushion for me head. Sometimes Ma and Da slept in the drop down bed in what we called the bed'ole. They had a proper tickin' mattress what Da had bought off a man in the market, real cheap, and a bolster! Ma was very proud of these. They had sheets as well as blankets and Ma had said that 'one of these fine days' she was goin' to get herself 'a real feather eiderdown.' Molly Aitkins had a real feather eiderdown, Ma and I had seen it when we took some broth to her when we was moored up together.

Molly had been real bad with the 'flu and her Arthur had gone for the doctor 'cos he was worried it might be the 'monia'. Ma had made some of her special broth and we took it along and I sat with Molly until Arthur came back with the doctor. There was just the two of them, they had no kids and Da said that's why they could afford Doctors for the 'flu!

"And where does this child sleep?" the government 'ealth inspector was now pointin' to our little sister Flossie. I could see Ma was getting' to the 'end of her tether' with all these questions. I could tell 'cos she had pushed the kettle all 'round the stove and was now fidgeting with the teapot.

"Our Florence sleeps with us" she replied.

"By whom do you mean 'us'?" the man looked down his long thin nose once more.

"Me man and me" Ma said, puttin' her hands on her hips.

"What all three of you, in that tiny bed!" the man almost shouted and was again writin' away on his paper.

"And the child is how old?" he said without looking up.

"She's four" Ma replied and sighed "But if 'E fancies stretchin out like, or if our Sammy or Jessie wants to go to bed early, then one of them'all..."

"I think I've heard quite enough" the man said lookin' down 'is nose yet again, as he began to put 'is paper away in 'is black bag. I could tell Ma thought it was high time this man was on his way. I knew she thought 'E 'ad no right to come into our cabin and ask a lot of stupid questions. Our Josh and me didn't know why she were puttin' up with it. Ma was usually very plain speakin' we couldn't understand it, it was just not like her. And we said so just as soon as the man 'ad gone on his way up the towpath.

"Why didn't you just throw him out Ma?" our Josh said.

"'Cos 'E's an inspector from the Government or so he says," Ma replied.

"I don't understand why 'E were askin' us all personal questions, t'aint right!" I said hotly.

"Yer Da says we 'ave to give 'im no trouble 'cos he has to write us all down and make a report about the way we're 'livin', though the Lord only knows why!".

Well it wasn't long after that we found out why! We was just tyin' up at our 'ome wharf when Smiffy comes out of Mr Griffiths's office wavin' a paper. Da was for getting' the cloths off so we could start unloadin' but Smiffy wasn't havin' none of it, he wanted to speak to Da – now! They went off into Smiffy's 'ole, a small 'lean to' at the side of the main wharf building. Smiffy had stacked barrels at the back to make a wall and stuffed the gaps with old sacks and straw to keep out the wind. At the front he had set up what he called a 'brazier', a rusty old oil drum with 'oles punched in the sides, wot 'E kept a fire burnin' in, to keep 'im warm in winter.

We watched Smiffy and Da sit down on the packing cases wot served as desk and chair in the 'lean to', and Da took out his pipe as he read the paper Smiffy was holdin'. Then Ma said, as she did so often, "Stop yer gawkin' girl!" and I stepped down into the cabin and busied meself mashing tea 'cos Ma always made me feel real embarrassed when she said that. Our Josh and Sammy set about the unloadin' so as to save time, but when Da came back to our boat, he didn't join them he came straight into the cabin, lookin 'like thunder'.

"Well of all the........." he began "That man from the Government, nosey bugger!" Now I knew this must be serious for Da rarely used what Ma called 'Language!' unless he was real mad.

"He's gone and reported us for livin' in wot 'E calls, overcrowded and un'ealthy conditions"

"There's no need to shout Joe" Ma said tryin' to calm 'im down. But 'E wasn't for calming down, 'E was real mad.

"E's wrote a letter to Mr Griffiths sayin' that it's against the law to have so many livin' in a back cabin, that somethin' has to be done about it ,immediate like! And if nothin' is done that he, Mr Griffiths, will be put up before the law! 'cos its his boats and he's responsible!"

Ma raised 'er eyes to the cabin roof and sort of smiled as if to say wot Da had just said was beyond belief!

"But we all live's in our back cabins, all the boaties" Ma said "And there's some, 'as more kids than us, there's nowt wrong with that, we've always done it, what else would they expect?"

"Mr Griffiths says they are havin' a crack down. Laws was made years ago about how many people could live in a back cabin, but no one took no notice. Now some nosy parker Lady wots-her-name in the government wants somethin' done about it. All the barge and narra'boat comp'nies are bein' investigated by this 'Ealth Inspector and Mr. Griffiths says they've all been given three months to sort it out". Da finished his 'speech' and sat down with a bump onto the side bed, puttin' 'is 'ead in his hands as he did so.

"Well" said Ma "What can they do about it? Boats has cabins and people lives in 'em" Ma sat down beside Da with her arms folded across 'er chest as though that was an end to it, but I could see by Da's face that it were n't. He looked out through the cabin doorway and sighed, then began again

"Look Flo, the government can do what it likes, say what it likes and people like us and Mr. Griffiths has to do what they says. Its not just us, Mr Griffiths has been given the names of *all* 'is boats wots overcrowded. There's the 'India' and 'Persha' the 'Rosemary' Frank Carter's lot on the 'Credence', that new man on the 'Nene' and Freddie an' Maizie on the 'Dabchick' as well. Smiffy says he has to speak to all of us to see what we can come up with. Mr Griffiths don't want it to cost him no money!"

Da sat with his head in his hands for some time. Ma just sat beside him as though she was findin' it 'ard to take in. Then suddenly she said "Well Mr Griffiths can't do without us, so he'll 'ave to do somethin' for us!" she said triumphantly.

Da looked at her and sighed again "Flo, we don't mean *that* much to Mr. Griffiths, he could find plenty of other people to work his boats. There's men queuein' up to work the boats these days!. When we was up North last week two or three of the factory men was askin' how they could get jobs on boats. They said they was sick of working inside, they'd been born on farms and was fed up bein' cooped up all day long, wanted the freedom of bein' their 'own men'. They seemed to 'ave some strange notion that we 'ad it easy, livin' and workin' on a narraboat."

Da stood up now and reaching out through the open doorway, tapped out his pipe on the gunn'all. "And to think I even gave them Mr. Griffiths name and told 'em to write to 'im at the wharf."

Just then our Josh stuck 'is 'ead over the side of the boat and called down into the cabin "Is that right Da, what Smiffy's just told me, about us bein' overcrowded and all?"

"Aye son, that's what they're sayin' ."

"Wot we gonna do about it?" our Josh asked.

"Don't know what we can do about it just yet" Da replied.

"We could allus get another boat" Josh said, quite natural like, as though 'E 'ad already thought it all through.

"What get a bigger boat!" Ma exclaimed. I could see she would not be for changin' the 'Isis', not for nothin', it was 'er pride and joy.

"No Ma, two boats! Now that I'm on the Company books, what's to stop me 'avin' a boat of me own? I could 'ave our Sammy with me, then there'd be room for you and Da and the girls on 'Isis'."

Well I thought, our Josh certainly 'ad it all worked out. I could see that Da was takin' it all in, though the look on Ma's face said she thought 'E 'ad gone quite mad! It was true Mr. Griffiths 'ad put our Josh on the books a couple of months back, but only after 'E 'ad kept on pesterin'. 'E was only on half pay mind you, but then 'E *was* only just seventeen. Da 'ad told our Josh that if 'E could get Mr. Griffiths to take 'im on proper so to speak, it would be easier for 'im to get his own boat later on, when 'E was twenty or so. Da said 'E'd done the same thing his self, when 'E'd worked on *his* Da's boat, before he married Ma. 'E had told 'is Da that 'E wanted to get wed and they'd gone straight to Mr. Griffiths and he'd given 'em a lovely old wooden boat named 'Dolly'. We'd all 'eard the story many times before. Both Ma and Da were allus tellin' us how good Mr. Griffiths 'ad been to our family and that 'E was a 'fair man and a boss worth workin' for. Our Josh had been so excited when we'd tied up at the wharf, not two months before and Da 'ad taken 'im into the office to see Mr. Griffiths. 'E 'ad taken some persuadin', 'ad Mr. Griffiths, ever a man to look for ways of savin' money. Though to be fair, 'E 'ad allus said how our Josh was the best man in the fleet when it came to lookin' after horses. Eventually however, 'E 'ad agreed to take our Josh on, but only on 'alf pay and now 'ere we was, 'ardly two months later and Mr. Griffiths was tellin' Da that 'E'd have to let us all go, unless we could come up with a solution to get 'round the 'government's new laws about overcrowding on boats.

Now I remember thinkin', if that inspector chap thought we was 'over crowded' what must 'E 'ave thought of the likes of the McGuire's or the Haskin's what 'ad ten and twelve kids each! Now it 'ad long been a practise of boaties, to 'elp them get 'round the problems of large families, for them to 'loan out' their children to other boaties, 'specially to them wot 'ad none of their own, or who's family was too young to be of any 'elp at all. Ma's brother Jim Farley and 'is wife Ada had nine children, but only four lived with them on their boat 'The Duke'. Their two eldest boys James and Nathaniel, were old enough to work on 'Fellows Morton' boats, and they'd promised James a steamer when 'E turned twenty one. Nellie their eldest girl 'ad gone off to work in a big hospital in Brum. Ma said she wanted to be a nurse and nothin' else would suit her. She was just turned sixteen and 'ad been told that if she worked 'ard as a 'ward orderly' she might get the opportunity to train as a nurse in time. Then there was Marg, who from bein' fourteen, lived with the Jacobs's on their boat 'Baltimore' Mrs. Jacobs 'ad been ill for years, she could 'ardly get off and on the boat, 'er legs was so swollen and sore. She'd asked Aunt Ada if Marg would 'elp 'er out a bit, 'til she got better. But everyone knew she wouldn't never get no better, 'er Mother 'ad 'gone' the same way! Then there was Monica, she was just eleven months younger than Marg and she was livin' with Aunt Ada's sister Maudie over a shop in Leicester. Maudie 'ad married a townie, Mr Ezeriah Mordicay. 'E 'ad inherited a pawn brokers business from 'is Father. Maudie and Ezeriah didn't 'ave no children of their own and Monica 'ad been a sickly child all 'er life and so they'd offered to give 'er an 'ome with them. Ma said that Ezeriah didn't 'old with children bein' on boats, but 'E said very little to the rest of Maudie's family 'cos they was all boaties. So Uncle Jim and Aunt Ada was left with Sadie, who was the same age as our Sammy, Tilly who was nine, Bella who was six and baby Thomas who was just two years old. Da explained to us that the 'government' would allow Aunt Ada's remaining four children to stay on their boat for now, 'cos they was all girls, except for baby Thomas and they was all under twelve years of age. I couldn't see what difference that made!.

Well it seemed that Da was quite taken with our Josh's suggestion that we should speak to Mr. Griffiths about takin' on another boat. This would double cargo space as well as our livin' and sleepin' space. Da said that me and our Josh and our Sammy could sleep on the second boat and he Ma and Flossie would stay on the 'Isis'. He and Ma talked of nothin' else all the rest of that day. I was glad 'cos I didn't want our family to be split up like our cousins. And I couldn't imagine life without our Josh!

That night Da worked out how much more cargo we could carry and before we all went to bed 'E'd put together all the reasons why Mr. Griffiths should let us take on another boat and how it would benefit everyone and how it would make more money for 'im. Da said 'E knew that money would be the only 'consideration' as far as Mr. Griffiths was concerned. Next mornin' we was supposed to be off early to collect another load of supplies for the Colliery at Newdigate, but Da wasn't for movin' off the wharf 'til 'E'd spoken with Mr. Griffiths. Smiffy came down to our boat twice to tell us that we should'ave left already, but Da said 'E wasn't budging 'til 'E'd seen the Gaffer! Smiffy said we'd be late loadin' up if we didn't get off soon and that he, Mr. Griffiths, hadn't come down to the yard yet, that sometimes it was eight o'clock and gone before 'E'd get there. Da just sat on the back deck with 'is arms folded across 'is chest, smokin' 'is pipe. In the end Smiffy couldn't do no more so 'E walked back up to 'is 'lean to' shakin' 'is 'ead. But 'E knew that Da were deadly serious, 'cos 'E wasn't usually that difficult. It seemed real strange to me, just hangin' about waitin for the Gaffer when we was usually away from the wharf at first light. Time spent 'tied up' was time wasted Da allus said.

Long Buckby on the Grand Junction Canal. Photograph taken during the Whitsun (enforced) stoppage in 1911 (Note: Longton is the 2nd boat in the picture).

CHAPTER SIX

Sugar for the Jam' Ole

As it happened, when Da did get into the office to see Mr. Griffiths later that mornin', things didn't go badly. Well, what Da didn't know, was that old Ma Sutton 'ad at last decided to give up. She'd worked for Mr. Griffiths and his father before him and when 'er husband Billy was alive they 'ad worked all up and down the country for the Griffith's. Now, Ma Sutton must 'ave been seventy if she was a day, well that's what everyone said, and 'though she was fit for her age, most of us boaties did worry about her, all on her own. Though Mr. Griffiths mainly gave her short stretches and her 'orse 'Tansey' was a good old mare, she knew the run so well she'd probably have done the job all by 'erself. Well Ma Sutton 'ad got word to Mr. Griffiths that she was givin' up. She 'ad delivered 'er last load to the stocking factory in Hinkley and she and 'er boat 'Bluebell' was moored up at Marsden Junction. It turned out that she had a daughter in Coventry and she was goin' to spend 'er last days with 'er. So, when Da had finally gone into the office to tell Mr. Griffiths 'ow he thought we could solve the 'overcrowding problem', well as far as our family was concerned, that it weren't difficult to persuade 'im. 'E could see the sense in letting us 'ave another boat 'specially as Our Josh was only on 'alf pay. Though some would think it was favouritism. Well that's what Da told us afterwards.

Mr. Griffith 'ad told Da to go off and do this trip up to Newdigate's and to see him again when we got back.. It were three weeks later when we was back at Griffiths's wharf again and Da and Ma 'ad talked of nothin' else but takin' over another boat, if Mr. Griffiths would get us one, all the time we'd been gone. The next mornin', when we 'ad finished unloadin, Smiffy came across to Da and said 'Mr. Griffiths would see him in his office - now!'

I always thought this was strange, Mr. Griffiths could 'ave walked the ten or so paces from 'is office to the wharf and talk to Da there, but 'E never did, 'E always sent Smiffy to fetch him. Da was in there quite some time, Josh and me 'ad hauled 'Isis' up to the turnin' 'ole and were tyin' 'er up opposite the wharf when we saw Da coming across the huge iron bridge that spanned the canal. We looked to see if he was smilin' or not, but it was 'ard to tell.

"Bet 'E won't have any of it" I said to our Josh.

"Bet 'E will!" returned our Josh as we finished tyin' up.

Ma was mashin' the tea when we stepped down into the cabin, we 'ad been 'ard at it since 'sun up' unloadin.' Partly to get on our way again as quickly as possible, we 'ad to keep the boats movin' or 'ahead', as the boaties would say. And partly to remind Mr. Griffiths what good employee's the Ridley family was! If Da was gonna have to persuade 'im, seein' us all workin' 'ard would do the trick, or so we thought.

"Come on Da, what did he say?" our Josh was impatient to know, well it were his idea!

"Let yer Da get his breath" said Ma as she handed out the tea

"What did 'E say, what did 'E say?" it was our Sammy now who was anxious to know the outcome of Da's meetin. Then for the first time in ages Da sat back against the cabin side and laughed, a good deep belly laugh and before we knew it we was all laughin' with him, but not one of us knew why! Then he looks straight at Ma an says

"The Gaffer says we can take on the 'Blubell' as soon as we like, but we'll have to fetch 'er 'cos she's moored up at Marsden Junction."

" But 'Bluebell's' Old Ma Sutton's boat" exclaimed Ma.

"That's right, she's givin' up" Da replied

"'Bout time too if you ask me " Ma said, "She must be gone sixty, 'tain't no good for a woman of her age, workin a boat on 'er own like that, not these days" Ma was for ever tellin' us that 'times had changed' and that when she was a girl you knew everyone who lived and worked on the Cut, but now the carrying companies was employin' any Tom, Dick or 'Arry, though some of 'em only stuck it for five minutes, you never knew who you was workin' alongside of.

We was all surprised to hear that Ma Sutton was givin' up, we'd known her all our lives and would often pass 'er boat or tie up alongside of 'er. She was a tiny woman with "ardly any meat on 'er' as Da would say, but by, could she work! She worked as hard as any man and still found time to scrub 'er cabin from top to bottom, she was a good'un.

Da carried on to tell us that the 'Gaffer' as 'E always called Mr. Griffiths, had been no trouble at all when he had thought it all over, it had made sense. Instead of 'im 'aving to find another crew or family to run 'Bluebell' with another full wage to pay out, he could let us work her along with our boat, and save his self money. I could see our Josh was disappointed when Da said that he would be wrote down as the steerer for both boats and Josh would still be the 'mate'. ' E said Mr. Griffiths didn't want to make our Josh the steerer just yet, as he thought 'e was still a bit young to be in charge of 'is own boat.

"Wanted to save money more like!" Josh said angrily "'E would've 'ad to pay me a full wage if I'd taken her on".

"Aye like as not Son" Ma said "But at least 'e 'as agreed to let us have the two boats and that'll keep the man from the Health Department 'appy. I wants to keep all me family all together" Ma went on "Not 'ave you all over the place and me not knowin' where you all are or what yer up to".

And so it was, ten days later we went up the North Oxford canal and took the 'Bluebell' in tow. Ma Sutton 'ad moved off, but she got word to us, through the other boaties, that she was leavin' 'er stove in the back cabin, as 'er daughter had no use for it. She wanted 7/6d for it and we could leave the money with Frank Beeton, the Lock Keeper, and 'er daughter would collect it. Of course Ma Sutton knew us well, but she would have trusted anyone who had taken 'Bluebell' on, especially any of the old boating families, we would never 'do another boater down,' as Da would say. And no one on a boat could survive without a good stove to cook on and to keep you warm. It was our only source of heating.

We was carrin' a cargo of sugar up to the Jam'ole, so it was easy for us to stop off at Marsden Junction to collect the new boat. Ma said she knew 'Bluebell' would be clean and tidy 'cos Ma Sutton was one of the old sort, she knew how to keep a boat clean as a new pin. Not all boaties was clean though, not by any means. We had heard of boats havin' to be 'fumey-gated'.

"What a disgrace" Ma had said "'ow could you live with yerself and wot would the other boaties think!"

'Cos news travelled fast on the Cut, specially bad news, you couldn't have no secrets. Well I don't suppose it was no different than people livin' in the same village or street, they would always have an opinion on their neighbours doin's.

It took a while for Hercules to get used to pullin' the two boats. It weren't so bad once we was underway, 'cos even fully loaded the two boats would 'swim' just fine, but stoppin' 'em, well that was another kettle of fish altogether! We all had to learn how to get the two alongside of one another in the lock and how long a piece of rope to have between them to make the steerin' easier. Ma wasn't too keen on Me and our Josh and Sammy sleepin' 70 feet away from her in Bluebell's cabin. Well she'd been used to havin' all of us together on the one boat every night of our lives, it was understandable that she would take time to get used to the idea. For our Josh and me it was like all our dreams come true, all at once. Our Josh was so proud and even though he was still only 'the mate', as far as Mr. Griffiths was concerned, Our Josh looked after 'Bluebell' as though she were his very own. The work was much harder for all of us but even more so for him 'cos we still only had the one horse and Hercules was our Josh's main responsibility. For me life changed over night for as I saw it, I was to have full responsibility for 'Bluebell'. I would steer her during the day and clean her from stem to stern whenever we was tied up. I was fifteen years of age and more than capable of steerin' a boat, I could work the locks and bridges, help with loadin' and unloadin'. Ma had taught me to cook and I was handy with a needle and cotton too and cleanin' was somthin' I'd done all me life so none of this was new to me.

But to have me own back cabin, well that was almost as good as getting' married and all young girls of my age wanted to be wed. The thought of sleepin' in a bed, with curtains was pure bliss, even if I was to share it with our Sammy. I had'nt slept every night in a proper drop down bed, not since before our Sammy was born, for when he came along I took over the side bed and our Josh moved onto the floor. But this was normal for boatin' families, we didn't know no better. I remember on one of the few occasions when I had gone to a village school somewhere up north, one of the girls laughed at me 'cos we didn't have proper beds. I told her we was better off than some kids I had met in Brummag'um, some of them slept four and five to a bed and up there in the north, the colliery day shift workers got out of bed and the night shift workers got in! I was to have a drawer of me very own, to put me things in. Not that I had much, but I did have two calico night gowns, heavily patched and darned. Two petticoats, one with real lace 'round the bottom, two pairs of drawers and liberty bodices. One navy blue serge skirt and two cotton blouses. I 'ad crocheted me own shawl with wool from a cardigan with big holes in the sleeves, that I 'ad un-picked. Most of our stuff came from second hand stalls in the markets of the towns where we tied up. Ma was always very particular about underwear tho'. She would boil up any articles we bought from the market before we was allowed to wear it, 'just incase,' she would say, 'cos you never knew where it had come from.

Sometimes Ma would order new stuff to be made by a proper seamstress. Mrs. Williams who lived in a cottage at Banbury Lock on the Oxford Canal was a well known seamstress, she made the typical bonnets the older boatwomen wore and had done for years. She also made shirts and blouses, but I can only remember ever havin one new blouse made for me by Mrs. Williams and that was just before I got married, but that's another story.

Our Josh was to have the side bed, opposite the stove. Ma said she would be happier knowin' our Josh was there with us at night, especially as you didn't know who was about on the Cut these days. We never locked our cabin doors, day or night, well, you just didn't. Mostly we never had no need to, but lately we had heard bad stories of boat women bein' 'interferred with' as Ma put it 'By drunken men from the towns' Mrs. Golding off the 'India' had said 'There was no smoke without fire, and the women must have been playin' up to the townie men.' Da had said that most boat women wasn't like that, Ma just said you didn't know these days, everythin' was changin'.

Our Josh said it would be nice to have a bit of 'eat at night, specially in winter. He had been sleepin' in the hold under the cloths for four years now, ever since our Flossie came along. Not that he ever compained, but I often felt sorry for him when it was real cold, in the snow or when it was lashin' down with rain, and the rest of us could just climb into our beds, with the stove banked up for the night, and our Josh had to go out into the cold. Still I was determined, now that we had the two boats, that I would make it up to our Josh. I would look after him like Ma looked after Da and the rest of us.

The weather had been particularly hot the last few weeks and Ma had been lookin' for a good excuse to tie up and get some washin' done. The problem was that we had a to keep goin' with our load of sugar for the Jam Factory and when we did get unloaded there, we had to go off somewhere else to load up again for the return trip. In the Summer months Da liked to be up and away each mornin' as soon as the sun was up. We would grab a mug of tea and a slice of bread for breakfast, on the way, usually at one of the locks while we waited for it to fill up or drain out. We would rarely stop during the day, Ma would again hand us a mug of tea and bread at a suitable lock, round about midday. Then we would press on during the afternoon and evening and get as far ahead as we could before it started to get dark. It weren't unusual for us to work fifteen or sixteen hours a day 'cos it didn't get dark 'til after ten o'clock. This bein' the case Ma had very little opportunity at the end of each day, to get out the dolly and tub which she would set up on the towpath, and even less of a chance to dry anythin' overnight. But the night after we had took 'Bluebell' in tow Ma had one of her 'ideals' as she called them. 'Isis' was fully loaded right up to the gunn'alls with sacks of sugar but the hold of Bluebell was completely empty. "If we ties up early tomorrow night," she said, "We can get plenty of water from the tap at Perkins's Yard, and me and Jessie can boil up the tub and get a good load of washin' done".

"Where you gonna dry it?" Da said

"You can rig us up a line on Bluebell" Ma said, "If this weather holds, and it looks as if it will, we can dry the lot as we goes along".

Ma was very pleased with 'erself and sat back with her arms folded, just to let Da know her mind was made up! We never argued once Ma's mind was made up, not none of us. We had made good time on this run and even stopping to take Bluebell in tow hadn't set us back at all. So Da was not too much against a short working day, 'specially as there was a nice little public bar just 'round the corner from Perkins' yard and Da liked a pint now and again.

So the following day we had a good steady run and even Hercules enjoyed the rare opportunity to stop and graze along the way. It was just after six o'clock when we tied up outside of Perkin's Saw Mill. I knew this 'cos I heard the church clock in the village, strike six times just as we was comin' up the Cut. Clive Perkins had done very well since he moved his business to the canalside. His Father had started the sawmill on the other side of the village beside the main road in to Coventry, but as the village grew and he became more prosperous Clive realised they would need a bigger place. The farmer who owned land on either side of the Cut was more than happy to sell a bit off to the Perkins's and Clive had already seen the advantage of shifting all their wood by boat instead of carting it, which was getting ever more expensive nowadays. He had given the carryin' contract to Mr. Griffiths, seein' as his boats regularly went up and down this stretch, and so we had often loaded up here and Da knew the men who worked in the Mill. Mr. Clive Perkins was a reg'lar Church goer' one of the few, so Ma said, who practised wot they preached! He had put up a water trough and pump outside his yard, right on the canal bank, for the 'Bargees' as he called us, to use. This was such a 'perk' for us boaters, it wasn't often that 'townies' ever gave us a thought, we was all so grateful.

There were two other boats tied up on the wharf outside Perkin's yard and as we wasn't loadin' or unloadin' Da pulled our boats up well clear of them. I waved to Margie Butler, a girl of about my age, as we passed their boat 'Sara'. Her Da and two brothers was unloadin' huge tree trunks one at a time, using the newly installed crane, and stackin' them just outside the yard gates. As soon as we was tied up Ma sent our Sammy and Flossie off to fill our water cans, the bucket and the dipper. Josh was unhitchin' Hercules and Da was seein' to the ropes and sheets at the front of 'Isis' makin' sure they was tied up tight as he didn't want to risk any of the village kids getting at the sugar in our hold. We was docked money on any sacks that was damaged or 'tampered' with. Da was always careful to keep just one sack near the cabin, wot he had opened, this was our own supply and if we was docked 1/-d, well it was worth it. Ma and me set about lightin' a small fire on the bank, there was plenty of wood chippin's lyin' about so I gathered some up and we soon had a blaze goin' under the galvinized wash tub which was now full of water. We 'steeped' all the 'whites' in the tub, givin' each item a good rub with carbolic soap before we left them to boil. Then back to our cabin and before long Ma was mashin' the all important tea. Lookin' back it seems we was always drinkin' mugs of hot black tea, laced with two or three spoonfuls of sugar, we didn't drink nothin' else, except water. But it was the tea and bread that kept us goin' we didn't stop long enough during the day to get anything else, keepin' the boats ahead was wot was important.

It felt like a holiday, tieing up so early in the day, and with the sun still smilin' down on us, we sat on the bank drinkin' our tea 'like royalty' Ma said. Margie Butler and her Ma, Rose, came along the tow path to join us. Ma brought out more mugs and the huge teapot which usually sat alongside of the kettle on the stove, we was havin' quite a time of it when Mr. Clive Perkins walks up

"A tea party is it?" he says.

Ma nearly choked 'cos she hadn't seen him coming and she began to struggle to her feet when he said

"No, no Mrs. Ridley, please don't get up, I saw you from my office window and just stepped out to wish you a good evening before I get off home".

Ma was standin' now and so was the rest of us, out of respect like, well he was a gentleman.

" Oh Mr. Clive!"

It wasn't often that Ma was flustered but her face was all pink now,

"We was just havin' a natter, it 'ain't often we gets the chance" she said.

"Of course Mrs. Ridley, you carry on, it's good to see you and your family looking so well and young Joshua tells me you have two boats now."

"Oh yes Mr. Clive, its old Ma Sutton's boat 'Bluebell', she's givin' up you know."

I'd never seen Ma so 'het up' she looked almost girlish as she stood awkwardly talkin' to the young Mr. Perkins.

"Yes I had heard that she's gone to live with her daughter in Coventry and not before time. She must be sixty years of age at least."

"Oh at least" Ma replied, for once in her life almost at a loss for words.

"Well I must be getting off home now, my wife and I are entertaining the new vicar to supper this evening and I promised Victoria that I would not be late. Goodbye to you ladies, Mrs. Ridley, Mrs. Butler"

And with that the young Mr. Perkins nodded to each of us and walked back into his yard where his men were just preparing to close the gates.

"Well" said Margie's Ma "E's never spoke to we like that 'afore, not never!"

"Oh" said Ma, still pink faced, "He's always been good to Joe and me, ever since we first met up with him. I think we was one of the first boats to load here, when they started to build the wharf.

"Well" said Margie's Ma again and carried on drinking her tea.

The wash tub was boiling away merrily, so I fetched the old bath tub that our Flossie could still fit into, well just. Our Sammy was playin' five stones with Margie's brother Thomas, but he looked up when I called and came willingly to help me get more cold water from the trough. Thomas came with him and together the three of us struggled up the towpath with the bath of water, to where Ma was now stiring up our washin'. Putting the bath down to one side of the tub, she then with a large stick she began to lift each garment steaming and dripping with hot soapy water, from the tub into the bath. Once the tub was emptied our Sammy was back down to the trough to fill our water cans, and when he returned, both was poured into the now half emptied tub. This made the remaining water cool enough to wash our heavier 'top' clothes in. I got on me knees and started scrubbing the 'whites' on the washboard while Ma set to with the rest.

Da came and sat down alongside of us on the bank, lit his pipe and lay back in the grass. Our Josh was down by the trough brushin' Hercules shaggy coat, or curryin' as he called it. He loved animals did our Josh, you could always find him in the company of horses, dogs, cats cows and the like, rather than people. He was seventeen years of age and showed no interest wot-so-ever in any of the lasses. Ma said it was 'cos he was shy in front of girls he didn't know. Da said 'e wouldn't ever get to know any, if 'e didn't speak to 'em. But our Josh was never a big talker. When I asked 'im, about girls 'e had said 'e didn't know wot to say to them. He said they wasn't like me, their heads was full of silly stuff and they giggled all the time. I said that 'cos I was his sister I knew wot 'e liked to talk about and that, 'cos we knowed one another all our lives we wasn't embarrassed nor nothin'. Sometimes we could work together unloadin', or walk up the tow path behind the horse for hours and not say a single word. But our Josh was always there to help if ever I needed him and he was never unkind, not to me or no one. Looking back, we was a happy family, not like some who argued and fought all the time, no we was happy and all helped to make things go along smoothly. I'm not sayin' we never fell out, well that wouldn't be natural, but when we did it never lasted long and none of us bore grudges. Ma always said she couldn't abide them as bore grudges.

We finished the washing and as it looked like being a fine night with not a cloud in the sky, Da and our Josh had rigged up a rope line between the masts in Bluebell's empty hold. We had some wooden pegs wot Ma had bought off a gypsy lady in a market down south, so she and I set about pegging it all up.

All the while we 'ad been seein' to the washin', the stew Ma had prepared earlier in the day, had been simmering away on the stove. Da and our Josh had strolled up to the 'Public' for a pint and they came back with a bottle of stout, a rare treat for Ma, who never went to the 'Public' 'Erself. It was still light and so we all sat out on the wharf side to have our supper. I found meself a nice pile of wood to sit on and balancing me plate on me knees, I looked down at me 'ands and thought, crikey, that's the first time they've been this clean in months! From where I was sittin' I could see the two rows of clean washin' blowin' gently in the evenin' breeze. I remember thinkin' how much I always loved the smell of clean washin' all that soap and clean water. And to see a line full of clothes blowin' in the wind, well somehow it made you feel real good inside.

CHAPTER SEVEN

Keepin' the Boats Ahead

The next day we stopped off at the Lock Keepers cottage to give Frank Beeton the 7/6d for Ma Sutton's stove. It was a common occurrence among the boat people, to leave messages and the like, with certain Lock Gate Keepers. So it came as no surprise at all, to find there was a letter waiting for us there from our Gaffer, Mr. Griffiths. Da came back from the lock cottage with the note in his hand. He said Frank had read it to him, it was 'orders from Mr. Griffiths, we was to turn off at Fazeley Junction and load 'Bluebell' with supplies for the Company shop at Stoke-on-Trent. 'Isis' was already loaded with sugar for the Jam Factory at Preston Brook and the Gaffer had wasted no time at all in getting' another load sorted, now we had the two boats. Ma raised her eyes to the sky, as she did when she couldn't find the right words to say.

"We'll have to work like the devil to load up the new boat and get on up to the Jam 'Ole, you knows what thems like up there if we don't make good time"

Da said "We'll have to make up the time we lose there, on the run up to Preston. If we don't get up to the Jam 'Ole by Thursday night, we'll never get unload on Friday in time to pick up the return load. We all knew how much Da hated to waste time tied up when we could be keepin' the boats movin'.

"I don't want to be kickin' me 'eels tied up there all weekend" he said as he pushed our boats off from the bank. First 'Isis', and then 'Bluebell'. Hercules took up the slack and soon we was under way. Da walked along the bank for a bit with Our Josh and the horse, then at the next bridge'ole he jumped onboard 'Isis' and took over the steerin' from Ma. She disappeared down into the back cabin, but I could just make out that Ma was still goin' on about the extra load!

I was behind on 'Bluebell' so I never heard what was said, but Da was still 'moutherin' on about it at supper that night. He had decided to keep going longer each night to try to make up the time we would loose, havin' to stop off and load up our second boat. We always got away as soon as we was awake in the mornin's, so we couldn't make up no time there. We 'ardly ever stopped during the day except for locks and bridges and occasionally other boats. Mugs of tea and slices of bread were handed out to us by Ma, while we filled or emptied the locks, so there was little chance of saving extra time there either. It was late Summer, and even though the nights were beginning to draw in, we would have twelve hours of daylight at least. Had it been during the winter months we would have been hard pressed to make the run from the City Road up to Preston Brook in three weeks anyway, as Da wasn't happy about us working the boats in the dark, he said it was very dangerous.

We hadn't stopped at the wharf in Fazeley for about two years. Not since Da had taken on the 'Northern stretch' when Mr. Griffiths got the contract up there, so now we didn't do the shorter 'Midland's run no more. Ma said she missed goin' into Brummag'um 'cos she liked the variety of shops and markets there. But our Sammy, he loved it 'cos it mean't he didn't have to go to school so often. 'Cos most of the boatie families lived and worked full time on their boats, there wasn't no time for children to go to no school. Da had explained that the government tried to keep some sort of control and boat children between the ages of five and twelve was supposed to go to local schools in the towns and villages where the boats was loading or unloading. This was not very popular with the boat families 'cos it meant the children couldn't 'elp their families with the work, as they would 'ave to go to school for the mornin' or afternoon session. Sometimes they would get back to the wharf to find their boat had moved off and then they'd 'ave to walk several miles along the towpath until they caught up with their family. This was quite a problem in winter when the nights drew in, but no boat family could afford to waste time, tied up waitin' for the children to come from school. At each school the children went to, they 'ad their 'School Card' signed by the teacher who stated the number of sessions the child had stayed for. The Government employed the hated 'Inspectors' who peddled their bicycles up and down canal banks 'spot checking' the children's cards, makin' sure that all boaties 'complied with the rega'lations.

We never had more than half a day's schooling in any one place and when we did, I can't say we learned much. Mostly we was too scared to speak, let alone ask questions. A lot of the teachers just stuck us at the back of the class and ignored us, then at the end of the session they signed our cards and sent us on our way. Our Josh and me never learned to read or write and neither had Ma or Da. Not that we needed to, we knew the stretches of canal by heart so no amount of sign posts was any good to us. Da knew the tonnages we carried by the gaugeing sticks and he counted sacks and barrels by makin' four marks on a paper or piece of wood, then crossin' them through so he would know that was five. The 'five bar gate' method Mr. Griffiths called it. We could all count up to ten 'cos we just used our fingers for that and Da had taught us. But we wasn't the only ones, lots of people wasn't able to read or write in them days and it weren't all boaties neither! Most of the people we came across in our working lives, the ordinary working folk in factories and mills, the grafters, as Da called them, they hadn't had a lot of schoolin' and they couldn't read or write much neither.

Most of our 'orders' from the 'Gaffer', Mr. Griffiths, came to us from Smiffy, by 'word of mouth' as you might say. It was rare for us to receive anything in writin'. Wherever we loaded we was given a 'loadin' note, we knew this was a paper to say what cargo we was carrin' and how much of it, so many tonnes, so many sacks like. And we would 'ave to show this paper at every delivery place and toll office along the way, it was called our 'ticket' and Ma always kept it safe in the 'ticket' drawer in our back cabin. We knew that our boat was 'registered' to carry 32 tonnes each, that was the absolute maximum. We also knew that with a full load on, the water would come almost right up to the gunn'all. We never liked to carry a full load, not on a long stretch, as it made hard work of the steerin'. The wharfingers and toll collectors used gauging sticks, which they stuck down the outside of the boats, to measure how much was under the water. This, Da told us, was how they knew what tonnage we was carrin' and tolls was charged on tonnage. It was years before I understood how it all worked, it was just part of all our lives, we used the words but we didn't always know what they really meant. There was a lot of trust in them days.

Now money, that was another thing altogether, we all know'd how to count money! Well sort of, not that we ever had that much to count, but you would know that two pennies would buy you pint of beer, three pennies would buy you a big bag of flour or a large cake of carbolic and in some places you could get two loaves of yesterday's bread for a ha'penny. Oh we never had no trouble countin' money. Da always got paid for each load when we delivered it. Some of the money 'ad to go back to Mr. Griffiths and Ma kept this in a tin box at the back of the drawer, under the bed 'ole in the back cabin, the rest was for us. Our money would have to 'see us thro' for the next run, keep us fed and watered as Ma would say. Out of it we would 'ave to pay for Hercules feed, new shoes when he needed them and any stabling along the way, 'though we tethered him alongside of us on the tow path, during the summer months and saved the stabling fee. The tolls came out of our money too, Da said that Mr. Griffiths had already reckoned on that, when the price was set. So we had to make sure we had enough to pay for these, 'cos they wouldn't let you through, not if you was carrin' cargo, if you couldn't pay the toll. Ma would want to 'put a bit aside', to get new stuff when the old was wore out, shoes and boots and our other clothes and a bit for Christmas as well. Mostly we bought things from the markets, from what Ma called 'second 'and stalls'. Da always said Ma was a 'magician' the way she always managed to lay on a good spread for Christmas day, he would laugh and say she had been at the 'golden goose' again. She would always smile back and say that Da didn't know everythin' she got up to and he would be very surprised if he did. I was never sure what she meant, but we all laughed anyway. It might not have been posh and all that, by some people's standards, but we always felt we had eaten a real feast.

Because of the way we was paid, the length of each run was very important to us, every day counted. If we took two weeks to get somewhere, when, with a bit of effort, we could do it in less time, that would mean Ma spent more money feeding us and Hercules, along the way. So the sooner we got loaded up, on our way and the job done, the sooner we got paid. This was the same for every trip. The longer you was tied up, the more money you was wastein', it was the boaties 'golden rule' and the old 'uns called it 'Keepin' the boats ahead'. Our family was real lucky 'cos we didn't have a Da who liked 'the bottle' as people put it. We saw many families struggle and go 'ungry while their Da's were spendin' all the money, and time, in the public houses. An' it wasn't only the men, there was plenty of women wot couldn't stay off the bottle neither! Ma said it was a disgrace and Da said it was a cryin' shame for the bairns, but although the boat families stuck together in times of 'ardship. We would never poke our noses into other folks business and the drinking 'abits of any boatman or women was strictly their own business.

When we reached the Junction and turned off the Coventry Canal and onto the Brum & Fazeley for the short run up to the wharf, we never expected to see so many other boats. There was boats and horses and people all along the canal bank for as far as we could see.

"Wot's all this?" I heard Ma shout to our Josh, who was leading Hercules up the towpath. "I 'ope its not a stoppage".

I couldn't 'ear the reply 'cos Ma was standin' in the well deck of 'Isis' and I was 70 odd feet away, steerin' Bluebell. I could see Our Josh leading Hercules to the far side of the path where he must have told him to 'Wait up.' He was a good 'orse and never needed telling twice, besides which he wouldn't want to miss the chance of an extra meal neither, he was straight into the tufts of grass, munchin' away even before our boats had stopped. Da threw the centre rope to our Josh and as 'Isis' slowed I sent our Sammy up to the front of 'Bluebell' to slip the cross straps so we would nudge up the side of the other boat. Da had walked along the top planks and was ready to take our for'ed rope when we came level, this he tied first to 'Isis' then throwing it to our Josh on the bank, where he secured it to the moorin' pin. Meanwhile I had thrown my stern rope to Ma and she took a turn on her back pin before throwin' the rope to our Josh on the bank. In minutes both boats was breasted up alongside of one another, I went down into my cabin and taking off the 'ob ring, pushed the kettle over the 'ole in the centre of the stove where it would quickly come to the boil. Like the 'orse, we never missed the chance of an extra cuppa, and it looked as though we was gonna 'ave a long wait, whatever the reason.

"Jessie, Jessie" it was Ma callin' me "Keep and eye on Flossie, I'm goin' with your Da to see what this is all about"

I stuck me head out of the open cabin doors just as Ma lifted our Flossie across from her boat to mine. Although I knew Da was the steerer of both boats, since the very first night I slept onboard Bluebell she had been *my* boat, as far as I was concerned, well mine and our Josh's. I stepped up to the well deck and me and Flossie sat on the gunn'all in the late summer sunshine, watchin' Ma and Da walk up the towpath to where a small crowd had gathered. I looked round to see where our Sammy had got to and just caught sight of him disappearin' in amongst the crowd ahead. Trust our Sammy to want to be in the thick of it – what ever it was. I didn't need to look for our Josh, I knew he would be with Hercules, and sure enough, there he was sittin' on the fence scratchin' the horse's neck and up behind his ears. Hercules loved this, he had even stopped eatin' and was rubbin' his nose up and down our Josh's chest.

"Want a cuppa?" I called out to him "Kettle's boilin"

And I stepped back down into the cabin to mash the tea. I felt the boat tip as our Josh came aboard,

"Wot's goin' on?" I called over me shoulder to him as he sat beside Flossie on the gun'all

"Don't know" he replied "Looks like trouble though, I'm stayin' right out of it, whatever it is."

I passed up two mugs of tea and stepped up to join them on the back deck with my own.

"Why're we stopped here?" Flossie was askin' now. She was always in a dream and never seemed to notice anythin' goin' on around her, still she was only four years old.

"We don't know yet Floss" Josh said "I expect Da and Ma will come back in a minute and tell us"

"Can't we go and find them?" she whinned in her baby voice

"No" said Josh "We're stayin' here with the boats, no use all of us trapesin' up the towpath".

"But I want to go!" Flossie said, raisin' her voice, she was getting all set up to have a tantrum. "I want to go to Ma! I want......"

"Look Flossie why don't you sit on top of the cabin and see if you can see Ma from here." Josh was tryin' to fend off the cryin' and stampin'of feet, which accompanied all of Flossie's many outbursts.

"I don't want to sit up there, I want to go to Ma, I want my Ma!" and she began howling.

"Well you can't." I said and straight away felt sorry for bein' so sharp.

Our Josh frowned at me, and picking Flossie up, stepped across the two boats, with her in his arms. I thought he was goin' to give in to her demands, but I should have known better. He carried her across to where Hercules was grazing, and they sat down together on the grass picking daisies to make a chain. I felt a stab of jealousy then, I wished I was just four years old and our Josh had the time to spend with me. Silly really, 'cos our Josh was so good to all of us. He was always 'elpful and kind, willin' to lend an 'and and never complained. He was a very special person, was my older brother.

I climbed up onto the cabin top and sat there drinking me tea in the sunshine. It was so unusual to have time to sit and do nothing and on such a beautiful day that me mind drifted off. I found meself thinking of what life would be like in the future. Our Josh was seventeen and would surely be courtin' soon, not that he showed the slightest interest in the lasses. If he got wed, he'd want a boat of his own and would go off to start a family of his own, I now thought with horror, I couldn't imagine life without our Josh. Then I remembered how I felt when Ernie Sparks, off 'Bedworth' had winked and smiled at me when we was waitin' to load at 'the Jam 'ole'. My stomach 'ad turned over and me legs turned to jelly and I knew I would want to get married some day. How could I not want the same for our Josh! Sometimes I just didn't understand what went on inside my 'ead!

Just then I looked up and saw the group of men and women gathered together on the towpath begin to break up and start to go back to their boats. I saw Ma and Da as they stood talking to a tall man in a suit with a bowler hat. They nodded gravely as they turned away and walked back to where we was waitin'. I knew then there must be somethin' very wrong 'cos everyone had walked away without smilin' or shoutin' there was no pattin' one another on the back, or callin after them, nothin'. This was very strange for a boaties gatherin'.

"I've got a pot of tea on" I called across as Ma and Da walked the length of our boats.

"Aye, we'd best have a cup" Da said and looking round called to our Josh "Best come inside lad, to hear what we've just been told".

"Where's our Sammy?" said Ma as she stepped across onto Bluebell.

"He followed you and Da" I replied "Didn't you see him up there?"

"No lass I didn't, I told 'im to stay with you and the boats! He'll get a good slapping when he does get back!"

Ma sat down in the bed'ole as Da and Josh followed her down into the cabin. Flossie pulled herself up onto the side bed sucking her thumb and curling a strand of white blonde hair around her forefinger. Everyone waited in silence as I poured the tea and handed round the mugs. I felt a bit scared 'cos Da looked very serious

"Well" he began "War has been declared!"

I didn't know what this meant, but Ma and Da obviously thought this was real bad and I didn't want to show meself up, so I kept quiet.

"Where, who…" began our Josh. Da looked back at him,

"The man from Brum' said the government declared war on the Kaiser two days ago. I don't know what this will mean for us boatmen, its too early to tell, but I can't really see how as it makes any difference to us. The man says it will all be over in a month or two, good of him to come along and tell us though".

I didn't know who this bloke Kaiser was and when later, I heard he lived in a place called Germany, I really couldn't see how it 'ad got anythin' to do with us.

Just then there was a call from the bank and Will Barrett stuck his head over the gunn'all,

"Aye up Josh" he said "What d'you say we go and volunteer to give this Kaiser bloke a thrashin'!"

"I'll give you a thrashin' Will Barrett, Our Josh is goin' no where, and neither will you if you've got a ha'peth of sense." Ma was on her feet, standin' in the door way, just incase our Josh had any ideas of going, but to where, I 'ad no idea!

"Aw Missus, you can't stop us lads goin' to fight for 'King and Country' now can you, think of all that 'honour and glory' stuff the man from the Ministry was talkin' about."

Will was grinnin' and we all knew he was windin' Ma up. Our Josh stood up and gently moved Ma to one side of the doorway as he stepped up into the well deck.

"Don't you be think of goin' off anywhere Our Josh!" Ma said as he stepped across the gunn'all to the bank.

"Aw Ma I 'aint goin' nowhere" he called back across his shoulder as he walked off up the cut with Will Barrett.

Ma sat down heavily on the side bed and Da put his hand on her knee

"Don't you worry about our Josh, he's a good lad, he wouldn't do anything as daft as joinin' up, not like that Will Barrett, he's a rum 'un".

"What d'you mean 'join up' " I asked, bursting to know what this was all about. I knew it was somethin' bad 'cos everyone was lookin' so serious.

"The Army" Ma said, "Goin' away to join the Army"

"But why would our Josh do somethin' like that?" I cried out in horror at the thought of our Josh goin' away, anywhere.

"The country 'as gone to War Jess" Da said lookin' at me real hard like. "The man from the Ministry was sent to tell us about it and to say that the country needed men who worked with 'orses to help with the transports and the like"

"But our Josh wouldn't want to go off and be a soldier! You wouldn't let him Da would you?" I began to feel frightened, though I still didn't really understand what it all meant.

"Well its not like being a real soldier, fighten' or 'owt like that, its to look after the 'orses what pulls the waggons and carts, not guns."

I still didn't like the thought of it. "But our Josh won't go will 'E?" I looked at both Ma and Da for them to say they wouldn't let him anyway.

"Im not goin' anywhere, and not off to join the Army you can be sure of that"

It was our Josh, he was standing on the back deck of 'Isis' and 'ad 'eard my out burst. I realised then just how close to tears I was and felt very stupid as I said "They probably wouldn't have you anyway!"

"Will's all fired up about it though" he went on, ignoring me. "He says he's off to the nearest barracks, he's goin' to join up but not as a horse handler, he gonna be a proper soldier, he wants to fight."

"Well he's daft enough to do it," Ma said, "Though what his Ma'll say I can't think!" she stood up and putting her mug on the shelf behind the stove stepped up into the well deck

"Well we haven't got time to sit around here all day, we'd best get on" she finished the rest of the sentence as she climbed across the gunn'all onto 'Isis' and disappearred down into the back cabin.

"Yer Ma's right, we should get on", Da said, but I felt that somehow he was reluctant to move. "Where's our Sammy?" he said as he too climbed across to the other boat.

"I don't know Da" I replied "I haven't seen him since you and Ma went off to see what this was all about."

"You seen him Josh?"

"No Da I haven't, p'raps he's on one of the other boats, I'll go and have a look." And with that Josh went off , walking past the line of boats all getting ready to move off, now that they had been told this terrible news.

I still didn't really understand what it was all about, wars and things didn't have no effect on us boaties, we just carried on doin' what we always did, no matter what. Our Josh eventually found Sammy playin' with a ball he'd found in a field, with some of the other boys and we were able to get underway again.

That night, as we all sat round in the back cabin, eating our supper, Da explained to us in more detail what wars was all about. How governments and kings had arguments, over land and boundaries and how men went off to fight one another, even though they didn't even know each other or why they was fightin'; and what it would mean for our 'Country'. I didn't really know what 'our Country' was neither. I had heard people talk of England, but at that time I never knew that was where we all lived. I had heard mention of 'the King' but as it didn't effect my day to day life I never gave him no thought. I still couldn't see no sense of it, or why boaties would want to go and get involved in somethin' that they didn't know nothin' about, let alone go killin' people, that I just could not fathom. But I went to bed that night, happy in the knowledge that our Josh had no intentions, whatsoever of joining up in all that madness.

*A cold winter's day! - Foxton Locks on
the Grand Junction Canal*

CHAPTER EIGHT

Christmas Shopping

It were funny, after we was told about the war havin' broke out, I didn't see that anythin' had changed very much, but everywhere we went, people was talkin' about it. Every time we went through a village or town I expected to see hoards of foreigners in uniform, fighting with our 'lot' in the streets. That was another thing, we had never called the 'townies' our boys or our anythin' before, we allus called 'em 'townies' and they called us 'Dirty Boaties' or 'Water Gypsies'. All of a sudden like, we was the same as them, or so we was bein' told. It must 'ave been two or three months later when I got me first sight of men in uniform.

We was late gettin' back to the City Road, havin' 'ad to wait at Town Wharf to unload our cargo of soap from 'Sunlight'. It was a Saturday evenin', just before Christmas and we would now have to wait 'til Monday before we could load up again. Ma said it would be a good time to go round the markets, as it wasn't often we had the chance, specially before Christmas. She decided that me and our Flossie would go with her and the menfolk would stay with the boats. We never liked to leave our boats, even if they was empty, you never knew what nosey parkers might want to see what you'd got. It was bad enough in the small towns but the City Road was so big and with so many people! Funny I didn't never call it London, to me it was always the City Road. Flossie and me was so excited to be goin' off with Ma to the markets. Da had slipped me a shillin' and told me to get somethin' nice for Ma and to be sure to get it wrapped in paper so she wouldn't see it. Then he gave Flossie a ha'penny to buy herself a lolly, this would be a real treat for her, 'cos we didn't get many sweetie things. Ma put on her best shawl and bonnet and we set off, leavin' the men on 'The Isis' and 'Bluebell' breasted up, alongside the wharf. It was early evening, and Ma said it were cold enough for snow, as we walked along the cobbled streets, under and over bridges with our Flossie huddled between us for warmth. It was dark, but the tall gas lights lined the streets so we 'ad no trouble seein' where we was goin'.

It seemed to me, it was Christmas already when we got to the market, there were so may people. Everyone pushin' and shovin' to get to the stalls, the barrow boys all competing with each other, callin' out what they had for sale, people everywhere barterin' and shoutin'. In a nearby 'public' someone was playin' a piano and we could hear singin' and the clink of glasses and roars of laughter. There was a strong fishy smell, as we passed a jellied eel seller and people stood about eatin' out of newspaper. Ma held on tightly to Flossie's hand and told me to keep close, else we would get lost. I didn't need to be told, I knew

I'd never find me way back through the maze of streets, to our boats, if I lost sight of Ma. As we pushed our way passed the stalls I was holdin' on tightly to the shillin' inside me apron pocket. Da said that places like this was rife with pickpockets and I wasn't about to let no one rob me of a whole shillin'. We stopped at one stall while Ma inspected the wares on offer, not 'appy with what she saw, we moved on to another and then another.

Eventually she settled on this particular stall where she rumaged through huge piles of second hand clothes. A tiny woman with enormous gold earings was sat on a stool watchin' everyone like a hawk. It wasn't in us to walk off and not to pay for goods, but not everyone was like us, we knew that. Da said there was more dishonest people livin' down south than there was livin' in the north. Ma pulled out a waistcoat with metal buttons and a velvet collar, then, carefully examining it for wear "I think this will fit your Da" she said in triumph. Then shoving it into my hand, carried on pulling out items of clothes and throwin' them on top of the pile when she decided they wasn't what she wanted. In this way Ma decided on two more items she thought good enough for her family to wear. A red woollen dress for Flossie, a bit big but it could be taken up, and a pair of blue serge trousers for our Sammy. They was too big an' all but Ma said he would soon grow into them. The tiny woman wanted eight pence for the lot, but Ma said she wasn't partin' with more than sixpence, take it or leave it and the woman grumbled but took the sixpenny bit Ma offered anyway.

We pushed our way past more stalls 'til we came to one sellin' crusty pies, I was so happy when she stopped and bought two big pork ones, cos' I loved the crusty pastry and tasty meat filling.

"When can I get a sweetie" Flossie was beginning to get bored now and wanted to have her promised treat.

"When we sees a sweetie seller" Ma replied without looking down at her, still intent on finding more treats to take back for her family.

"But I want a sweetie, Da gave me a ha'penny to get one and I want one now" Flossie wailed.

Ma stopped dead in her tracks and turned back to Flossie "Now don't you start that here madam" she looked cross but this didn't stop our Flossie, she was too used to getting' her own way.

"But Da said I could" Flossie's bottom lip was thrust out and I could see she was headin' for another tantrum. I didn't want Ma getting all worked up and spoil her buyin' spree, I could see how much she was enjoyin' herself so I said

"You carry on and get what you want Ma and I'll take Flossie over there," and pointed in the direction of a man selling taffy apples.

"Alright lass, but don't go getting' lost" she said and began to move off in search of more treats, but I caught her arm

"If I can't find you, we'll wait under the lamp post, just by the 'public bar' we passed on the way in".

Ma nodded her agreement, then called back over her shoulder "Don't go talkin' to no strangers Jess".

"No Ma" I called back, as Flossie took my hand and tugged me towards the taffy apples.

While my little sister was choosing the biggest one she could find I decided that I wouldn't go back and find

Ma straight away, as this would be a good time to look for the present Da wanted me to get for Ma, without her knowing. Flossie proudly took out her ha'penny and handed it to the red faced man who was holding a tray full of all types of sweets, with straps attached to it, which went round his neck. He smiled back at her, seeing her big blue eyes light up as she took the taffy apple on a stick.

"That'll keep you goin' for a while" he said and winked at me as he took Flossie's money

"And here's a piece of cinder toffee for your sister" he said as he handed me a little paper bag.

I was so surprised I couldn't think what to say "Ta, mister" Flossie said and the man winked at me again. I felt all hot and tongue tied

"Y-yes ta mister, ta very much" I eventually managed to say and pulled Flossie away into the semi darkness so no one would see my red face. 'Silly stupid girl,' I thought to meself 'He's only a sweet seller bein' friendly to make more money'. I looked down at Flossie, and was glad she hadn't noticed me gettin' all embarrassed, she was far too busy licking her sweetie.

I tried to look over the heads of the crowds all milling round a barrow selling meat and fish. I thought it funny that people were paying good money for the dead rabbits, hares and ducks, hanging upside down from the barrow. Surely they could set their own snares and catch any number of these any night of the week. Funny people the 'townies' I thought, as I walked over to a stall all lit up with fancy oil lamps. The small wooden barrow was covered over with a velvet cloth and I held my breath as I looked at the mass of sparkling 'jewellery' laid out there. Sparkley necklaces in boxes, broaches pinned to cards, glass beads hung up on hooks, silver chains with fobs, bracelets spread over cushions and what looked like hundreds of hat pins all stuck into an old straw hat with a large red feather. I had never seen such treasures! A little man dressed all in black, with a large black hat and tiny spectacles, stood behind the stall.

"And what can we do for you young Miss?" he said.

I looked 'round to see who he was speakin' to, but Flossie and me was the only ones there. I looked back at the man and the stall, the light from the oil lamps lit up every item on his stall everything glittered and twinkled.

"I-I w-want somethin' nice for me Ma." I couldn't think why I was so nervous. The little man leaned towards me,

"Might I enquire how much you would like to spend Miss" his whisper was exagerated.

I felt my cheeks go all hot for the second time but I wasn't gonna let it stop me, the sight of all these beautiful things spurred me on.

"Me Da's give me a shillin' to buy somethin' nice for our Ma, for Christmas"

I felt sure I had made a good impression on the man 'cos he looked carefully round his barrow and picked out two items.

"How about a pin or a broach?" he said offering me a tiny silver coloured bar with scrolls at either end and writing on. He must have known I couldn't read 'cos when I looked up at him he smiled and said " It says 'Mother'.

"Oh" I said, going all hot again. "Or what about this one" he handed me a small heart shape all covered in tiny stones which, as I turned it in my hand, glittered in the light from the lamps. Attached to the heart was a piece of blue ribbon sewn to a small pin at the back.

"It's marcasite" he said.

It looked so beautiful, I was sure that Ma would love it, and the heart, she would love to think Da had bought somethin' like that for her. I was then struck with fear, maybe the man hadn't heard me when I told him I had a shillin' to spend. This was so lovely, it might cost more than I had. I looked down at my boots for what seemed like a long time, tryin' to think what to do or say next. The man gave a little cough and I looked up. I was still holdin' on to the heart.

"Shall we say one shilling Miss?" his eyes was sort of smilin' at me, over his spectacles, but I didn't think he was makin' fun nor nothin.'

"Y-yes please" I managed to say "And me Da says, c-can you wrap it up in a bit of paper so Ma won't see it?"

"I think I can do better than that miss" he said "I have a little velvet pouch here" and he pulled out a tiny black velvet bag with a string into which he put the beautiful heart.

"Now I'll wrap that in paper for you Miss"

I couldn't believe this 'townie' was being so kind to me, let alone callin' me Miss! He handed me the package and I handed him the shilling. I looked down at our Flossie, she was still getting her teeth into the taffy apple and wasn't takin' no notice of me or the jewellery man.

"Good night Miss" said the man as I took hold of Flossie's sticky hand and walked away with my precious package tucked safely into me apron pocket.

I didn't know how long I had been, buyin' the broach, but I looked back to where I had last seen Ma and of course she wasn't there now. I couldn't decide whether to traipse round the market lookin' for her or to wait by the lamp post as we'd arranged. She might be ages yet I thought, but I might have been ages with the jewellery man so she might already be waitin' for us. Flossie was busy licking her sticky fingers now, having finished the sweetie.

"What we doin' now Jess?" she asked in between licks.

"We'll go over and wait for Ma by the lamp post" I said, having made the decision. I took hold of Flossie's shoulder, not wanting to take her sticky hand, and steered her through the crowds and past the noisy barrow boys still crying their wares. We stepped up out of the road and stood leaning against the lamp post. The piano player was still playing frantically inside the public bar and people was singing cheery verses and choruses of well known music hall songs. Shouts of laughter and the ring of many hobnails on cobbles made me look 'round towards the open doors of the 'public'. Eight or nine young men in army uniform had just arrived and were trying to push their way into the crowded bar. After several unsuccessful attempts, two of the uniforms was sent to the back of the premises with orders to buy the 'round 'for their mates at the offy. I watched as they leaned against the decorated glass windows of the bar, rolling, then lighting their cigarettes, their breath, like little plumes of smoke in the cold night air. One of them looked towards me, and embarrassed that he had seen me lookin' at them, I turned sharply round to Flossie who was still lickin' her fingers.

"Give me your hand Flossie" I said and began wiping it roughly on me apron.

"That hurts our Jess!" exclaimed my little sister, but I ignored her complaint and did the same with the other hand, needing to satisfy myself, as well as the young men in uniform, that I was busy minding my own business. I kept on rubbing Flossie's hand even when I heard the heavy booted feet walking towards me. I didn't look up, not even when they stopped right behind me, but when one of them put his hand on me shoulder I nearly stopped breathing.

"Hey you're a pretty girlie," the young man breathed down my neck, "Want to give a soldier a kiss on his last night, before he goes off to fight in the War!"

I wanted to scream and run! But didn't want to show meself up, and there was so many people about. I just looked down at my boots, thinking if I said nothin' they would go away.

"Yes" said another voice "Make that two kisses!"

The two young men in uniform behind me laughed loudly, my face burned so hot I thought it would burst.

"C'mon luv, whadd'ya say, just a little kiss"

I could smell they had been drinkin' and one of them weren't too steady on his feet, he was swaying about

"Tell them to go away our Jessie!" Flossie pulled her hand from mine and turned round to face the two young men.

"Go away and leave our Jessie be!" she shouted and stamped her foot as she always did to get her own way.

It was just as I turned to face the uniforms, having worked up enough courage to say somethin' to send them away when a third one came running up

"Hey you two! Marcus, Richard, leave the poor girl alone," he shouted

"Come on chaps we're off up the West End".

The two young men instantly lost interest and stumbled back towards the bar. My head was swimming, I felt so stupid, people was lookin' and I wished I had been anywhere but right under a lamp where everyone could see me red face. I looked frantically at the crowds millin' 'round the stalls hopin' to see Ma was comin'. A sea of faces seemed to be lookin' back at me, but there was no sign of her. I pulled me shawl up round me neck and pulled the brim of me bonnet down to hide me embarrassment. I nearly jumped out of me skin when another voice spoke behind me

"Excuse me Miss." I turned and looked up into a pair of clear blue eyes. "I just wanted to apologise for my comrades, you see we're off to France tomorrow and well, we're just having a bit of fun before we go."

I wanted to speak but my tongue seemed to swell up and stick to the roof of my now very dry mouth. The blue eyes kept on looking straight at me and I knew I was expected to make some reply, but I was completely dumb struck as they say.

"Well, no harm done, eh?" the young man was still waiting for a word from me, then he stepped back, stood upright, saluted, turned smartly and walked away.

"Eeh, our Jessie, wot's got you?" said the four year old Flossie, as I gazed after the young soldier. I was about to tell my little sister that at her age she knew now't, when

Ma stepped into the lamplight, arms full of packages tied up with string.

"I think I've got all I need. Here Jessie, take some of these from me will ya"

I stretched out me arms and took several packages.

"Ma, Ma wot can I carry?" Flossie jumped up and down shouting.

"Well now, pr'haps you could manage this" Ma said and handed her a large cabbage. Flossie took it eagerly and I prayed she would not say anything to Ma about the young men in uniform.

"You was ages Ma, I thought you was buyin' up the whole place." I said as we walked off up the street the way we had come.

"Well I had to get boots for our Josh, 'cos his are leakin' like sieves. Then I wanted to get a nice bit of fresh fish for supper, it's real cheap here if you goes to the right stall. We haven't had a nice bit of sea fish in months."

Ma was in good spirits, she always enjoyed a good shopping spree and chattered on about what she had bought nearly all the way back to the her own little world, while our Flossie set about pullin off bits of leaf from the cabbage and eatin' 'em. I was grateful for the dark, not wantin' Ma to see my red face, which was by now cooling off. I was glad too that Ma's chatter needed no answering and I went off on a day dream of my own.

Then just as we walked under the bridge and our boats were in sight, I heard Flossie's little sing-song voice "Guess wot Ma!" me heart sank as I waited for her next words

"What love?"

She'd got Ma's attention now and went on "There was this man," Flossie liked the attention so she would make the tale last as long as possible. "He smiled at our Jessie".

"Did he love?."

I wanted to strangle my little sister.

"Yes Ma he did," I could see her angelic face smiling up at Ma. "And d'you know what he did then"

"No love what did he do then?" Ma was humouring her.

I could hardly breath, not knowing how Ma would take it, she might think I had been bold.

"Well Ma" Flossie was savouring every word "He gave her a lump of cinder taffy!"

I let my breath out slowly, painfully.

"Did he now, well that was kind, and did you get your sweetie?"

"Yes Ma, I had a taffy apple and the man gave our Jessie some cinder taffy in a bag and she put it in her apron pocket." Flossie was triumphant having told her tale, but she wasn't finished and I held my breath again "Ma" she went on in her whiney voice "Will you tell our Jess she's got to share it with me!"

For once I was so glad that Flossie's love of sweets and spoiled selfish ways meant she was only thinking of the cinder taffy in my apron pocket. I smiled to meself as I curled up in me bed'ole on Bluebell that night, thinkin' about our Flossie. She was so spoiled but I had given her the whole bag, well I was just so glad she hadn't told Ma or the others about the soldiers. And Da had been so pleased with the little marcasite heart, he couldn't believe I got it for just a shillin', with the velvet bag an all . We both knew Ma would be as 'appy as Larry' when we gave it to her on Christmas mornin.'

CHAPTER NINE

Ruth's Secret

The wind had been howling and the rain lashing down all day, in fact the weather had been pretty bad on and off for several weeks. We was carryin' 'China Clay' up to the Potteries, which was a difficult enough cargo in the wet. It was packed in large canvas sacks, and was the devil's own job to keep dry. Da had put extra planks on top of the keelson in the bottom of our two boats, to keep the sacks out of the water wot collected there. Then he got Mr. Griffiths to let him have some spare cloths, tarpaulins Mr. Griffiths called them, to go the 'ole length of each hold, over the top of the cargo. Even with our own boats' cloths over the top of that again, we still had our work cut out to keep the wind from whipping the top cloths up and the rain pourin' in. We had to tighten the ropes at nearly every lock and bridge 'ole along the way. We was travelling with two other families and their boats, up the Grand Junction canal to Norton Junction, then on to Braunston 'turn' and up the Oxford and Coventry canals and on to the Potteries. Mr. Griffiths was trying to get a reg'lar contract with a company called Wedgewoods. He had been offered this special run 'cos they was tryin' out a different sort of clay, wot came here from the low countries, and not from Cornwall where they usually got it from. We 'ad to get there real fast like to prove we could do the job just as well as Fellows Morton and that lot. So there we was with our two boats, 'Isis' and 'Bluebell', the Jonas family and their two boats 'India' and 'Dab Chick' and George and Mary Higgins and their boats 'Lily' and 'Dipper'. Albert and Olwen Jonas had eight children on the boats with them and two more what had gone off to work for Ovaltine's. We had known them all our lives, 'cos they had worked for Mr. Griffiths as long as Da had. George Higgins was an older brother to Daft Freddie, but they was like chalk and cheese, and Mary Higgins, his wife, wouldn't have nowt to do with Lizzie and Freddie, in fact wouldn't never have them on her boats. Mary was very partic'lar like and kept their four small children very clean and tidy. They 'ad taken on Mary's brother Tom for this trip, so that he could work their second boat then we would all get up to Wedgewood's much faster. Mr. Griffiths 'ad promised Tom a boat of his own, when he had 'proved' his-self, so this run was very important to Tom. Smiffy had brought a letter from Mr. Griffiths, he stood on the tow path and read to Da, telling him he was 'in charge' of this 'fleet' of boats and it was up to 'im to make sure we all stayed together and made good time. He wanted the bosses at Wedgewoods to think he had a fleet of boats good enough to take on a contract from them to deliver china clay reg'lar like. Ma allus said she didn't care what we carried as long as it weren't coal, but that was before we had ever carried china clay –and in the rain !

The first two days out from 'Limehouse' we made real good time, the weather 'ad miraculously dried up and we had a good 'tail wind'. We set off at first light and carried on 'til well after dark, even though Ma never liked to work the 'orse at night, especially with the two boats, but we was under strict instructions to get up to the Potteries in under two weeks so we 'ad no choice. I could tell Ma was feelin' all important like, Da bein' in charge of all the other boats an' all, 'cos she kept turnin' and smilin' at George and Mary Higgins whenever they was close enough for her to see 'em. We could put both our boats in the locks together on the Grand Junction 'cos they was double 'uns. Da and our Sammy stayed bankside with Albert Jonas, his lad Jacob and one of their twin daughters, Ruth. They worked the locks so we could all get through without wastein' time. Our Josh was leadin, Hercules and I was steerin' Bluebell. I was glad that our Flossie hadn't made a fuss and stayed on 'Isis' with Ma. Lately she had taken it into her 'ead that she wanted to come onboard 'Bluebell' with me and no amount of persuadin' would make her change her mind. She was so crafty, she knew that if she 'ad a screaming tantrum, Ma would give in to her and let her do what she liked. So some days I had to put up with her incessant chatter and whining. I liked it now we 'ad the two boats and I could spend hours alone in the well deck steerin'. There was somethin' very satisfyin' about steerin' a boat up the Cut on yer own, especially when you 'ardly ever got chance to be on yer own and think yer own thoughts, without interruptions. Sometimes, when the weather was cold and there was a good long stretch between locks, I would sit on the cabin roof with me legs dangling over the hatch 'ole, down inside the cabin. Then with the back doors closed, I could stay as 'snug as a bug' with the warmth from the range wafting up around me. I could manage the tiller arm real good from up there, I got a good view of all the countryside around and I thought I was the 'bees knees'.

We 'ad been on the 'run' for eight days and during the last six the rain 'ad been pouring down day and night. Da was very concerned about the cargo and kept checking all the boats to make sure no water was leaking in. Mr. Griffiths 'ad promised all three skippers a bonus if he managed to secure a reg'lar contract on the strength of this run, so we all 'ad what Da called a 'vested interest'. Each night when we tied up the men inspected the 'ole length of their boats, tightening ropes and adjusting cloths, then each morning they did the 'ole thing again before we set off. Because we was tryin' to make good time we wasn't too fussy about where we tied up each night. It was April and we was workin' very long days, the nights bein' much lighter now, so by the time we 'ad moored up and 'ad our supper we was all ready to fall into our beds. Consequently even though we was workin' the boats altogether, we 'ardly had time to pass the time of day with any of the other families.

So when Albert's horse 'Dolly' went lame, just outside of Braunston and we all 'ad to wait up while he and our Josh took 'er off to the farrier, which luckily was quite close by, we suddenly 'ad time on our 'ands for the first time in our journey. Ma took no time at all in inviting Olwen Jonas and Mary Higgins into the back cabin of 'Isis', where she sat like Queen Vic herself, holding court, while she got out the best china and served them tea and slices of fresh baked lardy cake. The rain 'ad stopped, though the heavy grey sky was threatening more as Da sat on the roof of 'Bluebell' and packed his pipe with the strong tobacco he had bartered for from the skipper of a Dutch 'gaff rigged' barge, moored up in Limehouse basin. I sat on the gunnal waiting in anticipation for the pungent smell to come wafting my way as he lit up.

"You not joinin' the 'tea party' Jessis lass? " Da said in between puffs, "Yer Ma's pleased as punch, havin' the time to jaw with the rest of the women"

"I know, I replied, "She's been itchin' to show off the new china, ever since we left the basin" .

"Poor Olwyn and Mary'll never get a word in edgeways, now yer Ma's got them inside our cabin" Da said.

"They'll probably have to drink both Buckby's dry before Ma lets them out again"

I said and we both laughed, sharing a rare moment of closeness that I wanted to last forever.

But just then Rachael Jonus came along the towpath carrying her baby sister Martha in her arms.

"Hello Jessica, Our Ruth's mashed a pot tea if you'd like one" she said as she swapped the baby from one hip to the other.

I was about to decline the offer, not wantin' to break the spell of this special moment of closeness with my Da, when he said

"That's a good idea Jess, you go and have a natter with Rachael and Ruth, you don't get to see them much".

"I was just about to brew up meself," I said in the hope that Da would want me to stay, but he caught hold of my arm and tugged me across the gunnal and onto the bank sayin'

"You go off and enjoy yerself Jess while you've got the chance. I'm not above pouring a drop of water onto a few tea leaves you know. I looked after meself for many years before I married yer Ma!"

I could see it was no use arguing, and the spell was broken now anyway, so reluctantly I went off down the tow path with Rachael and Martha and on to their boat 'India'.

As I stepped down into the back cabin, there was a chorus of 'Hello's' from the Jonas children. They was all sitting round the range, mugs of tea in hand waiting for Ruth, the eldest of the twins, to finish butterin' large doorsteps of bread, before handing them round to her brothers and sisters. Rachael followed me down the step and promptly deposited baby Martha, into Miriam's lap.

"Aye our Rachael, I was just about to eat a piece!" she protested as the baby grabbed for the large slice of bread in Miriam's hand.

"Give 'er the crust to chew on, she likes that" Rachael replied as she pushed Issac and Jacob aside, making room for the two of us to sit down on the side bed. "Just make sure she don't choke".

"Aw, we was sittin' there!" Jacob protested, as he and Issac found themselves pushed off their seat.

"There's plenty of room on the floor !" Rachael retorted, "And if you don't like that you can allus go outside"

Jacob and Issac, who were obviously used to being 'bossed' around by their elder sister and knew they'd not win an argument with her, obediently, though somewhat reluctantly, sat themselves down on the bare wooden floor of the cabin.

"How are you then Jess?" said Rachel, "How d'you like steerin' the new boat then?" And before I 'ad time to reply……….

"You don't get no fatter do ya"

"D'you think yer Da'll get us all up there on time?"

"Is them new boots you've got on?"

"Can we come on your boat?"

The 'ole family was firing questions all at the same time and me 'ead was spinnin' 'cos I could 'ardly think of an answer for one, before another was being voiced.

I opened me mouth to reply, just as Ruth said

"Come on you lot, give 'er a chance, she's just got through the door!" Then turning to hand me a mug of tea she carried on, "It's nice to see you Jess, we don't often 'ave the chance to sit and natter."

I took the tea and sat gazing 'round at the Jonas family and remembered Ma sayin' that all of their names came out of the bible.

"I get up?" It was Isiah, he was the second youngest, about three I think and he was trying to climb up onto my lap.

"C'mon Izzy" I said as I hauled him up with my spare hand.

"Aw Jess, you don't 'ave to nurse him an all, I bet you gets enough with your Flossie." Ruth said

I was about to say I didn't mind when she went on "And what an 'andful she is, she wouldn't last ten minutes in this family!"

I opened my mouth to reply that she wasn't that bad, when Rachael cut in

"Yeh, we saw her 'avin a tantrum with yer Ma, before we set off, if she'd bin one of ours, she'd have got a clout and no mistake!"

"Well" I said, "She can be a bit........." and I was cut off by Jacob who put in

"We don't none of us 'ave temper tantrums, Ma 'ud clip us round the ear!"

I felt that I should defend our Flossie and Ma for allowin' her to behave badly, they probably didn't realise how Ma and Da felt about her, after Ma had lost so many bairns before she came along. I felt I should tell them how precious our Flossie was to them, especially when two winters back, she nearly died of the whooping cough, just like *our* little Issac 'ad. But looking round at this rudely healthy bunch of kids, who all fought for recognition and their place in this large family, I doubted that any of them would understand why Ma and Da spoiled our Flossie so much.

"Ah well, she is the youngest " I said "And I expect little Martha 'ere gets all the attention too".

"Yeh," said Miriam as she wiped buttery fingers down the front of 'er smock, "Martha just 'as to cry, and we gives 'er anythin' to shut 'er up!"

Miriam was a quiet little thing of about eight years old, and I judged that she, more than any of the others, got lost and almost forgotten in amongst this larger than life family. Isiah was getting' all fidgety on my lap and I was glad when he decided to crawl off in the direction of Jacob, who was playing with a tiny kitten on the floor beside the stove. Ruth, who had now finished dishing out bread and tea to the rest of her family, wiped her hands on her apron and came and sat between Rachael and I on the side bed. Everyone said they were identical twins, Ruth and Rachael, but I could see the difference. Whether it was because I had known them all my life, or because I took the trouble to really see them, I don't know, but I'd never had any bother in knowing which was which, except perhaps from across the cut or two boat lengths away. But up close you could see that Rachael had greeny coloured eyes, which were further apart than her sister's definitely brown eyes. And Ruth's nose had a slight bend in it, half way down and she was about half an inch taller than her sister. She said that was 'cos she was twenty minutes older, and that makes a lot of difference to a twin. The rest of the Jonas family 'ad no trouble at all in knowing which twin was which. I thought it was funny 'ow some people said they couldn't tell the difference, even our Josh, but then he didn't take no notice of people. Now animals, that was a different thing altogether. You put two horses side by side and even if you or I thought they was identical, 'e would know the difference. Just as well we're not all the same I suppose.

"How's your Josh?"

My thoughts was suddenly interrupted by Rachael's question.

"Our Josh?" I repeated stupidly "He's – um, he's fine, why?"

I looked at Rachael and was surprised to see that 'er face was going all pink. The others all laughed and I could see that this embarrassed her even more.

"Cos she's sweet on 'im!" Issac and Jacob chorused together

"I am not!" she snapped "It's Ruth, she can't stop talking about him that's all"

"I do not" Ruth cried, "It's you Rach, you go all silly every time you see him"

"Silly, me go all silly, what about last night, you must have brushed your hair ten times before you went out in the rain, just to see if he was on the tow path seein' to their 'orse!" Rachael went on.

"That's a lie and you know it" Ruth was almost shouting now.

"Here they go again!" Issac said in a sing-songy voice.

"And you can shut up!" Rachael rounded on her younger brother. "Why don't you lot all go and find yourself somethin' useful to do, instead of sittin' around earwiggin' on other people's conversations" Rachael indicated the door as she spoke.

I thought it unreasonable that she should expect her family not to listen in, 'specially when you all live in a cabin eight foot by six foot, it's a bit difficult NOT to listen to whatever is bein' said.

"I've 'ad enough of this anyway" said Issac as he pushed past the others and climbed up into the well deck "You comin' Jake?" and not waiting for an answer he stepped over the gunn'all onto the bank and was gone, leaving Jacob to follow in his wake.

Martha was falling asleep in Miriam's lap as Ruth lifted the baby and tucked her up with Isiah, who was already dozing noisily, curled up in the bed 'ole. She covered both children with her shawl before returning to the stove

"I'll make another brew" she said to no one in particular.

I sat in silence with the other girls, watching Ruth refill the kettle from the buckby can and putting it onto the stove to boil. Then Rachael took me by surprise a bit when she said

"Take yer bonnet off Jessie"

"Whatever for?" I said, not quite knowing why she would want me to take it off.

"Cos you've got lovely hair, it's a shame to keep it covered up"

I felt myself going all hot and put my hands up to my face to cover my embarrassment.

"Eeh, our Rachael, leave off, you've made Jessie feel all daft" Ruth said as she turned 'round from the stove. "Take no notice of 'er Jess, she's got a thing about hair, she just likes brushin' it." The other girls laughed and Ruth went on, "She'd 'ave us all lined up together, with our 'air all let loose so she could just brush it all day long if she 'ad 'er way".

My moment of embarrassment passed, but Rachael didn't let up

"Go on Jess, let it all down and let me brush it for ya!" and she reached across and pulled off me bonnet. "Its such a 'luvelly' colour, all red and shinney, like our copper kettle. I wish I 'ad 'air that colour"

I was still not comfortable with the idea of Rachael brushing my hair, I don't know why I thought it was so strange, probably 'cos my only sister was a lot younger and brothers never did that sort of thing. I 'ad always looked after meself, washin me hair and such like, Ma was not a person for fussing over any of us, except, of course, for our Flossie.

"You might just as well give in Jess and let 'er do it, she'll only keep on 'til you do" Ruth said laughing. "They won't be back with the 'orse for ages yet and yer Ma'll be chattin' all day if our Ma's got anythin' to do with it."

And so I took the pins from me hair and let it tumble down me back.

"Ooh Jess, look 'ow the light shines in it!" Rachael said as she set to work teasing out the tangles.

I couldn't remember anyone ever brushing me 'air for me, but it felt strangely nice and after a while I relaxed and we girls just carried on nattering. I 'ad never really considered what I looked like, but the Jonas girls obviously 'ad for they kept saying things about me.

"Eeh yer so pretty Jess, don't you think so Ruth?" Miriam said as she gazed up at me from the small wooden stool where she was sittin'.

"Give over!" I said, feelin' meself goin' all pink again

"But yer are" Rachael said from behind me, "I bet you 'ave all the boys wantin' to walk out with ya"

"I certainly do not" I retorted

"Go on, I bet they're all queuein' up, 'ave you got yer eye on anyone special?"

"Rachael!" I said, getting all annoyed now, "I do not 'ave any boys wantin' to court me and I am certainly not lookin' at any boys neither. I've………….." I was about to say 'never met no one,' but just then a little thought crept into me mind. I 'ad seen a boy, a lad a bit older than me, 'e 'ad given me a look 'up an down' at the City Road. We'd been loadin' sacks of sugar and one had split just as I were tryin' to lift it up onto me back. Our Josh was down in the 'old waitin' for me to hump it over the gunn'all, when I 'eard a ripping sound and felt the sugar pouring out onto the wharf. I 'ad tried to lower the sack to the ground, but just as I turned, the weight shifted and I toppled over landing with the sack on top of me, inches from the wharf's edge. The fall took me completely by surprise and I lay there for a second or two wonderin' what 'ad 'appened. Then I 'eard someone sayin'

"You all right there girlie?" and when I looked up, there was this lad standin' over me.

"I-I think so!" I said feelin' real stupid as I hoped me skirt and petticoats was coverin' me legs. I couldn't move me 'ands to make sure, 'cos the sack of sugar was on top of me, pinnin' me to the ground. The lad bent down and began to pull the sack off me when our Josh jumped over the gunn'all shoutin

"Wait!"

The lad turned round and quickly backed away, as if half expecting our Josh to take a swing at him.

"If you give me a 'and, we can move the sack together and not spill any more sugar"

Our Josh, ever the practical one, was more interested in saving the contents of the sack, than in seein' if I was 'urt or anythin'. The lad obeyed our Josh's instructions and between them they carefully lifted the sack and layed it on the ground beside me.

"I think we've managed to save most of it" our Josh said, "Thanks mate, I'll just go and get an empty'un to put this lot in" and he walked off up the wharfside and disappeared onto our other boat Bluebell, to get the empty sack.

It all 'appened so quickly and I was still lyin' on the ground, I remembered thinkin' that our Josh could've helped me up. I turned onto my side and was about to stand up when I realised the lad was still standin' there .

"Here girlie, give us yer 'and," And with that he thrust his large hands nearly into my face, then catching me two hands in his, he pulled me to me feet.

"Not hurt are ya?" 'E said and I felt real embarrassed, 'specially as he was still holdin' on to me 'ands. He seemed to be lookin' down at me for a very long time, not speakin' just lookin' and I just sort of gazed back up at 'im. 'E 'ad a real friendly face, with straight black hair stickin' out from under his cap. He was wearin' a smart double breasted waistcoat with brass buttons down the front and white corduroy trousers. I remember thinkin' 'fancy wearin' white trousers 'round 'ere", but my thoughts was interruped as I 'eard our Josh's voice

"C'mon Jess, don't just stand there, get this sugar shovelled up before we lose any more"

I quickly pulled me 'and away from the tall young lad and turned, all flustered like, to face me brother.

"Thanks for yer 'elp mate, we can manage now" our Josh said, sort of dismissing the lad. I thought it was a bit unfriendly of me brother, when this lad, who we didn't know from Adam, 'ad stopped to help. I was about to say somethin' of the sort to our Josh, but instead I turned intendin' to apologise to the young man for my brother's rudeness, only to see him walking off, 'ands in his pockets, under the bridge and out of sight.

I 'ad thought about that lad quite a lot since then, mostly when I was lying in bed at night, but I didn't know who he was. All I did know was that he worked for Fellows Morton, our Josh had said as much as we shovelled up the sugar

"Flash Boys, them 'Fellows Morton' lot, with their fancy wess'cuts and white trousers. Don't know wot real work is, they gets all their cargo loaded and unloaded for 'em, all they 'as to do is steer the boats!"

It wasn't like our Josh to pass comment on other people and their boats. I didn't know what 'e 'ad against this lad, p'rhaps it was just the fancy uniform. I decided not to say nothin' and just carried on scooping up the spilt sugar.................

"You still with us?" Ruth's voice brought me suddenly back from my thoughts.

"You bin day dreamin' Jess?" Rachael laughed "You was just tellin' us 'ow you wasn't interested in any young lad, then you went off all dreamie eyed, now c'mon tell us, wot's 'is name, 'ho is 'E?"

I felt the heat rising from the back of my neck creeping up to my cheeks then me 'ole face seemed to be burning.

"I-I don't know w-what you m- mean!" I stuttered, trying to hide me intense embarrassment.

The Jonas girls just looked at me, then burst out laughing

"Eeh Jess, he must be somethin' real special to make you go all gooey eyed an' romantic like!" Rachael said as she put her arms 'round me and gave me a sort of squeeze.

I knew it was useless trying to explain that they'd got it all wrong, for they obviously wanted to believe that I *had* met a boy. But what could I tell them, I hadn't even decided in me own mind what I thought about him.

"Aw c'mon Jess let us into your little secrets" Ruth laughed

"There's nothin' to tell" I replied, but knew they would not let it rest there, so I went on. "It was just a lad who stopped to 'elp when I fell over with a sack of sugar on top of me!" I knew this sounded stupid, but that's all it was.

"Who was he, do we know him?" Rachael was impatient to know more.

"I don't know who 'E is", I replied, "But our Josh said he works for Fellows Morton, 'cos of his uniform"

"Aw Jess, a Fellow Morton boatie, they gets a lotta money, 'specially the 'fly boat' boys, you could get married and live in an 'ouse – bankside!" Rachael said nudging me from behind, where she was still brushing my hair.

"Don't be stupid" I said jumping up, "I've never met him before or since, so just stop all this nonsense!" I don't know what made me so upset, but I pulled me hair over my shoulder and began twisting it back up into a bun. "I'll 'ave to be getting' back to our boat," I said, "I've got things to do!" and I put me bonnet back on me 'ead, and began tyin' the strings.

"Don't be so tetchie Jess." Rachael tried to pull me back "We was only 'avin' a bit of fun"

"No really" I said, determined not to stay a moment longer, "I've got a lot to do and Ma will expect........." I didn't get a chance to finish what I was sayin 'cos Rachael cut in.

"Don't go Jess, not yet, we wanted to ask you somethin' - well important like."

There was something in the tone of her voice that made me stop and think I should listen to what she 'ad to say.

"Go on then" I said, "Ask me."

"Well, its not that easy. I mean well it's really for our Ruth."

It was Ruth's turn to look embarrassed now as 'er twin sister seemed to be talking about her as though she wern't there.

"We thought, well, she wants to know if you would, I mean if you could........"

I 'ad no idea what they was getting at and now I was impatient to know.

"C'mon Rach out with it" I said.

Rachael took a deep breath and swallowed, then pulled herself up to her full height and began

"Its our Ruth, she's getting herself in a real bad way, 'cos she doesn't know what to do or what to say"

"Go on," I couldn't imagine what was coming next.

"She loves 'im, your Josh I mean, she just can't think of nothin' else. There I've said it now!" Rachael got up and took hold of her sister's hand and the two of them stood lookin' at me as though I would know what to do. I couldn't think of nothin' to say, I just 'adn't known, 'adn't thought. Wot could I say? The two Jonas girls just carried on lookin' at me, willin' me to say somethin'. I just sat there desperately tryin' to think of somthin' *to* say.

"Ave you spoken to our Josh?" I realised how stupid that sounded as soon as I said it. Course they 'adn't said nothin' to our Josh, that's where *I* came in, that's exactly what they wanted *me* to do. "I mean, does 'E know?"

"Oh Jess, E's never said nothin' to me, well nothin' more than 'ello or somethin' like that!" Ruth was twistin' the corner of her apron, like she was wringing out washing.

"I don't even know if 'E likes me!" she was nearly in tears now. "Does he ever say anythin' about me?"

How could I answer that, our Josh rarely talked about anythin' and when he did it was certainly not about girls. Now horses, that was a different matter, infact if our Josh 'ad to pick between a girl and an 'orse, the 'orse would win every time. But 'ow could I say that to Ruth. She obviously 'ad it real bad for our Josh, I 'ad to think of somethin' to say, so as not to 'urt her like.

"I-I don't think our Josh 'as really thought about, well, girls" I said, knowing that it was all comin' out wrong.

"That's good" said Rachael "At least we know there's no one else then."

Ruth managed a thin smile, "W-would you speak to him for me Jess, just sort of sound 'im out. Don't tell 'im wot we've said, just sort of find out if he likes me, will you do that Jess, will you?"

What could I say except that I would. I couldn't find it in me 'eart to leave 'er with no hope and to be truthfull, I really didn't know what our Josh thought of 'er, he'd never mentioned 'er. But as I walked back down the towpath towards our boats, I didn't 'old out too much 'ope for 'er................Poor Ruth!

Photograph taken in 1910 of two horse drawn F.M.C.boats waiting to enter Islington Tunnel.

CHAPTER TEN

The Judgement

Life on the canals went on as usual, although whenever we went into the towns along the way people was talking about the war, it didn't really affect us boaties. We still worked the same route, from the City Road to Preston Brook with our main cargo of sugar and tea and on the return trip picking up loads from factories and potteries where ever we could. Sometimes the Gaffer would get word to us to pick up a full load from this place or that and sometimes Da would stop off on the way up to fix up return loads. These could be just short distance stuff, like loading with cases of Jam from the Jam factory and taking it into Birnigum, or picking up crates of earthenware from the potteries and off loading in several towns all the way down to the City Road. Da always said he didn't like the short runs as there was too much loadin' and unloadin to be done. But I enjoyed stoppin off at different places, seein' new and different types of work. Sometimes we had to turn off the main canal and go off up an arm to a mill or factory or colliery.

Lately we had been given several loads of vitals and supplies for the mining companies in the Midlands. Most of these had their own wharfs and their own company shops. Da said that lots of these companies paid their workers in tokens and not proper money. These tokens, called Tommy Notes, could only be changed for supplies in the Company shops. Da said this was bad for the workers 'cos they had no choice in where they bought their vitals and prices was often much higher than in the village shops. Ma said it were a cryin' shame that workers was done down by the bosses in this way, but there was now't they could do about it. If you worked down the mines the companies owned you she said, they even owned the house you lived in. I couldn't see that it was too different for us, the Gaffer, Mr.Griffiths owned both of our boats, he told us where we had to load and unload, how much we would get paid and how long he expected the trip to take. He never took no notice of the weather, if we got froze up and couldn't move the boats for a week or two, we still got paid the same however long it took us. But Da said we was much better off, we had more freedom than the mine or factory workers and we did get paid in real money. We did own Hercules however and the cast iron stoves in the back cabins of both 'Isis' and 'Bluebell'. Ma seemed to think this made us better than some of the other boaties that she called 'Rodney Boaters' 'cos some of them hardly owned the clothes on their backs! Ma could be very vocal about other boaties, especially if she thought they was not 'particular'. By this she meant they did not keep their cabins nor themselves as clean as she would have liked. Water was something we was constantly thinkin' about. Clean water for drinkin', body and clothes washin' had to be collected from pumps and stand pipes along the Cut and carried in tin cans called Buckby's. These was placed on the cabin roof while we was travellin' and had to be got down whenever the kettle needed fillin'. We was always very careful with the water we used 'cos it had to last, so we never let a single drop go to waste. We all shared bowls of water for washin' and even after two or three of us had used the same water it could still be used to wash down the cabin sides or floor. So Ma said there was no excuses for not bein' clean. Ma said it was 'cos some boaties wasn't clean an' tidy that the town's people didn't like us, they thought we was all the same. I couldn't never understand that 'cos it weren't difficult to see that not all townies was the same neither! A lot of towns we passed through on the Cut, where the houses backed onto the canal, we could see for ourselves that they wasn't all that particular. I always thought that if I ever 'ad a back yard I'd want to keep it lookin' nice, not piled high with junk like lots of them as we passed by. I tried not to look at people wot was standing in their back yards, didn't want them to think I was nosey like. Well a person's back door was sort of private, we boaties never stared into anyone's back cabin door, it wasn't considered to be proper. If you had to knock on another boaties door we always stood to the side and looked up the towpath a bit, so as not to be rude.

That the townies didn't like us was a fact, we didn't know why, they just didn't I s'pose, so we tended not to 'ave much to do with them, we was just different. Because of this we never got to know places we passed through along the Cut, we had no need 'cos we wasn't gonna go there. We knew the places where we was welcome and so we 'ad regular stopping off places. I never knew the proper names for the towns we went through, most of us couldn't read and write so we wouldn't recognise the name even if it was writ down. We 'ad our own names for places, like Sutton Stop where we bought vitals, the Jam 'Ole where we off loaded sugar and loaded up again with pots of jam, the City Road, somewhere in the middle of a big town. I made up names for some of the smaller villages we went through like, the Crooked Church, the Windmill, Broken Down Bridge. All of *us* knew where we meant by these names, but I don't s'pose anyone else would. But as I grew older I could see all sorts of problems this could cause. From bein' quite young, Ma had told us the story of her Great Aunt who's sad fate had been caused by 'er not bein' able to read an write and by prejudice.

Often of a winter's evening, if we was tied up early, after supper we'd all sit round the stove with mugs of hot steaming tea and that's when Ma and Da would tell us about things. Things that had 'appened to them when they was young, things that had 'appened to other members of their family, or just other boaties and they wasn't all 'Fairy Stories' neither!

"Go on Ma, tell us again about poor Great Aunt Annie" we kids would ask.

"You've heard that story before" she would say.

"Please Ma, go on, just one more time"

"Well just you make sure I don't go on all night then 'cos we've got an early start in the mornin'................"

"Your Great Aunt Annie was my Gra'ma's sister and she was just eighteen when she married Josiah Cartwright.

'is family worked the boats for Matthew Brassington, They did the 'Cheshire run' mainly carrying salt out of the 'Works'. Gra'ma Mayhew was four years younger than Annie so she was still on 'India' with her Ma and Da. 'India' was a George Thomas boat, they 'ad a fleet of twenty odd boats carryin' all sorts of everything all over the Cut. They never knew where they was gonna be sent, George Thomas never turned 'is nose up at any type of cargo. It's a wonder that Great Aunt Annie ever got to meet Josiah 'cos Brassington's boats only ever did the Cheshire run. But they did an' I s'pose fate had to run its course. Gra'ma Mayhew, Florence, that's who I was named after, and me Ma before me, well she would always tell how pretty her sister Annie was. She 'ad beautiful auburn hair, just like you Jessie. "She could've 'ad her pick of any man on the Cut" she would say "But she was courted by Josiah Cartwright. He was a good man, don't get me wrong, 'E never had a bad word to say about no one, very quiet 'E was too, not a drinking man neither, no Josiah was a good man, 'ard worker too!"

We knew that Ma was well into her stride, when she settled back against the bolster in the bed 'ole and crossed her arms across her chest. Her eyes sort of glazed over and she stared over our heads as though she could actually see all that she was tellin' us.

"Well 'cos they was working all up and down on the Cut, Gra'ma didn't get to see Annie too often, one time it was nearly two years before they met up and Annie was so happy 'cos she was expecting her first baby. Gra'ma and her Ma started crocheting matinee' jackets right away! And 'Torie' Gra'ma's other sister started on a shawl. They was all pleased for Annie, specially 'cos she and Josiah was so happy. But as ever they didn't 'ave much time together 'cos their boats was bound in opposite directions, but Josiah promised to drop off a message to George Thomas's Boatyard to let them know when Annie's baby was born. In those days, that was the only way you could send messages, by word of mouth."

I remember thinkin' that things hadn't changed much 'cos that's what all of us boaties did. If it wasn't the boatyard, we sometimes left messages with a Lock Keeper or Toll Collector, if we was all workin' the same stretch. I reached over and quietly filled Ma's mug with more tea from the pot, being careful not to interrupt her thoughts.

"They didn't know, when they waved her off, that they'd not see her nor Josiah ever again. It must have been a good year before news got back to them and they was all so shocked and sad. Gra'ma always said that her Ma never did get over the shock of it, she was never the same woman again, grieved the rest of 'er life she did.

****

"Annie dear, put on another shawl today, the wind is blowing in from the East, I think we could be having snow before the day's out".

"Aw Josiah, you do fuss so!" Annie pretended not to care, but inside she felt so happy that Josiah wasn't like many other boaties, he was always showing how much he cared for her by trying to make life easier for her and especially now that they had the baby. The birth had been difficult and there'd been no one around to help, the night David Arthur Cartwright had decided to be born. Annie had been in labour most of the day but wouldn't let Josiah tie up until it was nearly dark. By the time he realised how far on Annie was, there

was no time for him to go for help, they were miles from the nearest village and no other boats were tied up along that stretch, so they had to manage on their own, just the two of them. Whether it was that had brought them closer together Annie didn't really know, it wasn't somethin' they talked about, but she felt that Josiah was extra 'specially attentive since baby David had arrived. And he was so proud of his son, you would think that no man had ever had a son before, the way he looked at him and held him. He would happily show him off to all the other boaties they met on the Cut.

"This is my son, David Arthur Cartwright" he would say proudly as he held him in his arms for all to see.

And Annie would sit on the gunn'all and look on with pride, not only at her beautiful baby, but at her very kind and considerate husband too. Everyone who met them said what a wonderful couple they was and that their marriage must've been 'made in heaven' 'cos they was so happy."

Ma was well into 'Er stride now and I could see we was gonna be 'in' for a long night, so I quietly mended the fire, so as not to interrup 'Er,

"It was the same then as now", she went on "You could be working yer boat anywhere up and down the country, it never mattered much . Gaffer would tell you where to go and load yer next cargo and where it 'ad to be off loaded. And they never knew the names of the canals they was working, 'cos like us, they 'ad never learned to read or write neither."

I remember thinkin' I 'spect they 'ad their own names for places, like Sutton Stop, where we all stopped over to go to Sutton's shop for supplies, an if the menfolk was lucky, an 'alf in the 'public' if you was tied up over night. It wasn't 'til I was nearly thirty that I found out it was really called Hawkesbury Junction! And even though you had family livin' and working the Cut you didn't know when you was likely to see them, we didn't send no letters, well no point really, there weren't no posting boxes and we 'ad no addresses anyway. Mostly people got in touch, when they needed to, through the 'Gaffers' or if it were real urgent, messages could be left with Lock Gate Keepers, that's if you knew they was working the same stretch. But often as not, unless you was both working a reg'lar run, it could be months or in some cases, even years before you bumped into yer relations. I finished mendin' the fire and gave Ma me 'hole attention, 'cos she were 'Off at a gallop' now.

"It had been a partic'lar 'ard winter and Josiah and Annie would 'ave found it more so now they 'ad baby David to look after. Once 'e started to crawl about it would 'ave been too dangerous to leave him in the back cabin with the stove goin' full blast, while Annie steered the boat and Josiah walked the towpath with the 'orse. In them days it was common for boaties to wrap their babies up warm and 'tie' them round the waist, to the smoke stack on the cabin top. With a cushion to stop them from getting too hot of course, but it meant you could see 'em all the while and they was kept warm too. People don't do it so much now, 'cos we knows the dangers."

* * * * * *

"We'll tie up after the next lock Annie, and 'ave a cuppa so you and David can get warm."

"I could do with a bit of a warm Josiah, an David'll go down for a sleep when 'e's had a drop of somethin' warm in his belly"

"That wind's raw, shouldn't be surprised if we don't 'ave snow later" And so they pushed on through the bitin' wind to the next lock. The Cut wound round in a big arch so you couldn't see the lock gates 'til you was nearly upon 'em. Annie remembered havin' seen another boat go past them, not five minutes before, so the gate only needed a little shove as the lock was 'set' in their favour. Josiah waited at the lock gates while Annie turned the rudder hard over then he gave the 'nose' a kick to help get the boat lined up to slide up the side of the lock, before closing the lock gate behind them. The horse was waitin' patiently on the lockside and Josiah gave his nose a scrub as he walked past him, to begin opening the sluices on the far gate The paddle gear was stiff and so he had to lean hard on the handle before it began to move. He had just cracked the first paddle and was halfway across the lock gates when he heard Annie's tortured scream! He stopped and turned in his tracks. At first he couldn't see what it was had made Annie cry out then she let out another howling scream and pointed to the water. He still didn't quite understand what was happening. The noise of the water gushing out from the opened sluice made it impossible for him to hear anything that Annie was shouting and she was jumping up and down in the well deck of the boat like something demented. It was then he realised that David was no longer to be seen on the cabin top and neither was the familiar smoke stack. In that split second he took in what must have happened, the chimney, with their precious son tied to it had somehow become dislodged and fallen into the water! Without further thought, Josiah leapt into the lock's 10 foot deep icy water. He couldn't see the baby anywhere and at first he hung on to the gunn'all while frantically pushing the boat away from the lockside. Then realising that the child *must now be under the water, he took a deep breath and pushed his himself beneath the surface of the chilling black waters. Annie's screams subsided as she waited anxiously for Josiah to return to the surface with David in his arms. She leaned over the side trying to peer through the receding murky waters. She waited and she waited and she waited. At one point she thought she could see the top of Josiah's now capless head, his hair floating out around his ears. It might have been just her imagination, it was so dark down there and with the boat gradually descending ever deeper into the lock it became even more difficult.*

Annie didn't know how long she had been leaning over the gunn'all, gazing into the dark waters, until a shout from above stirred her from her mesmerised trance. At first she couldn't make out where the voice was coming from......it was a man's voice....It must be Josiah, she couldn't quite focus on the face of the man looking down at her, she had been bent double staring into the dark muddy water for such a long time.

"Here Josiah, I'm here" she called up

"Are you gonna sit there dreaming all day Missus or are you gonna get the gate open and move yer boat outta there!"

It wasn't Josiah's voice, Annie was certain of that now, he would never speak to her like that, so if it wasn't Josiah then who was it, and where was her husband? Surely he must be up on the lockside with the 'orse, waitin for the levels to go down in the lock, til he could open the gate.

"Are you listenin' to me Missus? Get yerself outta there, I've got two boats to keep movin' I can't afford to sit around all day even if you can!"

Josiah, he MUST be up on the lockside, why was this man shouting at her? If he was getting impatient surely Josiah was there to tell him they would be through as soon as they could, they didn't want to waste time either, they had a load to keep movin' too!

"Oye Missus, you deaf or somethin' the rude man invaded her head again.

Annie tried to straighten up, she felt so stiff and cold. She tried to shade her eyes from the bright sunlight so that she could better see him.

"Josiah, me Man, is he not there with the 'orse " she called up.

"There's no man 'ere Missus, just the 'orse. What are ye waitin' for anyway!"

"Josiah, not there!" she replied trying to clear her head from the fog that seemed to be engulfing it.

"No Missus, no one, just the 'orse........... Look, if I opens the gate the 'orse'll walk on and you can tie up just beyond the bridge 'ole and wait for yer man there, I can't wait around 'ere for 'im to turn up, I've got to get a move on, I've lost a day already this week!"

Annie was still struggling to clear the fog from her mind, Josiah, not there! Where could he be, it wasn't like him to go anywhere without tellin' her, 'E was good like that. Surely 'E must have been there when they came into the lock, 'E had been there in the back cabin with her this mornin' when she woke up. He'd been mending the fire while she fed David.............. David, her baby............. Where was David! Suddenly the protective fog that had been clouding her brain lifted and the memory of all that had happened that morning came flooding painfully back. A long agonising, primeval sound escaped from her throat. The man on the lockside almost fell backwards so taken aback was he by the chilling sound of Annie's wailing.

"Look Missus, I only want to get you and yer boat outta the lock, no need to wail like a banshee!"

Just then another boater came up onto the lockside to see what was causing the hold up. The two men gazed down at Annie in disbelief as she continued to keen and wail. In between the sobbing she was trying to give voice to her now, clear mind.......

"Me baby! Me Man! In the water........... in the water! Ohhhhhhhhhhhh!! Me baby!!

Not being able to understand what Annie was saying between her sobs, the two men decided to get the boat out of the lock anyway and they began to lead the horse down off the lock top. As Annie realised the boat was beginning to move, she let out another loud howl

"Josiah....... me Man, 'E's 'ere in the water I'll not leave him.......Me baby!!

The horse, who knew his job well, was all ready taking up the slack on the rope and as he strained gently forward the boat moved accordingly. This movement in the now more shallow water, stirred up a little ripple and Annie reached down into the water believing she could see Josiah with David, just below the surface

"Give 'im to me Josiah" she cried "Give 'im to me!"

The two men looked at one another in amazement, then back into the murkie depths

"By God he must've fallen in!" said one to the other.

"Baby and all" said the other, realisation having over taken him.

And they rushed down the slope and through the bridge 'ole to catch up with the horse.

"Woah there boy, easy now" said the first man as he took hold of the halter and brought the horse to a standstill, while the other man tugged on the lead rope to bring the boat to a standstill at the towpath's edge. Annie was still wailing incoherently.

"I'll fetch me Missus to 'Er, she'll know what to do" said the second man to the first and he walked off up the towpath to where his pair of boats were waiting.

The first man made the boat fast and saw to it that the horse was safe, then he ran back to the lock and stood helplessly on the bottom step, gazing into the gaping mouth of the now empty lock.

"There ain't nothin' livin' down there! " he exclaimed as the second man joined him.

"No I fear you're right" said the other "I've left me Missus with the lass and sent me boy Will back into the village to get help".

Annie was oblivious to all of this, the painfull knowledge of the mornings events, hidden for a while until her brain could fully take in the severity of the situation, now hammered rawly inside her head! Josiah, David….gone! How could that be, one minute they had both been there, with her, and now………gone! No there must be some mistake, she'd have to walk back down the Cut to find them, Yes that's what she should do! And she stood up unsteadily from her seat beside the stove.

"C'mon lovey, drink yer tea, you'll feel better with somethin' warm inside you!"

Somewhere inside Annie's head a light seemed to go on. 'Somethin' warm in side you' someone had said that *to her earlier today, who could it have been? What did it mean? Why did it seem to be so significant? Again the fog seemed to be closing down inside her head..........! Then she remembered.... Josiah was waiting for her down the towpath, with David.....she'd go now and find him. She moved towards the cabin back door, a large woman she did not know loomed up in front of her......!*

"Now c'mon lass, sit yourself down, there's now't ye can do"

Who was this woman? What was she doing in their back cabin? Annie tried to search her mind for clues as to who she might be, but there were none. She was sure she didn't know her. Annie tried to push past her

"Josiah, David I've got to go to them!"

Two strong arms held her fast "Aw lovey don't be daft, you know they're not here any more, you know they've both been drownded".

The words didn't seem to make any sense at first.... drownded.....what did that mean? Annie rolled the words over and over in her befuddled brain......Her Man and her baby, drownded? No it was all a mistake, Josiah was just going to open the lock and then they would tie up the other side and have a cuppa. He had old her that, just a minute ago. She would put David down for a sleep when he'd had a feed, then they could push on for a few hours uninterrupted. But David must be still strapped to the chimney stack, he'd be cold if she didn't go now and bring him in. But why was this woman standing in front of her, trying to prevent her from going to her son! Annie mustered all he strength and pushing the woman deftly aside stepped up into the welldeck. She turned and looked up at the smoke stack, but there was something very wrong because......... it wasn't there……….. it had gone! How could……? The fog in her mind swirled and opened just enough to allow a single memory through…. David! her baby!, her six month old son! had toppled, smoke stack and all into the deep waters of the lock! Another agonising wail gave forth from her throat as strong arms surrounded her and pulled her back into the warmth of the back cabin.

"Aw Lass, dear lass, don't give on so! It pains me heart to hear ye, truly it does!" The big woman sat her down on the side bed and taking her into her arms as though she were a child cradled her until her sobs died away. Annie had no knowledge of how long she'd allowed herself to be rocked gently to and fro by the stranger. At one time she thought it must be her Mother or even her Gr'ma, she remembered being rocked by her Gr'ma when she was a little girl…..was she then a little girl again? Then she thought it was Josiah, he had cradled her like this when they were first married and she was so frightened, being away from her family for the first time, all the familiar things she'd been used to. He had been so good and understanding, and patient too, even when she'd been so silly on their wedding night. No one had told her what to expect. Josiah said her Mother should've or her older sister, but no one had and she'd been frightened and confused. But Josiah had tried to explain, as best he could and he'd been so gentle……

Suddenly there were voices outside, strangers. She didn't recognise any of them. She looked up to where she expected Josiah's face to be and was shocked to see a middle aged women she'd never seen before. She pulled herself away from the woman's embrace and stood up.

"Who are you, what're doin' in our back cabin?" Annie demanded to know.

"Me Man's just down the Cut a way, he'll be here soon........"

She didn't have a chance to finish her sentence, two men had pushed their way into the cabin and were talking to her. These were complete strangers too. Annie couldn't understand what they were saying to her. The strange woman seemed to be arguing with them, their voices were very loud. Other voices could be heard from outside of the cabin, by the sound of it there must have been quite a crowd. Annie couldn't quite hear what was being said. She looked at the two men who were addressing her, they were both wearing some sort of uniform. Who could they be, what were they saying to her? The woman still seemed to be arguing with them, she took hold of Annie's arm and tried to push her to the back of the bed'ole, one of the men took hold of her other arm and was pulling her towards the cabin door. For a few seconds there was a sort of see saw action taking place with Annie in the middle. They were hurting her now and then the second man in uniform got between her and the other woman.

"If you don't let her go, we'll have to arrest you too!" he shouted

"But she's done nothin' yer honour, it's not her fault" the woman's voice rang out loud enough for the voices outside on the towpath to hear and comprehend.

They all seemed to take up the same cry "It's not her fault.".......".You can't be thinkin' of takin the poor lass away!"....... "What you gonna charge her with?"...... "She didn't do nothing, it were an accident." ....".Let the poor lass alone!"

None of this made any sense to Annie and being totally unaware of what was happening to her, she did nothing to prevent the two policemen from pushing her up into the well deck and pulling her onto the towpath. Annie was surprised to see that it was snowing heavily. The fields on either side of the Cut were completely covered as were the cloths covering the hold of her boat. She marvelled at how clean everything looked, pristine and white, everything that is except for the footprints on the towpath. Men and women, other boaties, crowded around her as one of the two men in uniform tied her two hands behind her with a strip of leather.

"Surely there's no need for that" she heard one of the women say.

"She's in no state to go running away"

"Who can say what she might do" the constable replied

"Look here" the other one addressed the small crowd, "We are just doing our duty, two people have come to an untimely death here today and someone has to be made accountable, now step aside and allow us to continue."

"At least let 'er have this…." It was the strange woman from the back cabin, Annie recognised her, she stepped up to her and tenderly wrapped her own shawl around Annie's shoulders…

"You'll be cold lass, without this to keep you warm" Her face was kindly and she sort of hugged Annie and held her close to her for a second, then the constables pulled at her arm and led her away up the towpath.

It was sometime later that Annie became aware of her surroundings, she looked up from the wooden bench she was sittin' on, to the high brick walls around her. She noticed for the first time, the tiny window with iron bars and the huge black door with metal studs. There was straw on the hard earthen floor and in one corner a tin mug hung from a chain attached to the wall. Where was she? What was she doin' here? Surely she should be on the boat with Josiah and David.........David, he'd be needin' a feed. She knew it must be ages since he'd had the last 'cos her breasts were swollen and engorged with milk. And Josiah, where was he? He would be lookin' all over for her. But how had she got here? She got up from the bench and went to the door. She looked for some kind of handle or latch, but there was nothin'. In the dim light she could just make out a small square hole in the door, but it was too high up for her to look through. Then she spotted the key hole, bending down, she closed one eye and tried to peer through, but it seemed even darker on the other side of the door. Was it night time? No how could it be, there was light coming through the window on her side of the door. She decided to call out,

"'Ello! 'oose out there?" she tried to say but the noise that came from her cracked dry throat was only a whisper. "Ello" she tried again, "Can ya let me out of 'ere? The door's locked or somethin'?" Again she could hardly recognise the sound she was making. In her head the thoughts were booming out, but she knew that by the time it came out through her mouth it was more like the squeek of a mouse. She felt confused, weak at the knees and very, very tired.

The fog was beginning to cloud her brain again, she walked slowly back to the bench and sat down, pulling her shawl more closely around her shoulders she folded her arms across her chest, gently rocking herself to and fro...............!
She didn't know how long she been sitting there, when she first heard the sound of footsteps coming closer and closer. At first she didn't recognise the sound, but when the huge door was pushed open and a man in uniform came striding through the gaping doorway, she made a mental note that it must have been the sound of his approach that she had heard. Strange that she could not quite clear her mind enough to

remember perfectly normal sounds she thought. But the man was speaking to her now and she was having difficulty understanding his words, it was like he was in a tunnel calling out to her from the far end. His face seemed very close to hers, too close, she turned away and the fog in her brain swirled around and closed down around her once more.

She awoke with a start, feeling a strong urge to pass water. It was blacker than Stan'edge Tunnel and she had to feel her way around the walls to the door. Again she called out and again there was no reply. Somewhere deep inside her head she felt she had done this many times before, but the urge to pass water overtook all other thoughts. She knew there was no other furniture in the room other than the wooden bench she'd been sitting on, and no bowl or pail. What was she to do? Then she remembered seeing a pile of straw in one corner of the room and made her way in what she thought was that direction. After relieving herself she stood for a while with her back resting against the cold brick wall. Her mouth was so dry and her throat ached!..... The tin mug.......yes she remembered now, there was a tin mug attached to a chain on the wall.....now which side of the room was it. She began to feel her way around the wall, then frightened that she might trip over it she got down on her knees and crawled, feeling with both hands just infront of her for the mug or its chain.

Her left knee found the chain first when she painfully put her whole weight on it. But her need to find the mug, which hopefully would contain clean water was too strong for her to give any attention to her knee. Annie traced the rest of the chain with trembling finger tips until they came in contact with the mug. It felt very cold. She gently slid one hand up the side and found the handle, ignoring this, she carried on to the rim of the mug and carefully tipped one finger over the edge...........cold liquid met her cold finger..........she instinctively put the finger to her lips.....ah water! Afraid that her trembling hands would not lift the mug without spilling its precious contents, Annie lowered her head until her mouth came in contact with the rim of the mug and she sucked in a mouthful of pure cold water! It stung the back of her throat and she coughed involuntarily almost choking as she fought to breath at the same time. Lucky she hadn't actually picked the mug up she thought, otherwise some of the water might have been spilled. She sat up straight, resting her back against the wall waiting for the coughing to subside and her breathing to return to its normal pace before attempting the whole procedure over again. She took several sips from the mug, then realising that she had no idea how or when it might be filled again, decided to save the rest.

As she sat there on the floor in the darkness Annie's tortured mind drifted, this time the fog didn't close around her, this time she could see her Mother's face, smiling at her as she sat on the cabin top.....the sun was shining and the sweet smell of freshly cut hay was coming from the field they were passing. She looked down at her hands resting on her smock, they were tiny and plump......like a child's hands......and the fingers of her right hand were wrapped tightly around a small bunch of wild flowers.

"Now Annie" her Mother was saying to her "You mind you don't fall off the cabin top, while I go inside and mash the tea" Her Mother smiled at her again and Annie thought 'Tea' how many endless cups of tea had she drank? The fog swirled again in her head and protected her from further pain.

People seemed to come and go, things went on around her, she observed but did not feel they actually had anything to do with her, it was like looking in on a scene being acted out by a person who looked vaguely familiar, but had no real connection with. A dream, with no waking!

Then came the day that she was taken out of this room, or perhaps it was just later that same day, no it couldn't be 'cos she remembered it having been dark night at least once. She was taken to a bright room with very tall walls and lots of big polished wood fences and huge wooden benches. There were lots of men in black cloaks wearing funny woollen hats with pigtails at the back.....they talked a lot, but not to her. No one spoke to Annie!

She gazed around this amazing room, the ceiling was so high she could hardly see the cobwebs. And the lights around the walls seemed to splutter with a sort of greenish glow. They weren't candles she knew that, but she couldn't see where the oil was being kept...how could they burn without oil? The man in the big chair was saying something now and everyone seemed to be listening. Annie tried to make out what he was saying, but he sounded as though he was at the end of a tunnel and she could only make out a few words, none of which made any sense.

Then he said 'Cup able Homy Side' She liked the sound of that! What was it again.....'Cup able' or was it 'table' Cup-Table, was that what he said...and what was the other......'Homy Side'....was that a place like Wharf Side, or a type of boat or something meaning 'Cabinside'. Annie had never heard anything quite like it before, but she liked the way it felt in her mouth and she whispered it to her self all the way back to the underground room which had become the centre of her world .....

'Cupable and Homyside', ... 'Cupable and Homyside'.

A woman came into her room and gave her a bowl of porridge.......she now had a table and a chair in her room and a straw mattress on the bench to lie on....was it the same room, she couldn't remember......if this was a different room, what had the other one been like...had she lived here all her life, no somehow she didn't think so. Faces came to her, of people she must have known once, and places with bright sunlight, or had she just dreamed it all.......!

The porridge tasted good and warmed her inside. The woman stood looking at her.

"Won't be long now dearie! Must be aweful.....just waitin' here" and she was gone.

Waiting.......... waiting? Is that what she was doing? But waiting for what? Annie decided it was just another of those things she didn't quite understand and she went back to that place inside her head where she was a little girl playing in the sunlight and her Mother was always smiling at her. And there was a man too, he smiled at her. He looked familiar and Annie felt she ought to know his name, but just at the point where she thought it was on the tip of her tongue it would go again. She would try to keep his face in her mind for as long as possible, he looked kind and gentle...she wished he would just hold her hand, like he used to........did she ever hold his hand?

Then one day two different women came into her room and looking up Annie felt she wasn't going to enjoy knowing these two....they looked hard and mean!

"C'mon number 97 today's your lucky day" and they sniggered at one another.

Annie felt nervous as they approached her.

"Lets get rid of all these disgusting smelly clothes shall we?" They seemed to be talking to one another and not *including Annie at all, but they laid their hands on her and begin tearing off her clothes*

"Stop! What're ya doin' to me!" Annie let out a pitiful cry.

"We're gettin' ya ready for yer Big Day!" said the larger of the two women.

"Dressin' ya up in all yer finery" said the other and they both laughed cruely.

"What big day, what's happenin, leave me alone!"

The women ignored Annie's protests their rough hands tearing her clothes from her back.

"I wants the bonnet" said one "It'll look fine once its been boiled up".

"Why should you 'ave it Gerttie, I'm more senior to you, I'll 'ave it" and with that the larger woman tore the bonnet from Annie's head.

"Bit smelly in't it, 'ope you ain't got lice" she said as she stuffed the bonnet into her apron pocket.

"Don't take me bonnet" Annie cried as she tried to retrieve it "Not me bonnet please"

"Well you won't be needin' it where you'm goin', will she Gertie" the smaller woman laughed right into her face.

"Where am I goin'?" Annie implored

Both women stopped suddenly, looked at one another then burst into peels of laughter

"Well if ya don't know dearie, were not about to tell ya"

Annie felt a chill run down her spine and she crossed her arms over her breasts. One of the women produced a grey garment of rough material which she proceeded to put over Annie's head and pull over her naked body.

"Stick yer arms through here dearie" she indicated arm holes as she pulled the garment on down to Annie's knees.

"She won't be needin' they boots neither" said the other woman "Can I 'ave they Gertie, can I? go on, they'll do a treat for my Kitty an they're far too small to fit you!"

The larger woman shrugged

"S'pose so, I've got no use for 'um.

The smaller woman looked so pleased with herself as she knelt down and unlaced Annie's boots and removed them. Then taking off her apron she said "I'll 'ave to wrap 'em up in this. If Constable Smiff catches me 'E'll 'ave 'em in the furnace, an they're too good to be burned!

Annie stood observing all that was going on around her, not understanding, but somehow this was unlike the other dreams she had become used to. There were no smiling faces, no warm feeling inside, no sunshine, what was it that was so different today? And then the big door was being banged shut and the two awful women were gone. Annie sat down on the chair. In the fight to drag all her clothes away from her, the two women had forgotton her shawl which had somehow got kicked underneath the bed, one corner now stuck out, a bright shade of blue against the dark of the floor. Annie pulled it out and wrapped it around her.......... "Funny" she thought, "It looks familiar, but its not my shawl, mine's brown with a fringe of the same wool, I know 'cos I crocheted it". This shawl was knitted in blue wool and didn't have a fringe. From somewhere deep in the recess of her mind Annie thought she remembered when she'd seen the shawl before..........yes, yes it was coming to her now.......it was on the day that..........that, oh what happened on that day" Annie knew that she ought to remember. Then it came to her the shawl belonged to that kind faced woman who made her cups of tea in her own back cabin. Why would she do that? Annie was now frantically trying to regain control of her brain. The fog had gone but things seemed to be all mixed up. Her back cabin! She, Annie, lived in the back cabin of a boat on the Cut! If that were the case, what was she doing living in this room. She seemed to know that she had been here for some time.....but she knew now that this was not her home. She ought to be there, on her boat with......with...... and the face of that wonderfully kind man she remembered from her dreams came flooding into her mind

"Josiah!" she said his name softly as though trying it out for the first time "Josiah my husband! I have a husband!" she cried out, the sound of her loud voice echoing around the room. So if she had a husband, where was he now, why was he not with her. If she was married they should be together, Annie knew this was right, but where was he? Another face came flooding into her mind and with it the smell of baby softness.........she let out a gasp......David, her baby. Frantically she looked around at the brick walls that once felt like home and now seemed totally unknown to her. What was she doing in this place when she had a baby to look after and where was her husband. Annie could feel her heart pounding the sound of it was booming in her ears preventing her from thinking straight, trying to sort out this terrible mess. She took a deep breath and then instinctively another in an attempt to slow her heart rate.

Gradually she felt herself become calmer, she must try to sort out this muddle in her head. She was the mother of a beautiful baby named David, of that much she was now quite certain, that she was married to Josiah was also a certainty. So what had the woman with the blue shawl got to do with all of this. Annie shook her head as though that

would clear it. She tried to go back to her last memories......
She was sitting in her back cabin, the kind faced woman
was making tea, people were talking outside....but what
happened before that?

A noise outside of the big door brought Annie's thoughts
back to the cold room, the door swung open and a man
wearing a long frock came in, he was carrying a leather bound
book. Behind him walked two other men, one wearing a
blue uniform the other in a long dark coat carrying a top
hat and gloves.

"Stand up girl!" said the man in uniform "Show some
respect for your betters"

Annie dutifully stood up, though she couldn't think
why.

"Has she still said nothing?" the man in the dark coat
was speaking to the one in uniform.

"No Sir, not a word that anyone could make sense of"

"Well then lets get on with it Smith. There seems little
point in your trying to get any kind of contrition from the girl
Reverend, but I suppose you have to do your duty. "

The man wearing the long frock stepped forward opening
his book as he did so. "Annie Cartwright it is my solemn
duty to................."

Annie didn't hear another word, she had retreated once
more inside her head, frantically trying to remember...Annie
Cartwright, that sounded like someone she ought to know
...........Annie Cartwright...who was she? Please, please
let her remember! She knew it wasn't the kind faced woman
with the blue shawl but what was her name. Annie didn't
know but she was certain that it wasn't Annie Cartwright!

"In the name of the Father, and of the Son........" the
man in the frock was making strange signs in the air with

his hands. Annie looked at him blankly, she knew he was a complete stranger, she had never seen him before. He stared back at her, quite expressionless, then closed the book and stepped aside.

"It's all up to you now Constable Smith" he said "I've done what I can, God Rest Her Soul!"

The three men turned on their heels and walked smartly to the door. Annie wanted to say something, from somewhere deep inside of her she felt some sort of response from her was needed, but her befuddled brain could not put her feelings into words. She struggled to bring to the front of her mind anything which might help her to remember why she was here. Who were these people who seemed to have power over her, and why if she was married to Josiah with a baby of her own named David, was she in this place and not in the back cabin of her boat. She sat back on the chair once more tears of frustration ran down her face...she had to remember, it was so important, she just had to!

The big door swung open again and the two women who had deprived her of her clothes earlier came in looking very pleased with themselves.

"C'mon you, it's time for your long walk" said the one called Gertie and she reached out and pulled Annie to her feet.

"Stop, you're hurtin' me" Annie cried out as the large woman's grip tightened around her arm.

"Now don't you give us no trouble now" said the large woman.

For some reason Annie felt she didn't want to go wherever these two were intending to take her and she pulled her arm away, seeing the open door ahead of her she made a run towards it. The smaller of the two women got there before her and stuck her foot out causing Annie to trip and fall headlong onto the cold hard floor. She banged her head on the door frame as she went down!

"You little bugger!" The large woman kicked Annie in the stomach as she spoke through gritted teeth.

Annie curled up clutching her bruised stomach and gasping for breath,

"Get up ya bitch!" the large woman was shouting at her "Get up or you'll feel me other boot!"

Annie struggled to her feet while the two women looked on, once on her feet, still feeling' whoosie' from the bang on her head and the severe kick, Annie was unprepared for their next move. Pulling both hands sharply behind her they bound her wrists with rope, so tightly that she cried out. What was happening to her, Annie was panicking inside her head, what were they going to do to her now! She was dragged back to the chair and thrown down on to it.

"You hold the bitch good and tight Sissy, while I do the deed"

The large woman loombed over Annie and she saw to her horror that she was holding a large pair of sicciors. The next moment Annie felt her hair being pulled hard from behind and the snip, snip sound told her they were hacking off her long auburn hair. Snip, Snip... Handfuls were being thrown onto the floor. Annie tried to pull away again

"I said hold 'er Sissy or I'll chop your'n off too!"

The smaller woman nonly grunted in reply. Then both women pulled Annie's arms painfully over the chair back and tied them to the rung.

"That'll stop ya, you little whore!"

Snip, snip...more hair was falling to the floor. Big oily tears began to brim over and run slowly down Annie's face....

Why were they doing this to her, was this a bad dream, not like the lovely ones she had been having lately, but would she wake up and be back on her boat...was that it....was this all just a nightmare?

They eventually finished their gruesome task and untied Annie from the chair. They pushed her from the room and out into a long corridor.............so this is what the other side of the door is like, she thought stupidly. They pushed and prodded her past several other doors all looking the same then through a double door at the far end, two more corridors then they stopped in front of another door and knocked.

"Well this is where we have to leave you, little bitch, you won't be troubling us ever again." The large woman said and both women laughed maliciously.

The door was opened by a different man in uniform, he stood aside to allow Annie to enter. It was a large room, she could tell that, even though the lights were dim. Two other men came forward as she entered, one was the long frocked man she'd seen before and the other was a large muscle bound man who looked at Annie with malicious eyes. He grabbed Annie by the shoulder and turned her around, all the while looking her up and down.

"Hmm about eight an 'alf stone I recons" he muttered as he walked away towards a large platform positioned at the far end of the room.

In another corner of the room, Annie could just see in the dim light a group of about a dozen people all sitting on upholstered chairs and talking in low voices as they gazed at her. She caught the eye of a young man wearing a checked jacket, he seemed to be staring at her, then suddenly he realised that Annie was looking directly at him and he turned quickly away. Her attention was then caught by an older man as he came and stood in front of her and boomed out in a deep resounding voice:

"Annie Cartwright, of no known address, having been tried at Chester Assize on the eleventh day of February eighteen hundred and thirty seven and convicted of Culpable Homicide. ...."

"There were those words again, although they sounded a bit different this time. Annie realised she had been wrong before when she thought it was Cup-able, she now heard quite clearly the word 'Culpable' and the other, the Homy Side...that sounded right but she still had no idea of what it meant. The man was still droneing on and Annie used all her strength of concentration to try to focus on what he was saying next.

"........to be hung by the neck until dead. God Rest Her Soul!"

From somewhere deep inside the dark muddled recesses of her tortured mind realisation of what was happening to her began to filter through. She was Annie Cartwright and they were going to hang her, that's what all this was about, that's why she was here, in this place and not on her boat with, with Josiah! Suddenly it was as though a light had been turned on in her head and she saw the event of that fateful morning. She could see David strapped to the chimney stack and Josiah's smiling face saying they would tie up after the next lock and have a cup of tea to warm them....

Two pairs of strong hands took hold of Annie and projected her up the room to the platform. The man with the muscles came forward and pushed her from behind up the three steps and across to a door in the floor of the platform. Holding her tightly by one arm he whispered maliciously in her ear.

"Don't you give me no trouble, I can make this quick, or real slow!"

Annie looked past this awful man and saw instead the face of little David, her baby, lying asleep in her arms, her heart swelled as she looked upon his beautiful little face.

"Just you keep yer mouth shut, no squalking nor pleading, too late for all that now". The awful man invaded her thoughts again. "I'm putting this sack over yer 'ead now" He said again

"No!" Annie cried out "No please, please, why?" she tried to twist and turn her head to stop him from shutting her out to what was going on, she was afraid it would prevent her from seeing her baby"

"Cos I don't want to see yer ugly face!" the man whispered maliciously again into her now covered ear.

Despite the sack she could feel his hot smelly breath at the side of her face. He pushed her again and then she could feel him placing something heavy…a rope around her neck. He adjusted and positioned the knot and at that moment Annie opened her eyes and there was Josiah, her husband. Josiah with his fair hair falling across his face as he ran with open arms towards her.

"Josiah" she whispered as he picked her up in his arms and swung her 'round.

"Josiah" she whispered again as she gazed into his deep blue eyes………..

* * * * *

"There, I told you I'd go on all night if you didn't stop me" Ma said and she seemed to come back from a long way away. "And look the two little'uns is already asleep."

Flossie and Sammy were curled up together at the back of the bed'ole, Flossie with her thumb, as ever, stuck in her mouth.

"Aw Ma, don't leave it there, tell us what happened when Gra'ma Mayhew an' all the family found out what'd 'appened to Great Aunt Annie." Josh and I pleaded.

Ma looked at Da, who was sat on the back step, sucking on his empty pipe. He nodded.

"Just stir up the fire a bit and put the kettle on again" Ma said and I'll just finish the story."

I went to move towards the stove but Da signalled to me that he would mash some tea and so I settled down again to hear the end of the story.

"Well as I've told you so many times" Ma went on. "Things 'asn't changed that much since then, it still takes an age for news and such to get from one place to another, I dare say if it 'appened like that again today, we'd still all be none the wiser."

"It was old Bill Crouch wot bought a newspaper while 'E was up in Cheshire who first got wind of it, and then only by chance did 'E see Annie's name. 'E was heducated, was Bill, 'E could read and write. Though wot 'E needed all that learnen' for, livin' on a boat, working the Cut I don't know! But 'E were a good sort, Didn't cut no ice with 'Im, people bein' able to read and write. Well as I was sayin' it was Bill wot read in the newspaper that Annie Cartwright 'ad been tried and hung for wot they called 'Culpable Homicide', I'll never forget them words as long as I lives."

"But what does it mean Ma?" I asked tentatively.

"Search me" Ma replied "All I know is, them constables and court people seemed to think it was poor Great Aunt

Annie's fault that her husband and baby drownded in that lock. 'Ow they came to that conclusion nobody knew. But poor Annie couldn't read nor write neither. Me Ma alluss said she probably didn't even know who she could have to speak for 'Er. If someone 'ad'av got 'old of Matthew Brassington he'd have gone an spoke for 'Er, but 'E didn't know nothin' about it 'til it were all too late!Josiah allus carried the bills of ladin' and toll notes in his west'cut pocket and by the time they drained the lock and got 'Im out, well I don't s'pose they was readable. And the boat was in need of paintin' so no one could read the 'owners' name. No one knew nor tried to find out where Great Aunt Annie 'ad come from, nor where they was goin'. The Assize was meetin' a week after the accident, so Annie was put up before the Beak before anyone would've really missed them and once the sentence 'ad been passed .... Well it was all done and dusted long before Old Bill Crouch got back down to Limehouse. Someone did say they'd heard that Annie went mad inside that Gaol, well who could blame 'Er! She lost her baby and 'Er husband and then got the blame for it, don't make no sense, that's wot Gra'ma Mayhew allus said. She was never the same, died of a broken heart, ...never did get over grieving for her." Ma sighed and leaned back against the bolster with her eyes shut. And I thought I just saw the beginnings of a tear escape from between her eyelids, but she brushed it away with the back of her 'and "Now where's that cuppa tea, me throats parched with all this moutherin'."

CHAPTER ELEVEN

Hercules 'Took a Look'

Then came the day that our Flossie got the stomache ache and nothin' would pacify her, tho' Ma tried all manner of things. What she usually tried was bit of salt water, Ma allus sayes what ailes yer, cures yer and we'd 'ad a bit of salt beef for our supper the night before. Ma says it can sometimes give you a 'gippy' tummy on account of the salt being strong, so it seemed only right to give our Flossie salt water to drink. Well it didn't do neither, she didn't get no better and she didn't get no worse, she just rolled around on the floor clutching her stomach and making a lotta noise. I could hear her from the lockside where I was helpin' to wind the huge gate paddles, before we put the boats into the lock. It had been raining earlier but now the sun had come out and I was dreadin' Ma tellin' me to mind our Flossie down in the cabin on such a nice day. It had been rainin' on and off for weeks and this was the first dry day we'd had, and I was not about to spend the day indoors for no good reason. Well that's not strictly true, 'cos if Ma had of told me, I wouldn't have dared to argue. You only argued seriously with Ma at your peril!

Just then Da shouted at me to go across the gates and start windin' the other paddle, he said our Josh was walkin' Hercules on to the next set of locks. There was a short pound between the two sets of locks and it was easier and quicker for us to 'bow haul' the two boats up between them, rather than 'faff' around hitchin' up the 'orse each time. I was glad Da had given me somethin' else to be doin', so I could keep out of Ma's way and well away from our Flossie. These was single locks so we had to put each boat in separately, fill the lock, open the gates, float our lead boat 'Isis' out then close the gates again, empty the lock and start all over with Bluebell, the second boat. Our Josh had tethered Hercules under the trees at the next set of lock gates and had come back down the towpath to haul 'Isis' on up. Our Sammy was standin' on a box in the well deck steerin'. He could hardly see over the top sheet, even when he was stood on a box. Da stayed back to get 'Blubell' into the lock when it was set and when we had got her through, it was my job to shut the lock gates and set the paddles. I always looked about to make sure there was no other boats nearby, tho' like as not, they would give you a shout if they was wantin' to come through. Da was pullin' 'Bluebell' out through the top locks as I dropped the paddle and scampered up onto the balance bar and ran across the gates over the gapeing lock. Just as I landed on the other side, I saw Ma's head come bobbing up out of the cabin. She was looking straight into the sunlight and I knew she couldn't get a clear look at me. So I risked getting a pasteing, and ran for all I was worth past her, as she stood on the back deck of 'Bluebell', and on up to the next set of locks. When I got there, Our Josh was just manoevering 'Isis' in, so I was able to shut the lock gate behind him and get to work on lifting the paddles on the top gates. Then as I was clambering across to the other side our Josh was hitchin' Hercules back up, having given him a few minutes to have a drink and a chomp at the long grass at the side of the path. Our Sammy had got off 'Isis' and was away across the field towards the orchard.

"Da'll paste you if you gets caught" called Our Josh after him.

It took a short while for the lock to fill and I lay back across the balance beam with me boots crossed at the ankle, and me legs stuck out in front of me. Looking up into the clear blue sky, with tiny clouds high above, scudding across in all directions.

"Where's your modesty our Jessie I can nearly see yer garters!" it was Our Josh shouting across the lock, angry like. I felt so embarrassed, even if it was only me brother, but I didn't want to let on to him that I was.

"Shouldn't be lookin' then should you!" I retorted as I sat up quickly straightening me skirt.

"And you shouldn't be loungin' about like Lady Muck, showin' off yer drawers neither!" shouted Our Josh.

At first I thought he had been just moutherin' for fun, but when I caught sight of his face across the lock, it was very red as he wagged his finger at me and said

"You're a bit too big for tricks like that Missie!"

I opened my mouth to say something smart but he carried on

"I don't want to hear no foul mouthed boaties talkin' about my sister!"

My mouth stayed open I was so shocked, I hadn't done nothin',well not as far as I could see. Just then Our Josh caught sight of Da coming on up towards us, hauling 'Bluebell'

"I'll talk to you later Miss" he spat the words at me then stalked off down towards where Da was hauling on the lead towrope. I quickley set about winding the paddles as I caught sight of our Sammy comin' back across the field with a pocket bluging full of apples. How on earth he was gonna get across the towpath from the hedge without Ma or Da seein' him I just did not know. Most times I would create a small diversion or somat to distract them, so as Our Sammy could stash the apples under the clothes and get back on board without no one knowing no different. Da used to say it wasn't scrumping for apples that was the sin, it was getting caught, and that was by him an all! Ma would say she weren't touchin' nothin as wasn't bought and paid for. Our Sammy would say she wasn't getting the chance! Normally this situation would raise a smile between Our Josh and I, as we tried to get our Sammy back on board unnoticed. But today Our Josh was not for smilin', so niether was I! Eventually we all got goin' again and after that I was sort of wishin' that Ma would get me to look after our Flossie down inside our back cabin, out of Our Josh's way. I was still feeling upset that Our Josh had layed into me for no reason, but I felt embarrassed too 'cos our Josh had never spoke to me like before and I just didn't know why.

Our Flossie had gone to sleep and so Ma didn't want me to look after her now. Luckily she hadn't realised my scam in trying to stay out of the back cabin earlier, so she was happy for me to sit on the cabin roof or walk along the towpath in the sunshine. The weather being good, we didn't stop all day, Ma handed us out slices of bread and butter and good strong tea to keep us going. So it wasn't until we moored up for the night that I came close enough to Our Josh to whisper "What's got into you today?"

"You just wait there 'til I get back from stableing Hercules, then you'll find out soon enough"

Our Josh very rarely got angry and when he did it was usually quickly passed, but not today, he was still as mad as ever and I still didn't know why! I had a few jobs of me own to do before supper so I didn't hang around waitin' to be told, so when our Josh came and found me. I was cleaning out the stove on 'Bluebell'. Ma had taken Flossie off into 'Isis to cook supper and our Sammy was loungin' across the side bed, playin' with a stick and a bit of string, when I heard Our Josh's boots scrape the gunn'all

"Oye Sammy, go find yerself somethin' to do" he said as he ducked down into the cabin.

"Awh must I, I was havin' a rest !" Sammy whinned.

"Either make yerself scarce, or I'll tell Ma about the apples" Our Josh rarely threatened to tell tales on any of us, it seemed so out of character, I just did not know what was happening to my brother. Sammy didn't need tellin' twice.

"Now you Miss" he pointed to the side bed for me to sit on "Just you start telling me what you've been up to!"

"Me, what d'ya mean?" I cried out indignantly

"You needn't look the innocent neither!" he retorted.

"I don't know what you mean Our Josh, I 'aven't done nothin', well nothin' wrong that is"

"S'pose it depends what you means by WRONG"
Josh stood up and was looking down at me, threatening
like.

"Go on, hit me if you must, I ain't done nothin' I
swear!" I was nearly on the verge of tears, but I wasn't
going to let Our Josh see that. I was as strong as any boy,
I'd proved it many times and I wasn't about to let myself
down now so I said, full of bravado "I don't know what
you're tryin' to say I've done Our Josh, but whatever it is
it ain't true!"

Then Josh took me by the shoulders and stood me
up

" Look Jess, don't lie to me, or I'll...."

"You'll what Our Josh, tell Ma?" I spat the words
through clenched teeth, I'd had enough of this now and
was convinced that Our Josh must be completely mad. I
tried to shrug his hands off me shoulders, but he gripped
on tighter "Josh, you're hurtin' me!"

"Hurtin' you, Hurt you, I'll hurt you if I catch you
hanging around with rough 'Rodney' boys" and with
that Our Josh sort of flung me backwards against the
drop down.

It took a second for the words to sink in "Issac Dury!"
I exclaimed, then as the shock began to sink in, I started
to laugh, God knows why! Probabley it was that I could
not believe our Josh actually believed I would............
but what did he believe?, he hadn't actually said. Then
before I could stop laughing and ask him, our Josh fetched
me such a belt across the mouth.

"What's so Bloody funny Miss," I still didn't like
the tone of his voice and backed away "You may well try

to hide from me Miss " and Our Josh pushed me back against the drop down again. This time I kept my feet.

"Now Miss, what have you got to say for yourself that's so funny, will you be still laughing when I've punched your stupid face a few times!"

What was happening! Our Josh never spoke to me like this, he was always kind. He hadn't hit me in a long time, well not on purpose like. My whole world turning upside down and I still didn't know why!

"Why are you sayin' these things to me our Josh, why?" I tried to catch hold of his hand as he raised it above his head, thinking he was goin' to hit me again, but he leaned his elbow on the cupboard above my head and looked down at me and sighed.

"Jessie how can you stand there predentin' you don't know what I'm taklin' about."

"But I don't Josh, I don't!"

Just then Our Sammy stuck his head through the cabin door "Ma says you're to come for supper NOW!" and then he ran off.

"This will have to wait until I can speak to you on your own Jessie" Josh said as he

swung up through the open door. "But you just watch out ;cos I'll be watchin you my lady" and with that he was gone leaving me gasping for air, with a bruise down my face and arm that hurt so much I thought it must be broken. I would 'ave to think up an excuse for and still not knowing what it was I had done that had made my beloved brother turn against me so suddenly.

I didn't have no time to think much about it as I made my way to 'Isis' back cabin and climbed down inside with the rest of the family. Thankfully no one seemed to take no notice of me as I pushed between Da and our Sammy to sit in my usual place. Everyone was jabbering at once as Ma loaded the plates with hot stew and passed them around the tiny drop down table. Sammy and Flossie had theirs in bowls, 'cos they was messy eaters. There was a lull in the talking as everyone set too, eating the delicious meal. After a whole day of bread and tea, it was good to have somethin' to get yer teeth into. Not that this rabbit was tough mind you, oh no he was cooked to a treat. No fat and tender as you like. There was nothing left on those plates tonight or any night.

"Well I'm glad today's over" Da said as he leaned back against the cabin doors which were wide open, on account of the fine evening.

"Why's that then Joe?" Ma asked absently as she busied herself collecting up the plates.

"Well it's broken the back of this trip, we've got a good few extra miles under our belts on account of the fine weather today and if it holds for tomorra, we'll be in Gas Street by Friday afternoon." Da sighed as he packed his pipe with baccy. "If we gets unloaded early we could be away from there before night fall"

"Aww Da!" it was Flossie wailing from her corner on the drop down bed "Ma said I

could have a 'suck' from the suck shop when we gets to Brum!"

"Oh Flossie love, don't you worry we'll get you a sweetie, even if our Josh has to run all the way back out to Tamworth to catch up with us" Da laughed as he stepped up to the well deck and lit his pipe.

I watched him as he stood out in the clear moonlit night. I envied the way he always spoiled our Flossie, I could not remember ever getting special treatment the way she did, she only had to have a little cough or fall over and winge and Ma and Da would be fussin' 'round her. The rest of us? Well we'd have to be half dead before anyone would notice anythin' was wrong with us.

"You're quiet tonight Miss" Da said without even looking down into the cabin. It made me jump 'cos I knew he were speakin' to me, lately both he and our Josh had taken to calling me 'Miss'. I was confused, I didn't know whether this was good or bad. I didn't know if they was sayin' it to make fun of me or 'cos I was getting older. I couldn't think of nothing to say so I got to me feet and grabbed a dish rag off the hob and began wiping down the table, then I folded it back into the cupboard out of the way. Ma was pilein' the dirty dishes into the tin bowl

"If you pour in the hot water I'll take those out and do them" I indicated the dishes.

"A bit eager aren't you" Ma said "Got a young man waitin' for you, have you?" Ma laughed and everyone seemed to join in. My face went bright red and I was so angry. Normally I would have had a smart answer ready, but somehow tonight I'd had the stuffin' knocked out of me by our Josh's words and actions and I was still reeling from the shock of it all.

Silently I took the bowl from the stove and turning, caught sight of our Josh's eyes burning into me. I wanted to drop the bowl and run away, far away where I wouldn't have to look into those eyes once so kind, now so full of hatred. What had I done to make him change towards me, this beloved brother who had been my friend and soul mate, through thick and thin we had always stuck together. Our Josh had got me out of many a scrape, and me him. I couldn't think of a time when we wasn't 'close' – until now.

"Here, give us the bowl" it was Da, hands outstretched, looking towards me

"Jessie what ever's the matter with you, you're in a dream or somat" Ma said behind me.

Not finding any words to say, I handed up the bowl of dirty dishes to Da and followed up behind with the dish rags. It was a warm evening and the moon was already rising. A dark red glow spread across the sky far into the west.

"Red sky at night, shepherd's delight" Da said to no one in particular. He puffed away on his pipe for a few minutes "Pretty good for us boaters too" he said again.

I didn't turn 'round, I couldn't trust myself to say anythin'. I felt as though I would burst out cryin', so I just carried on with my chore. Just then our Josh pushed between me and Da and stepped over the gunnal onto the bank

"Just goin' to check on Hercules" he said and walked on alone, but Da stopped him

"I'll walk up with you Josh, need a bit of a chat" and with that the two of them walked off up the tow path together.

I felt a sinking feeling in the pit of my stomache, what were they goin' to talk about? What did Da want to say to our Josh that he couldn't say infront of the rest of us. Did Da know why our Josh had turned against me, was our Josh goin' to turn my Da against me? What had I done! I racked my brain to try to recall anythin' that I could have said or done that would have made our Josh hate me.

"You finished out there Jess?" It was Ma calling from inside the cabin.

"Yes Ma" I managed to say without her noticing the shake in my voice.

"Well I'm puttin' our Flossie to bed so you may as well go on back to 'Bluebell' and get yourself and Sammay away to bed, early start in the mornin' mind".

I was grateful that Ma did not expect me to join her in the back cabin as we often did, or sit out on the towpath. I felt so tongue tied and was sure she would ask about the bruise on me face and I hadn't had time to think up an excuse yet. Without getting back into the cabin I hung up the bowl on the hook over the stove.

"Here Sammy" I said "Take these plates, then we'll get off to bed."

Sammy took the plates and spoons from me. I didn't wait for him, I just climbed over the gunnal and began walking back to 'Bluebell', moored up behind. Ma had let the stove out earlier in the day, she said we didn't need two fires going, but the cabin was still warm from the earlier sunshine. I pulled open the doors, but didn't go straight into the cabin, instead I sat on the gunn'al gazing up at the clear star studded sky and the cream coloured moon. On such a beautiful night, how could my whole world be falling apart, it just did not seem fair!

Just then Sammy came slopeing along the length of the boat, dragging a small length of rope behind him. He was always fiddling with rope or bits of string, strange, I thought, how that could keep his pea brained mind occupied for hours, why couldn't life be that simple for me?

"You comin' to bed now Jess?" he said as he climbed onboard.

"No I think I'll sit here for a bit longer" I said "Maybe wait 'til our Josh and Da get back".

"You'll be there all night!" Sammy replied "I heard Da say to our Josh that he was gonna walk over to 'The Bull' for a quick one, that's a mile and a half at least, they won't be back 'til closing time."

"It's not like Da to go off without sayin' anythin'," I said, disappointed that I would not have the opportunity to speak to our Josh tonight, although I was still scared of by what he might say.

"He did SAY, just before supper. It must have been before you and our Josh came in." Sammy had pulled open the drop down bed and was about to scramble in

"And you can get undressed before you get into bed!" I exclaimed as the light from the moon lit up the cabin.

"Aww Jess, it only takes me twice as long to get dressed in the mornin' and you know how Ma goes on if I'm late getting' dressed"

"It's not getting' dressed that takes you the time, its wakin' up!" I was in no mood for a fight with our Sammy over whether or not he could sleep in his clothes

"Now get them clothes off before you gets into bed!" I said sharply.

"Alright our Jessie, there's no need to shout, d'you want Ma coming down on us?" Sammy was indignant and as ever would try to have the last word.

"Just do as I say Sammy" I said, quieter now, "And no arguments!" I put in again just as he opened his mouth to say somethin' else. But Sammy gave up and did as he was told.

I sat on the gunn'all for what seemed like hours before finally deciding to get into bed myself. I felt stiff as I tried to stand up straight, me arm was aching fit to drop off and the bruise on my face was throbbing. I had no mirror, but when I felt my cheek, it was hot and swollen. I opened the lid of the buckby on the cabin roof and dipped a rag into the cool clear water, pulling it out, I let the water ouse and run onto me face, mopping it as it ran off me chin. Then I held the damp cloth to me cheek as I lay down on top of the blankets. Still thinking I would stay awake until Da and our Josh returned, so that I could have it out with my brother, I decided not to get undressed and into bed. I left the back doors open and thinking that even if I dropped off to sleep I would hear our Josh when he climbed down into the back cabin to go to bed himself.

The next thing I was aware of, was the sun's rays pouring in through the gaps around the doors which were now closed. I sat up suddenly and realised that it was already morning and I must have slept all night. I looked straight across to the side bed where our Josh usually slept, but it was empty, his blanket and pillow were missing though, which meant he must have come back last night and took them to sleep somewhere else. Well if ever I had needed confirmation before that something real serious had happened between me and our Josh, I certainly had it now, he wasn't even going to share the back cabin with me! By God he must really hate me – but why?

Realising that I was still dressed from the night before, I swung my feet over the bedside and sat up. Our Sammy was still snoring away in the corner, so I decided to leave him for a while. If I was quick I might catch our Josh on his own while he hitched up Hercules. I pushed open the back doors and climbed out into the clear blue morning sky. As I stepped onto the bank I realised that I was too late to try to speak to our Josh before we set off, for Hercules was standin' with his nose can on, hitched up and waitin' for the off.

"C'mon girl" Ma said as I reached 'Isis' back cabin "Your're late this mornin!"

"Sorry Ma" I replied as I took a mug of steaming hot tea from her. Then as I began blowing it she said "By our Jessie, that's a shinner and no mistake!" and she pushed me head over to one side to get a better look at the bruise on me face. "What were you doin' to come by that?" she looked accusingly at me.

I felt myself go bright red and sweat seemed to pour from nowhere all down my back.

"Well" Ma was lookin' at me, straight in the eyes and waitin' for an answer.

"I-I fell over" I said awkwardly

"Fell over, fell over what?" she didn't let up on the stare.

"I slipped on the gunn'all" I lied, not able to return her gaze "Last night, when I went to bed, I –I slipped and fell against the back door" I put my hand to my cheek and dropping me eyes began to examine every knot hole in the floor of the back deck, hoping no one else had noticed, but as I raised me head I caught sight of our Josh, hands on hips, eyes burning into me, as he stood a little way off beside the horse. Just then Da came out from the hold, under the cloths, where he must have been leveling some part of the cargo.

"Mornin' Miss" he said smiling.

I wasn't sure if he was laughing at me again. I tried to speak but I was tongue tied and no words would come out.

"Speak to your father when he speaks to you!" Ma said sharply and I choked on my tea!

I thought I would get a chance to speak to our Josh alone, later that morning when we got to the locks, but Ma decided, as it was such a nice day, she would have a bit of a walk up the towpath and wanted me to steer 'Isis'. I couldn't believe it, Ma rarely walked the towpath, preferring to stay onboard one of the two boats, so why did she want to walk today. Everything seemed to happening on purpose to thwart me. I was sure now that my whole family was 'in' on the conspiracy. Even our Sammy had gone off to steer 'Bluebell' without a word.

I felt so miserable and alone, and all sorts of aweful thoughts was running through me head. You gets a lotta time to think when you're stood in the well deck of a boat steerin' all day, with nothin' but mile after mile after mile of canal to look at, and nothin' to interrupt yer thoughts. It was nearly mid day before Ma decided she'd had enough walking for the day. Our Flossie, had slept most of the morning on account of the stout Da had brought from 'The Bull'. Someone had told him that a drop of stout was good for a bairn's stomache ache and so he had brought a bottle back with him. They'd given her some last night and some more with her breakfast this mornin' and it had knocked her right out. I remember thinkin' they should give it to her all the time, I'd never known my little sister so quiet. But she was awake now and whingeing 'cos Ma was not there, so at the next bridge'ole Ma had hopped back on board of 'Isis'. Our Sammy carried on steerin' while Ma sorted Flossie out but Da decided to pull up just before the next set of locks. Hercules was playin' up a bit, which was unusual for him, and our Josh wanted to give him a lookin' over.

The sun was high in the sky and not a cloud to be seen, it was such a beautiful day, I thought I should be really happy, but of course I wasn't. I still did not know why my beloved brother had turned against me and it was breaking my heart. I couldn't remember a time when our Josh had been so horrible to me, and he'd hit me, he hadn't done that in a long time. We argued sure enough, like most brothers and sisters, but it never lasted long, once we'd had our say, it was over like, well you couldn't carry it on too long. Livin' together in such a small back cabin made it almost impossible to ignore one another so we just had to get along. But I knew our Josh was still angry with me, but for what I had no idea. I'd spent all moring and the day before trying to rack me brains, but was still no nearer to knowing what I had done to make him so angry. I remembered him sayin' somethin' about 'Rodney' boaters, 'rough Rodney boys' he had said, but why would he believe I'd have anything to do with any of them. Ma had allus made sure we all knew who, amongst the boating families, she considered 'rough' and we was told to stay away from them, they was dirty and lazy and generally no good. Ma always tried to make sure we never moored up close to any of them, and when we was small children we was told not to play with them. Most of the boating families were very proud of their boats and the cabins was kept spotless, but like any community there were some families who weren't 'partic'lar', infact they was downright 'flilthy' and some of 'em were 'drinkers' an' all.

The other boating families called these 'Rodney' boaters – don't ask me why! But our Josh had said somthin' about me and 'rough Rodney boys' how could he think that I......Well just what did he think.........? That, I had to find out, and right now!

Da was on the bank waitin' for me to throw the rope so he could tie 'Bluebell' up behind 'Isis'. I could see our Josh leadin' Hercules to a shadey spot under the trees and decided to go and have it out with him there. I knew I would be pretty safe, in full view of everyone and our Josh would not shout or do anythin' to spook the horse. Ma was mashin' the tea and our Sammy and Flossie were sittin' on the cabin roof with large slices of bread and butter. Da was packing his pipe with baccy, sittin' on Sammy's box on the towpath, so I decided this was going to be the best chance I would get.

"Come for another hiding have you?" our Josh must've known it was me, even though he was bent over Hercules's hoof, with his back to me.

"No Josh, I've come 'cos I don't know why you give me the first one, I don't know what I've done to make you hate me or want to beat me!" I realised I was near to tears and it must have been somethin' in me voice, 'cos our Josh put the horse's foot down gentley and turned towards me, then he put his hand on me shoulder

"Look Jess, you're not a child any more, you're growin' up, you're nearly fourteen, if I catch you with any of them 'Rodney' boys I'll......."

I pulled away from him sudden like "What d'you mean, I don't go near any of 'em" I was angry now! How dare our Josh even think it!

"That's not what I heard the other day!" he retorted

"Heard, heard what?" We was both shouting now. "And I suppose you believe everything you hear!"

"I didn't want to believe it, not the things they was sayin' not about MY SISTER!"

Suddenly Hercules' head went up, pulling the lead reign from where it was looped over the fence and he was off! Galloping up the tow path towards the lock.. Our Josh sent me a look of pure hatred and without a word was away, running for all he was worth after the horse.

Da and Ma, seeing Hercules, our usually good tempered and mild mannered horse, go bolting off, started shouting to know what had happened. Not wanting to have to explain and at the same time realising the danger of a loose horse on the lockside, I took to me heels after our Josh. I ran for all I was worth the hundred yards or so, hardly dareing to look ahead of me for fear of what might be happening. Half way along Da over took me running hard and cursing just as we both heard a loud splash! We had to run up a steep bank to the lock top and I could hardly breath, I was panting so heavily. But when we got up there it was empty and there was no sign of Hercules or our Josh! For a moment it seemed unreal, we'd heard the splash, so we knew the horse had gone in, but where was he? A boaters worst fears was that a horse or a person would fall into a lock, some of which were more than 15 feet deep and getting a horse out was damn near impossible. Just then we heard another splash and then I saw Da go plunging off down the other side of the lock, I quickley followed and immediately realised what had happened. Hercules must have run straight on past the lock, but at the sharp left hand turn had run out of towpath and plunged into the canal, our Josh, not seeing anywhere for the horse to get back out, had jumped in and was swimming alongside him to give him confidence. Although they can swim, a lot of horses drown 'cos they just give up. Our Josh was encouraging Hercules to come in close towards the bank further down where it was shallow. He had his arm under the horse's head and was talking to him all the while. Da and I walked slowly down towards the spot we knew our Josh was trying to guide him to. We didn't want to spook him again so we kept quiet, so he would just listen to our Josh's voice and go where he was being taken. There must have been quite a 'shelf' below the waterline 'cos suddenly Hercules lurched forward with our Josh hanging on 'round his neck, then two more steps and he was out! Shaking himself from head to tail and soaking us into the bargain. As we leaned towards this soggy pair, Da took a firm hold of Hercules' reign. I stretched out me hand to help our Josh up the steep bank, I had a moment's doubt just before he took it and pulled himself up to where Da was standing holding the horse. Just then Ma arrived, out of breath, with our Sammy and Flossie running behind her. Everyone seemed to be talking at once and not making any sense, there was hardly any room for us all on this narrow stretch of tow path and we were all getting in each other's way when Da said,

"C'mon we'd better get back to the boats and get these two dried out."

As we all walked back across the lock we met up with Bert and Benny Dobbs, coming up towards us. They had seen something of what had happened from way back down the Cut and having tied up to wait for the lock to empty, were coming to see if we needed any help.

"Your 'orse took a look then?" said Bert full of concern

"Aye Bert" Da replied "He took off when these two here were havin' a barny," and he nodded towards me and our Josh.

I felt me face go bright red and I suddenly burst into tears. The embarrassment and shame was too much and with everyone standing there, looking at me, I just couldn't bear it so I picked up me skirts and ran off down the tow path towards our boats. I didn't stop until I had reached the safety of 'Bluebell's' back cabin and once inside I shot the bolt across the back door and fell down sobbing into me apron.

I wasn't sure how long I had been locked in there, but me throat was aching from crying and me sleeve and apron were soaking wet from the tears, when I became aware of someone outside knocking gentley on the door. I couldn't be sure whether this was the first time anyone had tried to get me to come out, or whether me family had just ignored me, leaving me to 'cry it out' as Ma often put it, but I knew I must have been there for some time.

"Jessie, Jessie, c'mon open the door." It was our Josh and he was speakin' so quietly and kindly that I wanted to start bawlin' all over again.

"C'mon Jess, you can't stay locked in there for ever, you've got to come out sometime."

I wanted to speak, to say he was only going to shout at me again, but my throat was so tight I couldn't make a sound.

"Jess please, I want to talk to you............. no shouting, I promise"

I pulled me apron up over my head and dried my face, then fumbled to pull the bolt back. I didn't know if I felt relieved, or frightened or just exhausted, all I knew was that our Josh was being kind to me once more and whatever he had to say to me would be bearable as long as he didn't hate me. I pushed open the doors and immediately turned my head away from the bright sunlight which flooded in. Josh's large body was framed in the doorway as he bent almost double before climbing down into the cabin.

"What're doin' on the floor?" he said offering me his hand

I still couldn't speak but I let him help me up onto the side bed. Me head was pounding and I just wanted to lie down somewhere in the dark and go to sleep. I sat beside me brother, so happy that he cared enough to come and see how I was. I realised that he must have changed his clothes for he was no longer wet. Suddenly he jumped up and I didn't know what he would do next, but he reached up to the cabin roof outside and brought in two mugs of hot tea

"I nearly forgot these" he said as he handed one to me.

I took it gratefully and cupping both hands 'round me mug took tiny sips of the hot sweet liquid.

"I-is H-Hercules alright?" I managed to ask after the tea had loosened my throat a little.

"He doesn't seem to be any the worse for his dunking" our Josh replied

"A-and you, are you alright?" I said again

"I'm fine Jess, just as well it's a nice hot day though"

There was silence then between us until I plucked up the courage to say

"A-and a-are you still angry with me?"

Silence again. I looked up into our Josh's face and he looked long and hard back at me.

"Look Jess, the other day, when we was loadin up at Timony Wharf"

I nodded

"Well, I had to go over to Randell's to get some syz'all for Da and while I was in there two of Ma Dowse's sons came in. They didn't see me 'cos I was in the back room with Mr.Randall, measurin' out the syz'all. I didn't take no notice of them until, ...well, I heard your name mentioned."

"My name, the Dowse boys, but.....!" I was flabbergasted

"Well you can imagine, I didn't know why any of the Dowse boys would mention the name of My Sister, let alone in the way they was sayin' it"

"What d'you mean Josh, how was they sayin' it?" I still had no idea where any of this was leadin' but I knew I didn't like the way our Josh was tellin' it.

"Jess it was as though they both knew you!" Josh was lookin' at me strange like

"Well they *do* know me!" I exclaimed, "We've known them all our lives!"

"Yes, I know we see them all the time up and down the Cut, but that's not what I mean." Josh was getting irritated and I didn't want him to start shouting and getting all mad again. I wanted to understand what he was tryin' to say, but it made no sense to me.

"Look Jess, they was sayin' things about you, things that well, they shouldn't know about a girl. They were sayin' what they would, well like to do when they saw you next, you know!"

I jumped up suddenly! "No I don't know our Josh, but if your sayin' what I think you're sayin' then you should go and wash your mouth with carbolic!" It was my turn to be angry now! The Dowse boys, the filthy little..........! Well it just didn't bear thinking about. "How could you believe anything that came out of their foul mouths!" I cried, "Let alone anything about me! I haven't seen any of that bunch for months, how could they say ANYTHING, they don't KNOW anything about me.............!"

"I'm sorry Jessie, I know I shouldn't have believed anything they said, but they were talking about a pair of bloomers with pink ribbons and lace. I know Ma had two pairs of bloomers made for you, she collected them from Mrs. Williams last month when we was moored up near there, and garters, they said you had garters to hold up your stockings."

Our Josh was still sitting on the side bed and when I looked down at him with his head in his hands. I saw that his ears had gone all red and I realised he was embarrassed. I wanted to put my arms 'round him and hug him to me like a small child, but for some reason I could see the funny side of the whole situation and I started to laugh! I just laughed and laughed. Our Josh looked all confused

"Whats so funny?"

But I couldn't answer him 'cos I couldn't stop laughing!

"Its not funny Jess, I don't want anyone thinkin' that you and they………."

"Oh Josh, its your face, you look so serious!"

"It IS serious" he replied, standing up, "And you should take it serious, you should……."

"Josh" I interrupted, "All girls of my age wear garters to hold their stockings up! And I've just remembered that I did see the Dowse boys, two weeks ago. I was running down the top planks to fasten Hercules' lead reign to the mast, that mornin' when we was just setting off from the colliery wharf and it was real windy, d'you remember?"

I was holding on to our Josh's elbows and looking straight up at him. "Well the Dowse boys walked by on their way up to the stables. There was a huge gust of wind as I jumped down off the planks onto the towpath, it nearly took me skirt and petticoats over my head! Whatever they saw it must have been then, anything else is just in their dirty little minds." I looked hard at my brother, "And yours too if you believe them". I dropped my hands and stepped towards the door. But our Josh put out his arm to stop me.

"Jess, I'm sorry. I never thought, I mean I………"

"But you DID think, you thought what they were sayin' about me was true, you believed their foul talk, Josh how could you?"

"I'm sorry Jessie" Josh put his hands 'round my shoulders and pulled me close to him, "You're my sister, I care about you, but you're a pretty girl and you're growing up fast. I was afraid….."

"Afraid of what?" I put in

"I don't know, I was just afraid that one day you might want to go off with some awful bloke. That people would talk about you the way they talked about Lizzie Higgins, you know, before she wed Freddie."

"Oh Josh" I said as the tears welled up in me eyes once more, "You stupid big lout!" And I hugged my big brother and we never spoke about it again.

Photograph taken in May 1910 of two horsedrawn boats in the Brentford Gauging Dock, the India *and the unfortunate* Stockport.

CHAPTER TWELVE.

The 'Orrible Day

"Oh Ma, you know I don't like goin' up to no farmer's doors, least ways, not ones we don't know. Can't our Sammy go?"

"Jessie, just stop your moutherin' Flossie's not been well all night an a drop of warm milk'll do her the world of good"

"Couldn't I just ask our Josh......"

"Jessie, you could be there an back again in the time it takes you to argue, just do as your told!"

"But Ma….."

"Jessie…….!"

I knew Ma was getting real mad at me, it weren't often she raised her voice at any of us,Well not in an angry way. We all had to shout across locks and from one side a'cut to t'other. But Ma was never one to just bawl her head off, not like some I could think of. I finished lacing up me boots then reached over the dropped down table and opened the cupboard above, careful not to make no noise and wake our Flossie, didn't want her grizzling again! I took out the small can, then reaching for me shawl from beside the bed'ole, I stepped up from the cabin into the well deck.

"Don't take all day about it" Ma said as I went to step over the gunn'all to the tow path.

"We'll get goin' as soon as our Josh gets back with Hercules, if you cut across the north

field you should catch us up by Stockers Bridge."

"Oh Ma, couldn't you wait til I get's back, I'll run all the way and be back before our Josh gets the 'orse set on."

"Jess, why are you makin' all this fuss, all I want's is a can of milk for our Flossie from the farm and you're acting as though I've asked you to bring me the Moon, I don't know what's got into you lately, you used to be such a good girl, now all I get is back chat, and with yer Da still in the sanitorium, I can't be doin' with it.....do you hear me girl?"

"Yes Ma." I hung me 'ead in shame, I didn't want to make Ma mad at me. But she knows how I hates goin' to farms and the like, specially on me own. I'll walk the length and breadth of the Cut, in all weathers, with never a moan, she knows that, but goin' across the fields, up unknown paths, even into the towns and villages we passed through.....not for me......I likes to stay with the boats, well it's wot I knows best.

"Here Jess, take tuppence for the milk, they can't ask more 'un that for a small can"

I took the coins from Ma and holdin' them tightly in the palm of me hand, tuggin' me shawl up over he 'ead, I set off in the direction of the farmhouse we'd passed late last night before we tied up. I reckoned I could find me way there more easily if I stayed on the tow path 'til I came level with the wide track which looked as though it went right up to the farm, rather than cuttin' across the field. At least that's what I told meself, wantin' to stay on familiar ground for as long as possible. Goin' back would be a different kettle of fish altogether, as I'd have to get a move on to meet up with our boats at Stockers Bridge.

It had rained heavily overnight so I walked with me 'ead down, tryin' to avoid the deep ruts and puddles along the way, no sense in getting' me feet wet through now, they'd get wet enough goin' back across the fields. It was cold too, so I hunched over, keepin' me shawl tight under me chin with one hand, in the other I clutched the two pennies Ma had given me and the handle of the small buckby can, for the milk. So when this small dog appears beside me, sudden like, I felt a bit nervous.

"Good boy" I says, hopin' he's friendly, but carryin' on walkin' just incase. The dog sort of 'fell in' beside me, as though he knew me, but I knew he weren't a boat dog, well not off any of the boats I knew. He was black an' white with a large waggie tail and big floppy ears, 'E must 'of belonged to someone 'cos he 'ad a collar. "Good Boy" I says again, not knowing what else to say to 'im. Just then I reached the track which ran away from the Cut and up in the direction of the large farmhouse which I could just see between the trees about half a mile away.

"This is where I turn off" I said to the dog, thinkin' 'e would carry on down the tow path, but he followed me up the path, as though he lived there.....perhaps 'e does, I thought and carried on up towards the farm.

"Well, well, well! If it isn't one of those 'Dirty Boaters."

The words sent a chill all through me and I looks up to see this boy leanin' against a tree, holdin' two lifeless rabbits by their back legs.

"Don't you know this is private property" he says again.

I didn't know what to say. Yes I knew it was the farmers land, but I was goin' up to the 'ouse to buy milk, surely there was no 'arm in that.

"I knows that", I said, with all the authority I could muster, "Cos I'm up to the farm meself just now, to buy milk" that'll settle his hash, as Ma would say and I went to walk past him. But he stepped out right in front of me, grinnin' like some madman.

"Well maybe I won't let you go any further" he said

"You can't stop me!" The words were out before I even thought...... "I'm just goin' for milk" I said, not quite so sure of meself now.

He smirked "Bit high and mighty for a 'Dirty Boatie' aren't you" he said, still blocking my way on the path, "I ought to teach you some manners!"

"I don't know what you means." I said, beginning to feel real scared now. I didn't like the way 'e was lookin' at me. "D'you come from the farm then, I only wants milk for me sister, she's not been well, and me Da's got the monia, and Ma sent me..........!" The words sort of tumbled out of me mouth as I felt me stomach turn over.

The boy was laughing now...... "Got a lot to say for yourself 'Little Miss high and mighty.' Not bad looking either, underneath that filthy shawl......lets have a look at you" and he reached forward and grabbed me shawl, pulling it off and throwing it into the hedge. I tried to hold on to it, but he took me by surprise and I was aware of the can and the two pennies in me hand and didn't want to drop them.

" Ere, give it back!" I shouted and rushed to retrieve it from the hawthorn branches where it was caught up on the wicked thorns. Trying to untwine it, with one hand, I felt one of the thorns rake the back of my hand, but I gritted me teeth and carried on until it was free. He was laughing again and standing very close......too close, I could feel his breath on the back of my neck. I looked down at the trickle of blood running from my hand, not wanting to turn and look this boy in the face. I fussed over me hand, dabbing it with me shawl, hoping he wouldn't realise just how frightened I was.

"Now look what you've made me do!" I said in a mindless sort of way, trying to step back from the hawthorn without coming into contact with him. But it was the wrong thing to say......

"Oh dear, what HAVE you done?" he said and I knew he was mocking me. He caught hold of my wrist, "Let me see" and he pulled me towards him.

"Let me go, you're hurting!" I cried out, hoping that by raising my voice someone might hear, or at least make him think someone would hear.

"But you MUST let me clean up your hand" he said in a very deliberate, menacing way as he pulled me closer to him. He was strong, stronger and taller than me and I judged him to be a at least two or three years older. He was holding on to my wrist so tightly now that I could hardly feel me fingers. He held it up to his mouth, as I tried with all me might to get away, but he just held on. For a moment I thought he was going to bite me, as he opened his mouth, I was about to scream but his next action shocked me so much I just stood there with me mouth wide open …….. He licked the blood off my hand, with one long slow movement of his tongue ……..!

I stood rooted to the spot, sort of tranced as I watched in horror. Then from somewhere deep inside me came a shrill cry that scared me almost as much as it did him! I kicked his shin and at the same time pulled back my hand so swiftly that he let me go.

"You dirty 'orrible creature!" I cried as I set off running up the path for all I was worth. It all happened so quickly I couldn't be sure whether I was runnin' towards the Cut or the farm, all I knew was I wanted to get as far away from this monster as I could. What an 'orrible thing to do, was all I could think of and as I ran, I could hear the sound of his laughter ringing in me ears. I ran until I thought me lungs would burst and suddenly I was out of the lane and standing in the middle of the farm yard. I stopped to catch me breath, I bent over double in an effort to calm me breathing. Me heart was pounding clear up into me throat and I thought I'd never stop shakin'. I looked back along the lane to see if he'd followed me and was relieved to see that he hadn't.

I must have looked a sight as I trudged across the yard and up to what I judged to be the kitchen door. Da always told us to knock at the kitchen door and not go up to the front'un 'cos some folks got 'funny' if the likes of us knocked on their posh front doors. We boaties only 'ad back doors on our cabins, so there was no choice. Well, I thought this looks like the kitchen door, so I'll knock on that. I just wanted to get the milk and be on me way back to the safety of our boats. I waited, but no one answered, so I knocked again this time a bit louder.

"I'm coming, I'm coming!" I heard a voice from inside the house, and the door was opened by a large red faced woman, wearing a stiff white apron. "Well!" was all she said as she stood looking at me. I didn't know what she meant at first, so I just looked back, sort of stupid like. "What do you want girl?"

Oh I understood that all right but the words just wouldn't come out of me mouth, just a sort of strangled noise.

"What do you want?" The voice was louder now with more than a little annoyance

"P-please missus, me Ma wants some milk" and I held up the small can, in case her mind was as befuddled as mine. "Milk" I said again quite unnecessarily.

"We don't give it away" the woman said, crossing her arms across her chest.

"N-no, I've got money, Ma gave me tuppence, she said you wouldn't charge more than that, well not for just a small can." The words fell out of me mouth again, mindless mouthering, what must she think..........!

"Give me the can" the woman stopped me from making myself look even more foolish by holding out her hand and grabbing the two pennies from my outstretched palm. And with that she turned and closed the door in my face!

I stood there for what seemed like an age, wondering if she was in fact going to return with the milk, or whether she'd just taken the two pennies and shut me out. I was about to knock on the door again, when I heard footsteps and the door was opened, not this time by the woman, but by a girl of roughly my own age. She was dressed in a heavily patched blue dress, the sleeves of which were completely threadbare. The hem was halfway up her calves and I could see that her boots were badly worn, the toes having parted company with the soles.

"Missus says to give you this," and she held out the small can to me. I remember thinking, she looks awful poor for a farmers daughter, I thought they was all rich!

"Thanks" I said as I took the can, and just to show I wanted to be friendly like "Is this yer Da's farm?"

"No" she answered, "My Dadda's dead, I just work here"

I was about to say I was sorry about her Da, when a voice from inside the house boomed out "Shut that door girl and get back and tend to this fire!" and the door closed in my face a second time.

I turned and walked back across the yard, poor girl I thought, fancy havin' to be at the beck and call of that ferocious woman. I knew what being 'in service' was all about, Ma and Da had told us many times how lucky we was to be boaties, 'cos we was more or less our own bosses, well once we'd loaded up and got goin' we was. Then I thought I'd better get a move on, I had to find me way across the fields to meet up with our boats. I didn't know how long I 'd struggled with that 'orrible boy in the lane. It could have been hours or minutes, I just didn't have any idea. I stopped at the far side of the yard, where it met the dirt track and scanned the horizon. I would have to go off to the left to get back to the Cut further along from where we was moored overnight, up by Stockers Bridge. I could see a line of trees, away off in the distance and judged that to be the Cut and so I set off in that direction. I kept looking back over me shoulder to make sure I wasn't being followed. I didn't want no more encounters with that awful boy!

The first field was ploughed and planted with what Da called 'Winter Barley'. The deep ruts were full of rainwater, after the previous nights downpour and I was soon struggling ankle deep in mud. At the far side of the field I had to find a place where I could get over the low wall and into the next field. This one was all grass and I could see a herd of cows away off to the right "I'll keep out of their way," I said aloud as I jumped down off the wall. Halfway across this field I could see a small copse and knew I would have to go through it to get to the Cut. From where I was, I could see a well used stile between the hedge and the wall, "Well at least I won't have to climb over the wall" I said to myself, as I set off towards it. Thank goodness there was no sign of that 'orrible boy!

Then as I came up to the style, I saw the black and white dog again. He came straight up to me, as if he knew me. I remember thinking "That's funny, I saw him just before that boy appeared........." Then as I was goin' through the gap in between the bushes I felt meself falling forward, I must have banged me 'ead or sometin' 'cos I was feelin' sort of 'fuzzie' when I 'eard voices and felt hands on me arms and legs. Expecting to be raised to me feet once more, I sort of relaxed a bit. I don't know at what point I began to feel that things wasn't quite right. Me 'ead felt fit to burst an I couldn't quite tell where all the noise an curfuffle was comin' from. I tried to lift me hand to me head.........everythin' was black.....had I gone blind or somethin? From somewhere.....down a long dark tunnel, I heard a voice shoutin' somethin' I couldn't quite make no sense of. I tried to piece together what I thought I 'eard, to see if it'd make sense of why I couldn't move. It felt like somethin' heavy was restin' on me. I tried to recall what I 'ad been doin' just before…… but before   what, I just couldn't tell. P'raps somethin' very heavy had fallen on me, p'raps I'd fallen down an 'ole and was trapped and that's why I couldn't move me 'ands and legs, but it felt like somethin' was tied round them………What did that voice say? I couldn't quite make it out, I must try to clear the fuzziness in me 'ead, so I could hear what was bein' said.

I tried to turn me 'ead in the direction from which the voice was comin' from, then another voice close by shouted ….. I must try to make sense of what I was hearin'. All of a sudden it seemed that the cloud in my 'ead cleared and so did the blockage in me ears, I realised then that there was lots of different voices, all shouting, together like……!

"Hold her legs!"

''Hold her arms!"

"Don't let her move"

P'raps I was badly hurt, I thought, strange the only pain I felt was in me 'ead, but I couldn't move and everythin' was black.. Then suddenly the fog in me 'ead cleared and I was brought back to reality as the words I had heard shouted filtered through to me befuddled brain…………!

"Get her drawers off!"

At the same moment I felt several pairs of 'ands roughly tugging at me under garments. Deep inside me I felt the terror risin' as me knickers was torn off. I 'eard the material tearing and felt the grass on my now naked bottom. Please God, make this not be 'appening to me.make there be some other reason for what was bein' done to me, please God…..please! please! Me prayers died on me lips as an 'eavy weight fell on top of me , crushin' me.   More voices was shoutin', I couldn't 'ear what they was saying………Hot breath on me neck, in me face, claw like fingers rakeing me private bits….me 'head suddenly burst with the realisation of what was happenin' to me, as a voice screamed into my ear "Come on you bitch – open your legs!" From somewhere deep inside me I felt this wild animal stirring….then bursting to fight its way out. I 'eard a long low growl and then a high pitched sort of howl which went on and on getting stronger all the time, an' more an' more high pitched as I felt somethin' hard an' hot bein' thrust up between my legs. Hot! Dry! Agonisingly painful! Thrusting deep inside me….again and again…..deeper….deep inside ME!! "No, No, No! Please God, please….please not me, don't let this be 'appenin' to me, please! I didn't know if I was screamin' inside me 'ead or out loud, but with every ounce of strength in me body and every fibre of me soul I mustered all me power together. Again I 'eard this strangled animal cry and realised it was comin' from me own throat, as I tried to throw off me attacker. Still everthin; was black, tho' inside me 'ead everythin' was RED! But all me efforts was in vain…..I couldn't move a muscle somethin' or someone was pinning me arms and legs down, then whatever was holdin' me 'ead must have let go 'cos I was able to move it ….the hot breath on me neck told me where me attacker was layed heavily against me so I lunged forward with all me strength and

bit down as hard as I could into soft flesh.........All I felt was a mouthful of sacking and dry earth, but me teeth must have found their mark 'cos I 'eard a yelp and momentarily my attacker shifted his weight.....I tried to lift my lower body to shake him off, but his weight kept me pressed to the ground.......and all the while there was shoutin'......"Keep her down!" "Hold her feet!" "Stop her kicking!" Hurry Up!" "Can't hold the bitch forever!" Then the hot breathing in me ear got faster, the pain between me legs and inside me got worser an' worser until I thought me inards was bein' ripped out. I just knew I 'ad to stop what was 'appenin' to me.......again the wild animal inside of me took over and I felt all me muscles go tense, then I kicked out with me left foot for all I was worth and suddenly it came free, but not before it came in contact with somethin' solid but soft.......
I 'eard an agonised cry over to my left then "Hold the bitch 'til I've finished" my attacker screamed into my ear. I kicked out again and again, all the while screaming and howling bursting inside me 'ead. Then amid shouts and the sound of runnin' feet, I felt the heavy weight roll off me "Come on boys, run for it!" "Get away from here quick!" "Someone'all have heard the bitch!"

I don't know how I long I lay there, numb, detached, almost without thought or feeling, in a state of nothingness, me brain floating somewhere else quite detached from the rest of me body. Then slowly the realisation of what had happened to me begun to seep through, like the small drops of water weeping through a leaky keelson. With me now freed hands I dragged me skirt and petticoat down from over me 'ead, to cover me nakedness. As I squirmed on the ground I felt a sticky liquid running down me bruised thighs, stinging as it went, but still everything was black.....! The pain between me legs got worse as I rolled onto me side and tried to sit up. I lifted me 'ands to me 'ead and felt the roughness of the hessian sack........ "So that's why I can't see nothin." Feelin' around me neck I traced the string which held it fast until I found the knot. With fingers that was tremblin' uncontrollably, I fumbled for what seemed like ages before I worked the knot loose enough to release me from the eternal darkness. I tugged at the sack and pulled it off me 'ead.......the daylight blinded me! The throbbing in me 'ead turned to a blazing inferno and from somewhere deep inside I felt a tidal wave well up, like an 'ole lockful of water, built up inside of me. Somehow I knew I had to stop it from spilling over or I knew I would never stop the flow and it would drownd me. I took a deep breath in and realised that me throat was dry and sore, hot tears welled up in me eyes and I screamed inside meself "Don't cry, not now, don't you dare cry!" Two more rasping deep breaths and I nearly had meself under control. Then I began to shake violently, involuntarily, uncontrollably....little mewing noises escaped from my throat and I began to feel the full weight of that wave bursting to escape. Once more I told meself forcefully not to cry, I clenched me fists and then me jaw.....! I knew that if I ever let the flood gates burst, I would never stem the flow and would surely drown in my own self pity. 'Get on with life'..... I'd heard the phrase so many times, levelled at those who'd had disasters and tragedies and most boatie families 'ad seen more than their fair share of them! I tried to stand up, but the shaking was uncontrollable, me legs just wouldn't hold me weight. I slumped back into the dirt.

I lost all track of time. Strangely the Sun seemed to be in the same place, surely hours, even days, had gone by! Everythin' all round me looked the same …..but different. I saw me bonnet hanging in a bush, its ribbons fluttering in the breeze, was it really MY bonnet, it looked familiar, but how could it be MY bonnet when it looked so normal? How could things look so normal, surely the whole world had changed and therefore shouldn't things look different. How could that bonnet, the one now hanging on a bush, look just the same as it had this mornin' when I took it off the 'ook over the bed'ole in the back cabin. Was that only hours or days or weeks ago…..another lifetime even! As I looked around me, I saw a small buckby can standing on the step of the stile, it looked strangely familiar, and yet, why would it? Did it belong to me? Is that why I recognised it? It looked sort of brash, too colourful, sittin' there on the stile………..the stile ! Oh my God! The stile! I was just climbing over the style with the can of milk for our Flossie when……..! Oh God, did it really happen to me? ME, the girl who got up this morning, as usual, washed her face in cold water in the dipper….. as usual…..ME! Little Jessie, Our Josh's sister…..Our Josh! Oh my God! What was I to tell him, me brother, me big oaf of a brother, him what was the kindest and gentlest of all people. Him what loved birds and animals more than us humans. What could I say to him, how could I face him, how could I put all this into words. And Ma, what could I say to her. I felt dirty and wretched. I felt that somehow it must have been my fault. But how could it be, what did I do? Ma should 'ave never sent me on me own to fetch milk. I told her I didn't want to go, I pleaded with her to send our Sammy……why had she insisted that

I had to go, did she know this was goin' to happen to me? How could she know! Oh God, why, why? Why me, here, now.....its not my fault, I didn't do nothin'....please God make it all be a nasty dream, let me wake up in a minute and find it wasn't true!! Round and round in me 'ead I chased one thought after another. Nothin' made sense, nothin' seemed real and yet here I was, sitting in the dirt, me clothes all dishevelled, me bonnet in the bushes, me stockings 'round me ankles and me drawers....! Oh my God.....! I folded me arms tight across me chest, hugging meself, holdin' meself together, almost as though I thought I'd fall apart if I ever let go.........!

I became aware that I was gentley swaying, to and fro, backwards, forwards, backwards, forwards. Fine rain was falling on me upturned face and I realised that I was rocking meself, holdin meself real tight, as though I was holdin' a baby, but the baby was ME! I don't know how long I'd been sittin' there, but I was wet through. From somewhere way off in the distance I could hear a voice ....it was callin' out, yes it was definitely someone callin' out a name.....

"Jessie! Jessie! Where are you?"

It sounded familiar....Jessie! I knew I recognised it.......of course it was my name, Jessie! And who was it callin?......Our Josh, who else! Our Josh, oh no, he mustn't see me here, like this....! What can I do....! I tried to stand up but me legs weren't attached to the rest of me body, nothin' seemed to work. I rolled onto me side and bringing me knees up to me stomach, managed to pull meself to a kneeling position. Every muscle, every bone, every sinew in my body screamed out, the pain took me breath away! I must have cried out, coz the next thing I heard was

"Jessie! Jessie is that you?" and our Josh pushed his way through the hedge and stood looking down at me. "Jessie, I've been lookin' for you, where have you been? What's up? Oh no Jess, what's happened to you?"

It was more realisation than a question. He dropped to his knees and before I could reply he'd enfolded me in his arms. Just as well it happened real quick, 'cos I think I would have run away from him, or pushed him away. Not 'cos I didn't want to see him, but 'cos I felt so ashamed. But I couldn't do neither, he scooped me up in his arms and held me so tight I thought he'd squeeze what little life I had in me, out. He never said nothin' just held me tight in his strong arms. I felt the tidal wave rise up again inside me, but this time I couldn't stop it from washing over me. From somewhere deep down inside of me came this long low wailing cry, by the time it reached me throat it was overtaken by the wave and both seemed to burst out of me mouth at the same time!

I don't know how long I cried for, or how long our Josh sat there cradling me in his arms, all I knew was that I never wanted the moment to end. I never wanted our Josh to let me go. All the hurt and pain I was feelin' poured out from me throat and all the love I'd ever felt for him, all me life, turned to an iron like grip with which I held on to him. If anyone had seen us, they wouldn't have believe we was just brother and sister. But that's all it was….he was our Josh and I loved him. After a while I felt our Josh loosening his hold on me.

"Jess, Jess listen to me, stop cryin', stop cryin' please. Who did this to you?"

The sobs were still raking me body, but in-between the shudders I tried to reply

"I-I d-don't know!" I wailed "I-I d-didn't s-see them."

"Them" he almost shouted "Them, how many.....?"

"I-I don't know Josh! I d-don't know, they tied a sack over me 'ead!" I looked about me to try to find the offending article, as proof of what I was sayin'.

Our Josh stood up and pulled me to my feet, I swayed towards him and he put out his hand to steady me. "Hold on Jess, hold on to me, til you get yer strength, here come and sit on the stile."

I hesitated the sight of the can on the stile seemed to unnerve me.

"C'mon, you'll be alright, just sit here while I try to tidy you up a bit"

Josh led me to the stile, took out his kerchief and began wiping my face. Then satisfied that he'd done as good a job as he was likely to do, he got up and began looking 'round the area. He pulled me bonnet down from the branch where it'd been flutterin' in the breeze. He picked up the old sack from where I must have tossed it, once I was free of it. He crawled under the hedge to fetch out me shawl, someone must've thrown it there and then he spotted somethin' else in the nettles beside the wall. I watched as he pulled my ripped and muddied drawers from the middle of the nettlebed without flinching. Carefully and without a word he folded them until they were small enough to fit into his pocket. Then satisfied that he'd collected all the things he wanted, he came back to where I was sittin'.

"D'you think you could walk a bit now Jess? It's not that far to the boats an' you can hang on to me."

He gently helped me to stand up but never said another word all the way back to the boats. I wanted him to ask me again who had done this to me. I wanted to tell him how I felt. I wanted him to say he'd go after whoever it was. I wanted to tell him how dirty I felt. But we walked on across the fields in silence, his big strong arms around me. It wasn't until I could see our two boats moored up just beyond the bridge 'ole that reality struck me again and I felt fear rising up inside me! So powerful it was, that I had to bend over double and when the hot bitter liquid convulsed and stung my throat, it felt as though I was releasing all the bitterness and anger I had been feeling, pouring it all out onto the ground in front of me.

Ma saw us coming and I saw the recriminating words die in her throat, as she took in the 'ole picture. She was a wise woman was our Ma, she might never 'ave shown it, but each of us knew, and respected her for it. She didn't scream and shout like many another might 'ave. She didn't weep and wail, in fact she said very little.

"C'mon Jessie my girl, lets get you inside where its warm".

And she and our Josh helped me over the gunn'all and down into the safety of our back cabin. She didn't fuss me or ask what had happened, though I saw the glances she and our Josh exchanged. I hadn't noticed that our Sammy and Flossie weren't in their usual place in the bed 'ole until Ma said

"Take yer tea with you onto Bluebell Josh, and keep an eye on the little'uns".

I just sat beside the stove while Ma poured strong black tea into me mug and laced it with a drop of somethin' from her little bottle 'For medicinal purposes' she always said.

"Get that inside you love, then we'll get you out of those wet clothes."

CHAPTER THIRTEEN

A Big Mistake

I awoke from a restless sleep to the familiar 'drip, drip' drip, sound of water running off the back deck and dripping down into the coal box below. Rain and howling wind had lashed our boats all night, continuously rocking us to and fro, pushing Bluebell hard up against Isis, which in turn hit the bank then bounced back and hit us again, our planks creaking and groaning all the while. The wind got up under the cloths what covered the 'old, they thrashed and billowed, threatenin' to tear away from the ropes that 'eld 'em in place, while the rain 'ammered relentlessly on the cabin roof.

I pulled the blanket up around me ears and snuggled down into me pillow, listening to the morning sounds, tryin' to resist the thoughts of yet another day. I heard the steady 'Ping-hiss, ping-hiss' of rain hitting the inside of our chimney then spluttering on the hot embers inside the stove below. Every now and then the wind violently shook the branches of a nearby tree and thousands of droplets would rain down upon the cabin roof, making a thunderous sound. In the grey half-light that filtered through every gap and chink of the cabin's wooden planks, I could just make out the figure wrapped in blankets, curled up on the side bed. I thought me eyes was deceiving me, the figure looked so small, our Josh were a good height, even for seventeen years of age. Could he have shrunk in the night?

I rubbed me eyes with me knuckles and looked again, screwing up the lids in an effort to focus better in the dim light. Somewhere in the recess of my brain a thought began to take shape, somethin' had 'appened, but what was it, why couldn't I remember, was it yesterday or last week, what could it be? Then suddenly I sits bolt upright, as the events of the previous day blasted into my consciousness! It wasn't our Josh, sleepin' in his usual place on the side bed. It couldn't be, for the two men in uniform, the two soldiers who walked down the towpath towards our boats, the two men who thought they was so important, had taken our Josh, my beloved brother, away, to God only knew where! I sank back onto the pillow, hot tears stinging my eyelids before runnin' freely down me cheeks. How could they, why 'ad they? It didn't make no sense! Our Josh never wanted to be a soldier an' anyway his place was 'ere with us, with his family. 'E was a boatman, through an' through 'E didn't want to go an' get mixed up in their war.It were now't to do with us, why oh why! The thoughts just went round and round in me head as they 'ad all the previous day.

Then this thought came into me mind – of course, it had all been a big mistake, I could see that now and when they got our Josh to the barracks they would realise they 'ad got the wrong man, well boy more like! I smiled to meself now as I envisaged the tale our Josh would tell when he came back to us. We'd all sit on the back deck and laugh at their stupidity! Well all I 'ad to do now, was to keep everyone goin' for the next day or two until he came back! The previous day we 'ad all been so excited at the prospect of seeing Da, after 'is three week enforced stay in the Sanatorium. 'E were over the 'monia now and 'ad got word to us that 'E would meet us at Nuneaton where he 'ad arranged to pick up a cargo of earthenware, to take back to the City Road for shipment abroad. Ma, who 'ad sorely missed him while he were in the hospital, was 'over the moon' and 'ad baked a special fruitcake for the occasion. Pure extravagance she 'ad said, but Da were very partial to fruitcake and this was a celebration after all! But after the two soldiers had come to our boats that mornin' and taken our Josh away, everthin' had gone flat. Ma had said "I don't know what we're gonna tell yer Da. He'll be mad as hell, …they've no business interferein' in our lives,….. we never wanted no war, it's now't to do with us!" For meself, I just could not and would not believe it were anythin' else but a huge mistake. They had somehow got it all wrong. I convinced meself that as soon as our Josh arrived at the Army barracks they would realise he was the wrong person and would send him back home to us.

Of course Ma told Da all about it as soon as we met up with him at Boot Wharf. I spotted 'im right away, as we came under the bridge, Isis and Bluebell 'long lined' behind as Hercules and I trudged up the tow path. He was leanin' up against the wheel of one of the carts, with his pipe in his mouth, his coat collar turned up and 'is cap pulled down around his ears. 'E was wearin' a scarf and gloves, I'd never seen 'em before, I thought, as I pulled on the 'orses rein and shouted 'Woa Boy! 'E looked so much better than when we last saw him. I had been so frightened when he hadn't come back from the doctor that day. And when our Josh told me they'd taken him away to the Sanitorium 'cos he had the 'monia, well, I thought it was the worst day of me life, well, until yesterday it was. But Da was better now, and 'ere he was, all smiles and hugs. As soon as he saw us comin' into the wharf, he jumped forward to grab the rope from off the nose of 'Isis'. Hercules had come to a stop, so I ran back to 'Bluebell and shouted to our Sammy to throw me the 'stern' rope. Sammy pushed the 'elum arm over, to turn 'Bluebell's' nose in, then he jumped up onto the cabin roof and ran down the planks the whole boat's length, to grab hold of the front rope. By the time 'e got there, Da had already pulled 'Isis' to a standstill, so 'e walked back, took the rope from our Sammy and together we pulled 'er to a stop an all.

The next minute we was all on the wharfside. Da put out his arms to Ma but Flossie got in between and begged to be picked up. We all crowded round him, tellin him how well he looked and how glad we was to 'ave him back. Then we all just stopped dead in our tracks when 'e said

"Where's our Josh?"

Suddenly I couldn't speak, I opened me mouth, but now't came out, I just held on to 'is arm and shook me head. Da looked first at Ma and then at me.

"Flo" he said "Flo what's 'appened, where is he, where's our Josh?"

Ma caught 'old of his 'and as he set our Flossie down on the ground.

"Oh Joe, I'm sure it's all been a big mix up, two soldiers came along early yesterday mornin' and took him off to the Army. 'E were tackin' up Hercules in the stables behind the Barge Inn, they went and fetched him from there." Ma were getting' all het up again, 'er cheeks was all red and there was tears in 'er eyes as she carried on.

" They said the Company 'ad signed a paper wot said 'E could go! We didn't know now't about it….. it must be a mistake, our Josh didn't want to go and ……"

The words seemed to fall out of Ma's mouth and Da shook her gently by the shoulder

"Now, now Flo, c'mon don't be getting' yerself all worked up, stop gabbling and start again at the beginning, tell me exactly what happened."

Da led Ma back up the wharf and they sat together on the back deck of our boat 'Isis'. I felt they should be left alone to sort it all out, so I took Flossie and Sammy into the back cabin of Bluebell. I pushed the kettle into the middle of the stove to bring it to the boil and got out the teapot from the 'dropdown'. It was our instant 'cure all' and all our lives seemed to revolve around thousands of mugs full of hot, sweet, black tea!

"I wanna see our Da!" whined Flossie "Why can't I, I want Ma!" she carried on.

I could see that she were for startin' another tantrum, things was bad enough without 'er screaming an' throwin' herself about. I looked about to see what I could give her, just to shut 'er up. The sugar can was the first thing to catch me eye……..

"C'mon Flossie, let Ma and Da have a bit of time to their selves, tell you what, if you promise to be a good girl, you can dip yer fingers in the sugar." I wasn't sure that would work, you never could tell with our Flossie, sometimes there was just no quieting 'er, but she 'ad a very sweet tooth, so I could only hope……..!

"Can I lick 'em first?" she said, slyly lookin' up at me with those big blue eyes, as though butter wouldn't melt in 'er mouth.

"Can I 'ave some too Jess?" This was our Sammy

I didn't 'ave to answer 'im, I just gave 'im one of me 'looks', 'E knew exactly what that meant.

"Just get the mugs out" I said to him, as Flossie stuck her wet sticky fingers back into the sugar can for the fourth or fifth time. I took two steaming mugs of tea out to where Ma and Da were sittin'. They was still deep in conversation so I reached across the gunnal and put 'em down on the cabin top and walked quickly back to 'Bluebell'. Our Sammy had poured two more mugs of tea and we sat in the 'well deck' drinkin' it, all the while keepin' an eye on Ma & Da, not knowin' what was likely to 'appen next.

By the time Ma had finished her story, Da was real mad and went off to have 'words'! With who, we wasn't quite sure. I 'ad left them alone together for a while before taking their mugs of tea, but Da didn't stop to have his, he just upped and went off, returning shortly afterwards sayin' he couldn't find no one who knew anythin'. He decided we should load up as arranged and head off towards Braunston. He grumbled on all day sayin' 'The cheek of it, taking our Josh, don't they know we can't be doin' without our Josh!'

We had loaded our cargo of earthenware pots and then set off. Da planned to make enquiries that evening as soon as we tied up in Braunston. 'E was gone most of the evenin' and Ma 'ad to keep his supper warm as the rest of us had eaten ours long before he came back. We all sat in the back cabin of 'Isis' not knowin' what to think.

"Can't get no sense out of anyone!" he exclaimed as he stepped down into the cabin. "We'd best get a good night's sleep tonight and press on to Stoke Bruerne tomorrow, we'll sort it all out then."

We was all so sure it had been a big mistake and in a day or so the army would send 'im back and everything would get back to normal. I imagined our Josh running towards our boats down the towpath. If we was movin' he'd leap onboard and give Ma and me a big hug. Or if we was tied up, he'd stick his head through the cabin door and say "Got the kettle on Ma, eeh I'm famished!"

Now, as I lay in the bed'ole on 'Bluebell', the grey light of morning filtering through the gap between the top of the doors and the hatch, I was aware of a queezie feelin' in me stomach. It wasn't like me to be off colour I thought, as the first feelings of doubt slid uninvited into me head. Could it be that Mr. Griffiths had actually agreed to let our Josh go, 'ad 'E actually signed a paper condemning our Josh to the Army. No, I decided, Mr. Griffiths might be a strange sorta chap, but he would never do a thing like that…. not to us…… he liked us! Smiffy always said so.

No it 'ad to 'ave all been a big mistake. I pulled me knees up to me chin and hugged them, happy now in the knowledge that all would be well and our Josh would be home soon. Then we could tell Da together …… about…… about wot 'ad 'appened to me……..and with our Josh beside me, I knew it'd all turn out right…..He 'ad promised he'd be there with me an our Josh never broke a promise, not never. Everythin' was gonna be just fine, I now told meself. And with that I swung me legs over the side of the drop down bed and pulling the blanket 'round me shoulders, went to stoke up the stove. I pushed open one side of the cabin doors and gazed out into the grey wet morning. I was heartened to see that the rain had eased off and the wind, although still gusty, was changing direction. At least we wouldn't be headin' straight into it all mornin' I thought.

I could hear low voices and the faint sound of the stove being raked next door on 'Isis' and knew that Ma and Da was up and about too. I went back to the bed 'ole and pulling the 'modesty' curtain across behind me, quickly got dressed. I was rolling up the mattress and stuffing it into the cupboard with me blanket and pillow, when I 'eard our Sammy stirring behind me

"Whatcha leave the door open for, it's freezin" he grumbled as he pulled his blanket up over his head.

"C'mon our Sammy, shake a leg!" I called to him as I pulled back the curtain and smoothed out the crocheted blanket covering the day bed.

"The kettle's on, tea'll be mashed by the time you're up and dressed."

"It's cold" he groaned from under his blanket.

"You'll be a lot warmer when you starts movin" I replied.

"You two up in there?" it was Ma callin'. I stuck me 'ead out of the door and looked across to the back doors of 'Isis' where Ma was just peeping out.

"Aye Ma, we're up. I'm just drinkin' me tea then I'll go and see to Hercules".

Ma nodded and went back inside the cabin.

"C'mon Sammy, don't let Da know I had to nag you again to get you up" I spoke quietly as I really didn't want Ma and Da to hear me.

"Oh all right!" he said between gritted teeth "One day, when I grows up, I'm gonna stay in bed all day!"

"One day when you've got yer own boats you'll realise just how much time gets wasted, lyin' in bed, when you could be up and out and 'alf way up the Cut before some as I knows gets outta bed! Just get your clothes on Sammy." I said, as I eased me feet into me boots.

The leather had gone all 'ard where I'd dried them out beside the stove overnight. Then, tyin' on me bonnet and pulling me shawl around me shoulders, I stepped up to 'Bluebell's' back deck, ready to face another day. I thought Hercules gave me a funny sideways look, as I pulled the wet sacks off 'is back and attached his nose can for 'is early mornin' feed. For as long as I could remember it had allus been our Josh who saw to Hercules. 'E did everthin' for 'im and you could see 'ow they was 'attached' to one another. Hercules would nudge our Josh with 'is nose, to get 'is attention and to get 'im to scratch 'is neck. When 'E was in a playful mood, our Josh would elbow the horse back, then pretend to ignore him, pretend he didn't know what the 'orse wanted. Hercules would try again, and again until our Josh gave in and gave him a good scratchin' all up and down his neck and behind his ears, he liked that best of all.

"I'm sorry old boy" I spoke to the 'orse while I rubbed him down, "You'll have to make do with me 'til our Josh gets back". I'm sure he understood me 'cos he sort of nodded his head up and down "Yes, I miss 'im too" I whispered, as I gently scrubbed the course hair on his forehead, right between his eyes. Hercules blinked in answer, as he continued chomping the oats from his nose can. Just then I heard the sound of Da's heavy boots as he jumped off the gunn'all onto the towpath.

"Water level's up this mornin' should be an easy run to Stoke Bruerne" he called over to me, as he pulled on the ropes to make sure they was good and tight over the cargo.

"With all the rain we 'ad last night, I'm surprised we 'ain't up on the bank this mornin" I called back.

The rain kept off for most of the day and we did indeed make good time. With so much water in the Cut our boats swam well, even though they was both fully laden. Da decided to tie up overnight at Stoke Bruerne, so he could make enquiries about our Josh., Constable Watkins, the policeman there, was very 'elpful and kind to us boaties. If ever we went to 'im with a problem 'E would always take the time to explain things and try and sort them out for to us. We mostly tried to stay away from the lawr 'cos some of 'em didn't like us, but Constable Watkins was different. Da said if 'E went to the police 'ouse, maybe 'E'd be able to find out where our Josh 'ad been taken. Then we could get this mess sorted out and let him know where to meet us, 'cos we knew they would let our Josh go, once they realised the mistake they'd made.

We was all onboard 'Isis' with supper bubbling away in the pot, when Da came back from seein' Constable Watkins. I could see from his face 'E wasn't 'appy. No one spoke 'til 'E was seated on the side bed then Ma turned round from the stove,

"Well Joe, what did 'E 'ave to say ?" she asked, rubbin' 'er 'hands down the sides of 'er apron.

"'E says he will 'ave to make some enquiries, but most likely its not a mistake. 'E says lots of young men is bein' taken off to the Army!"

I didn't want to hear this, I had convinced meself yesterday and all day today that our Josh would be sent back to us, as soon as they found out 'E wasn't meant to be in the army. I wanted to put me fingers in me ears when Da was speaking again, so I wouldn't 'ave to believe what he was sayin'.

"Apparently things havn't been goin' as well as they'd expected...... at the 'Front' like. They've lost a lot of men, ...regular soldiers like, and now they needs more, and 'orses too. Constable Watkins says they've took 'orses as well as men."

"But they can't have our Josh!" I blurted out suddenly "He's not a man anyway, he's only seventeen, he's too young".

"Hush girl" Ma said "Let yer Da finish".

"Well there's not much more to say really, I'll go back in the mornin' to see if he's found anythin' out, but he doesn't 'old out much hope. He says communications is all in chaos, sometimes people don't get to hear for weeks where their 'usbands and sons have been sent to".

Ma covered her mouth with her hand, but I could see she was bitin' her bottom lip. She looked across at me, but I didn't want to meet her eyes so I pretended to be looking for somethin' behind the cushion. No one spoke. Then Flossie who was playin with Ma's button tin on the floor said

"I'm starvin' I want me supper!"

Trust Flossie to be thinkin' of her stomach I thought, and even though I felt me 'eart would burst, I knew that life would still 'ave to go on ....somehow!

We ate our supper in silence, no one darin' to look each other in the eye, only our Flossie seemed totally oblivious to what was goin' on, I s'pose the rest of us just hoped it'd all been a nightmare and we'd wake up soon and find our Josh was still with us.

Da went off quite early the next morning and none of us mentioned our Josh until he got back. We all just sat in the back cabin of 'Isis' eatin' bread an' drippin and drinkin' tea 'til we could stand the silence no longer. Rain was comin' down in 'rods' and there was now't to do except wait for Da to return. So I took our Sammy back across to 'Bluebell' with me and was pretending to do important jobs around the cabin to keep meself busy, when I heard the sound of Da's boots as he walked up to the boats. I flung open the back doors of 'Bluebell' and was across into 'Isis' cabin before he could begin to tell Ma what 'E'd found out. We all knew from the look on his face that it wern't to be good news.

"Constable Watkins says 'E 'as made some enquiries on our be'alf and it would appear that our Josh 'ain't the only boatman to be taken away yesterday to the Army. Apparently the government says they needs more men who're good with 'orses an' lotsa boatmen are bein' sent to Flanders, that's some place in France I think. All the Carryin' Companies 'ave been told they must sign over as many able bodied men as they can, for the War effort."

Da must have gone on talking for quite a while, but I didn't want to hear no more. All I knew or cared about was that our Josh would not be coming home soon, it hadn't all been a mistake and our Gaffer, Mr. Griffiths, 'ad actually signed my beloved brother over to the army. How could he, why did he? I just couldn't think straight. An 'ard lump started to take shape deep inside my chest. I knew it was like nothin' I had ever felt before, it just sort of grew and grew this hard lump of hate for everyone who had a part in our Josh's bein' taken away, and most especially for Mr. Griffiths. Into this lump I poured all me emotion, all me thoughts and memories of our Josh, all the tears I wanted to cry, all the words I wanted to say. Everythin' got swallowed up inside of this lump and I made up me mind to hold it all there for as long as I needed to. I knew then that we would all have to get on with life 'til our Josh came back, but at that moment I didn't know 'ow it was gonna be possible. Our Josh was such a big part of all our lives. I knew too that I must not break down and cry for I felt that if I started I would never be able to stop, the flood gates would open and I would drownd us all in me tears.

"We'll just have to keep goin' without him, til this war thing is over"

I began to hear Da's voice once more.

"Constable Watkins says it can't go on much longer, they'll soon 'ave this Kaiser fellow brought to his knees and our boys'll be sent home."

But some'ow I didn't really believe it, not even then.

*Photograph of soldiers being trained to work
with boat horses. Taken at Devizes Wharf on the
Kennet & Avon Canal, during World War I.*

CHAPTER FOURTEEN

Keep the 'Ome Fire Burnin'

The next few weeks passed by in a haze of 'ard work and bad weather. We all seemed to be at each other's throats for no good reason. Da's 'omecoming from the sanatorium should 'ave been an 'appy time for us all, but it was 'eavily over shadowed by Josh's havin' been took from us. I tried with all me might not to think about our Josh. Every time memories of him slipped into me mind I felt the hot tears stinging the backs of eyes and I was determined not to cry, ever again! I kept meself busy all day, from when I woke up to when I fell exhausted into bed each night. The weather was bad too, it just rained and rained. Somehow I felt it was right, the sky was crying the torrent of tears that I refused to. I was grateful for it. We all went about our business with 'eads and shoulders bowed to the wind and rain, a good excuse not to look anyone in the eye and far too wet to stand about chattin'. And so we survived those first few weeks without our Josh, no one mentioning 'is name, in fact 'ardly talking to one another at all, even at meal times which we shared in the back cabin of 'Isis'. Even Flossie, for the first time in her short life, 'ardly spoke at all.

Then one day as we was passin' the Salt works near Marston, we saw Ma Baker with 'er two boats 'Grebe' and 'Water Lily'. They was both low in the water and must 'ave just left the works with a cargo of salt bound for the City Road. Ma Baker was steerin, the second boat and she frantically waved a piece of paper when she saw us coming along be'ind her. Da was on the bank with Hercules, but he ran on ahead of the 'orse when he realised she was tryin' to shout through the driving rain. The wind was all the time carryin' her voice away and I could see Da was holdin' his hand to his ear to catch the sound. I was two boat's length away, and then some, steerin' 'Bluebell' and 'ad no chance of hearin' what she was sayin. So I 'ad to wait 'til we got to the next lock before I could find out what it was all about. My interest however was very short lived when Da told me that Ma's eldest son Billy Baker had suffered a similar fate to our Josh, 'E 'ad been commandeered for the Army just six weeks before. She was proudly waving the letter she 'ad picked up at Sutton Stop; it was from 'er Billy. Apparently 'E had also been sent to this 'Flanders' place to work in the stables with other boaties, but he didn't mention our Josh. Ma Baker said she would write back and ask 'er Billy to look out for our Josh, specially now that Da 'ad told 'er we'd had no word of him.

The lock gates was opening and I 'ad 'eard enough, so I walked back to 'Bluebell' and and began heaving on the

- 241 -

rope to pull her out of the lock. Our Sammy was workin' the locks with Johnny Baker, a lad of about the same age, so I worked the boat alone, with thoughts of our Josh pourin' into me 'ead as fast as the rain was pourin' down from the sky. I couldn't think how it was that Billy Baker, who everyone knew hadn't a ha'peth of sense, could write a letter to his Ma when our Josh, who knew all there was to know about narra'boats and canals, even though 'E was three years younger than Billy, couldn't read nor write. Then I got to thinkin' about 'ow a letter could get all the way from across the sea, from this place called Flanders where 'they' 'ad sent our boys. How would 'they' bring it? How would 'they' know where Ma Baker was? It was to me, totally unfathomable. I don't know for sure, but I think it was at that moment that I made up me mind that somehow or another, I was going to learn to read and write properly. I spent the rest of that day imagining what I would write to our Josh, if I only knew 'ow to write down the words. Before that day I never felt the need to do no book learnin' I couldn't see no point to it. Now, I wished with all me 'eart that when, on the few occasions I'd been sent to local schools along the way, I'd paid more attention, instead of sittin' at the back of the class all day dreamin'.

When we tied up that night I didn't rush off to join the others, I busied meself with the stove and other chores on Bluebell, takin' me time about it too! I was almost afraid to step down into 'Isis' cabin, afraid that Ma and Da would be talkin' about Ma Bakers' letter and about 'er Billy and the war. When finally I did pull open the cabin doors the rest of the family was sat around the tiny table eatin' supper. The smell of delicious hot stew filled me nose and made me stomach rumble, but as I squeezed down onto the coal box step beside the stove, I felt a huge pang of guilt. Here I was snug in our back cabin, about to fill meself up with Ma's wonderful rabbit stew, while our Josh was goodness know's where, far off in some foreign country, with people he did not know, townies most like. Who would look after him? Cook for him? Do his washin? I felt the hot tears threaten to fill me eyes again and bit down 'ard on me bottom lip in an effort to stop them. Again I felt the 'ard lump forming in me throat and chest and into it I poured all the unshed tears and all me thoughts and fears for our Josh and carefully placed a tight lid on it all!

"Is there to be no end to this blasted rain?" Ma said to no one in particular, as she ladled the stew into me bowl.

Da sort of grunted in reply, but 'E never lifted his eyes from 'is supper. Sammy was slurpin' noisily as he tucked into 'is food, but no one bothered to tell 'im to eat more slowly and Flossie was nearly asleep as she monotonously spooned up the stew. The heat from the stove, normally a welcome relief after the rain soaked day, threatened to stifle me and I ate me evening meal as quickly as I could. Then on the excuse that I 'ad to darn an 'ole in me stocking before the morning, made me way back to 'Bluebell' and the solitude of 'er back cabin. I stoked up the stove and took off the hob plate, then pushed the kettle over the flames and waited for it to boil. I sat gazing into the fire for a very long time, but when I 'eard our Sammy's footsteps coming along the towpath, I realized I couldn't remember a single thought and the kettle was boiling away furiously.

"You makin' tea Jess?" our Sammy said as he stepped down into the cabin.

"Aye" I said, "And you can 'ave a wash in the bowl after I've 'ad mine" I replied

"Awh! 'ave I got to Jess? I'm tired, I just wanna go to me bed." Sammy 'ated washing at the best of times, but 'ated to share anyone else's water even more.

"I won't be long" I replied as I poured water into our enamel 'washing' bowl "You can get undressed and drink yer tea while you're waitin'".

I took the bowl over to the bed'ole and pulled the 'modesty' curtain behind me, before taking off me skirt and blouse. I realised I must have an 'ole in me boot as one stocking was soaking wet and stuck to me foot. Oh well, I thought, it'll have to do for a few days yet, 'til we gets back to the City Road, when Da would have the time to mend it for me. My ablutions finished, I pulled me long sleeved calico nightdress over me 'ead and passed the bowl to me unwilling little brother.

"Give me your boots and socks and I'll put them beside the stove to dry off." I said "And you'd best 'ang your trousers over the rail too."

Neither of us mentioned Ma Baker's letter, not that night or any other. I didn't know what our Sammy was thinkin' as he curled up in the bed'ole beside me, but I knew it was a long time before his deep rhythmic breathing told me 'E 'ad finally fallen asleep. I lay for hours listening to the steady drip, drip, drip of the rain and wondered if it were rainin' in Flanders.

I awoke next morning early to the grey light filtering through the gaps in the cabin door and hatch. I lay there in the bed for a while, just listening to the morning sounds, birds singing, tree branches creaking, the light wind causing ripples on the water, forcing them up between the boats and the bank, making strange burbling noises. I sat up in the bed and hugged me knees, there was somethin' missing, some sound that was not there. I fought with me befuddled sleep ridden brain tryin' to work out what it was that I couldn't hear. Then as I rubbed me eyes with the 'eels of me hand the answer slipped into me 'ead, there was no steady drip, drip, drip – it'd stopped raining! I lay back in the bed and thought 'ow funny it was, you got so used to 'earin' the rain that you didn't know what was missin' when you couldn't 'ear it no more.

Our Sammy was still sleepin' so I pulled me nightdress over me 'ead and in the grey light and found me skirt and blouse at the end of the bed. As I stepped to the floor, I was again aware of a queezie feeling in my stomach, I tried to dismiss it, but as I reached for the kettle I realised it was not going to go away, in fact I was certain now that I was going to be sick. Luckily Sammy had left the washing bowl on the back step and I was able to make full use of it.

"What's up with you our Jess?" it was Sammy, the noise 'ad woken 'im up!

As I wiped me mouth with the back of me hand I said "Dunno, must be somethin' I ate last night".

"Not like you to be ill!" he said again as 'E lay back on the pillow.

I opened the cabin doors and stepped up to the well deck, bowl in 'and. I was just leanin' over the gunn'all washin' it out when I 'eard Da be'ind me on 'Isis'.

"What's up with you lass, not sickening for som'at are you?"

"D'don't think so Da" I replied, thankful that me back was turned to 'im as another unwanted thought slid painfully into me mind. I heard the cabin doors of 'Isis' close again and was thankful that Da 'ad gone back inside. I sat on the gunn'all breathing in the clean fresh air, grateful for a dry morning after all the rain. Thoughts of the terrible attack on me came floodin' into me mind once more. At the time, Ma and our Josh 'ad both questioned me about it and although I 'ad tried not to think about it, over the last few days, words they 'ad said to me then, kept on comin' back to me. I didn't want to think about it! I 'ad been dreading to tell Da and our Josh 'ad promised 'E'd be with me when I did. E promised E'd tell Da that it weren't my fault........well it weren't, I knew that, but some'ow I felt, when I did pluck up the courage to tell 'im, it would all come out wrong and Da would think that I had done somethin' wrong. I wondered if Ma 'ad spoken to 'im, but I knew in me 'eart that she couldn't 'ave, 'cos Da wouldn't let a thing like that go, without wantin' to know about it first 'and like. It seems strange, lookin' back now, that somethin' so aweful, somethin' that affected me 'ole life, some'how got lost in me mind after our Josh got taken away. Sure there 'ad been the odd moment when the enormity of the attack rushed into me mind, but in those few weeks following our Josh's being taken for the Army, the loss of him overwhelmed me. I couldn't never remember a time without our Josh bein' there, he'd always been there, 'E was me brother, there was just two and an 'alf years between us. I felt the hot tears well up and threaten to brim over again and it took all me strength and will power not to let go of the flood gates. I decided then that

I'd 'ave to speak to Ma on 'er own and between us we'd decide wot an' when to tell Da about the attack. I just 'oped 'E wouldn't want me to go into details, I'd pushed all the pain of that day deep inside, locked it there and didn't never want to re-visit it, not for no-one. I didn't want to connect this aweful sick feeling wot was comin' to me each mornin' with that event. I knew enough about life to know the signs and Ma 'ad been expecting several times between our Sammy and Flossie.....no I didn't want to give any of these thoughts breathin' space. So I stepped down into the cabin, and pullin' back the bed'ole curtain, I began to shake our Sammy.

"C'mon our Sammy, get yerself up, I'll mash the tea"

"Aw Jess, just another ten minutes" Sammy protested as 'E turned on 'is side and pulled the blanket up over 'is head.

I opened the front of the stove and began to rake the ashes so the fire would burst into life. Then taking off the 'ob plate, I pushed the half full kettle of water over the flames, which had now begun to leap up from the embers. Noisily I shovelled up some coal from the box beneath the step and throwin' it into the stove, turned to our Sammy, lying fast asleep again in the bed behind me. I was about to shout at him to get up, but then thought 'Where's the 'arm,' if he does stay asleep a bit longer, no one else was about, there were no sounds now from 'Isis', Ma was most likely still asleep too. The kettle boiled and I made us a pot of tea, then pouring the hot black liquid into me mug I sat sideways on the cabin step and gazed out into the early mornin' mist rising slowly from the canal. It seemed to cling on to the 'edges and trees, not wantin' to go like, but the gentle breeze which was blowin ripples on the top of the water, made the mist part and sort of swirl up. A bit like steam slowly rising from the kettle's neck, just before it boiled.

I sat there for a long time wonderin' if our Josh was lookin' out on the same scene in this Flanders place. I wondered if he was lookin at the mist risin' off the canal as he boiled 'is kettle for his first cuppa tea of the day. I wondered what kind of boats he was workin' and whether the 'orses was well kept. Well I knew they would be looked after once our Josh got there, but you never knew what people had done to horses, before you got 'em. Some of 'em was quite skittish and bad tempered, but Da always said it was the way they 'ad been tret, made 'em wicked. Not their fault at all, it was up to us to show 'em we cared, to make 'em trust us. Our Josh was good at that, he had a special way with 'orses. He said you 'ad to speak to 'em, quiet like and tell 'em all the time what you was goin' to do, so as not to fright them. I told meself that was why 'they' had took our Josh, I remembered then that one of the uniforms had said they needed men who were good with 'orses at the front! At the front of what I wondered? Then I realised, they was most likely pullin' lots of boats or even heavy barges, tied up together in long lines with big shire 'orses pullin 'em and they needed good 'orsemen like our Josh up the front leadin 'em! Then I remembered Joe Stoker sayin' to Ma the other day that the fightin was bad 'out there 'and I couldn't quite get me 'ead round that one. Then, as I remembered some of the hot disputes over who's lock or bridge'ole it was and 'ow some of the rougher boat men, and women, would be prepared to fight anyone who tried to go through before them, I decided that these

'Flanders people' must be a rum lot. I drained me mug and set it back on the 'ook beside the stove, then good-naturedly stretched out an 'and to shake our Sammy's shoulder.

"C'mon our Sammy, Look lively", I said in a deep voice, tryin' to imitate the uniform who had come for our Josh, "We've wasted enough time here, get yer gear togehter, we're off to the City Road!"

"By you'm in a good mood this mornin" our Sammy said as he sat up in bed rubbing the sleep from his eyes.

"Well it's stopped rainin." I said as I handed him a mug of warm tea. And with that I wrapped me shawl around me shoulders and went off to feed Hercules. Somehow I felt closer to our Josh when I was seein' to the 'orse. And now I'd put things straight in me 'ead, I was ready to face another day! I knew now that there was nothin' Da nor no one could do to bring our Josh back soon, so we'd just all 'ave to get along without 'im. I felt that whatever 'appened to me in the future, it could never be as bad as these last few days 'ad been. I felt that if our Josh 'ad to face up to whatever was goin' on in this 'Flanders' place, then the least we could do was keep goin' until 'E came back. We at least, did 'ave each other, poor Josh was amongst strangers and Da said they spoke a foreign language! Our Josh couldn't even write in 'is own language, so what 'ope 'ad 'E to learn another! No I decided, we must all keep goin' and do the best we could 'til our Josh came back 'ome to us.

The End

The End

ABOUT THE AUTHOR:

Suzie was born into an Irish-Romany family and is very proud of her Celtic heritage. Her connection with all things 'spiritual' began at a very early age, in fact she has profound pre-birth memories.When only four years old, she was found by her Father, holding hands and conversing with her 'dead' Grandmother, with never a thought that this could not be possible. She communicated telepathically with other children, whom she had never met. Members of her family and close friends, felt immediate benefit from her 'healing hands' when laid upon them......something her Father was anxious for her to keep secret from the nuns and priests involved in her very Catholic upbringing. That she has always walked and talked with Angels, will come as no surprise and may be not even her connections to the Ancient Ancestors. However her extra terrestrial encounters may take a little more understanding. Suzie will tell you that she is definitely not a 'Spiritual Medium' in the usual sense of the term, she believes that Spirits appear to her simply because she is open to the possibility, and that everyone has this ability, it's just that conditioning has made some people sceptical about all things paranormal. Likewise intuition is something that our 'logical' brain often over rides. If you still your mind and listen to your inner voice, all you will hear is loving truth.

Lightning Source UK Ltd.
Milton Keynes UK
31 January 2011
166695UK00001B/4/A